P9-DVV-424

Please Bless Marilyn

Gordon T. Allred

Bookcraft

Salt Lake City, Utah

Library of Congress Catalog Card Number: 89-61688

ISBN 0-88494-706-8

First Printing, 1989

Printed in the United States of America

To all who wait and wonder

One

She was driving fast, far too fast, and not really caring. Without any specific plans in that regard, she was nevertheless aware that her actions were almost suicidal. The lump of bitterness and self-pity in her throat was more than a lump now, pressing into her sinuses and squeezing moisture from the corners of her eyes.

Blinking rapidly, trying to clear the film from her gaze, she saw the moon swelling blurred above the nearby mountains north of Park City, incredibly immense, the color of magic in a lambent blending of pale pink and gold. She snuffled loudly, vaguely realizing that hay fever season was wafting in to help compound the problem. Wiping at the corner of one eye with her fingertips, she reached for a Kleenex in the glove box, glanced up, froze at the wheel, and braked desperately. Three deer had materialized on the highway fifty yards ahead, palely luminous in the headlights, eyes intermittently reflecting the beam like green stars. Frantically she bleeped the horn and saw them shift uncertainly for an instant, then scatter in opposite directions, leg muscles swelling to gain traction.

She slowed, half sobbing, half sighing. "Idiot . . . idiot . . . " It was a combination of relief and exhaustion, but a bad time to relax. Looming just ahead was a phosphorescent green road sign reading "Morgan 26, Ogden 48" and shortly beyond, another sign that simply said "Ramp," accompanied by a narrow turnoff that banked in a great curve like part of some gigantic amusement park —abruptly, infuriatingly ambiguous.

No time to adjust or consider, and she powered straight ahead, still travelling beyond the speed limit, hoping for the best, hoping that she was heading toward Ogden. It took only two or three minutes of doubt and indecision, growing emptiness in the stomach, for her to comprehend that she was journeying instead for the sagey expanses of Wyoming with no turnoff in sight. Furthermore, the highway at that stage was only two lanes. Angry with herself, with the stupid highway department for its irrational direction signs, angry at the world, rapidly becoming faint and dizzy, she eventually found a wide enough spot to turn around. Or so it seemed until she had almost completed her maneuver. Suddenly her right front tire slumped into an unreasonably soft shoulder of sand and gravel.

Cramping the driver's wheel to the left, she tried to swing out of it and simultaneously caught the flash of distant headlights in her rearview mirror. Panicking, she gunned the accelerator only to slump deeper into the treacherous softness. The headlights were approaching at frightening speed, and she seized the wheel, straining irrationally as though trying to break it from the column. By now it was too late to extricate herself without magnifying the danger greatly. The rear end of her car projected halfway into the lane of oncoming traffic—and she saw not only one set of headlights, in fact, but another not far behind.

By now, in fact, it was too late for anything, too late to get out and wave them around, and nothing to wave with but the pale palms of her hands. Too late even to exit the car, but she tried, lunging for the door on her right, praying that her taillights, tilted at their oddly oblique angle, would provide enough warning. Her dress caught on the gearshift, and as she released the door it sprang open against her weight, plunging her foot into the sand and wrenching her ankle.

Light swelled, glared explosively in the side mirror as the car vroomed by, buffeting her with its wind, only to be duplicated seconds later by the next vehicle also accompanied by a loud, long-fading blast of the horn. Inconceivable! They had merely swerved slightly without the least deceleration, hurtling on like demons into the night.

For a moment she clung to the open door trembling, then slammed it and limped her way around the car fast, not wanting any repeat performances. Once more in the driver's seat, she remembered to switch on her warning blinkers. Then, casting an anxious glance at the highway behind, she gunned with a scraping of metal and shrieking of rubber backward onto the asphalt. The possible damage to her new butterfly yellow Mazda added a moment or two of dismay, but it was outweighed by relief.

A few minutes later she had reached the Ogden turnoff and was heading northwest toward the little towns of Henefer and Croydon. Moonlight flooded the verdant hills and valleys, filling at last the meandering Weber River with silvery iridescence.

Opening her window, she smelled the freshness of the night, the faintly exciting and secretive odor of wood smoke, of slopes covered with sage. The initial turbulence had abated, and she could think a little more objectively about what had happened less than three hours earlier. "Since there's no help come let us kiss and part." Who was the poet? She knew most of the lines, though maybe not in quite the right order, and couldn't think of his name at the moment. "Shake hands forever, cancel all our vows. And if at any time we meet . . . " No, that wasn't quite it. How did it go? "And when we meet at any time again, be it not seen in either of our brows that we one jot of former love retain." Ah yes, and immediately the lump in her throat was welling again, spreading to her sinuses, even seeming to invade her very *brow*! Her eyes also began to brim again. She was torturing herself—now that the anger had ebbed a little—with a saccharine sorrow, and that was bad news. "Nay, I am done—ye get no more of me. And I am glad, yes glad with all my heart that thus so cleanly I myself can free." That was better, *that* was telling him. It put a little starch in her spirit.

Anyway, she wasn't going back to her apartment in Ogden for a while. She was going to stay with her mother in Huntsville a short distance away, visit there also with her brother and his wife. Half an hour later, having shortcut northward across the winding back road of Trapper's Loop, she had skirted the eastern portion of Pine View Reservoir and parked in the drive of her old family home on its quiet shore.

Inside, she mounted the stairs, feeling their soft-carpeted familiarity with a sense of comfort, entered the bathroom with its antiquated tub standing on legs like lions' claws. She looked at herself in the mirror—the vermillion of her dress and matching earrings, the shimmering, blond cascade of her hair—the badly smudged eye makeup.

And then a face much like her own materialized behind it in the mirror, lovely and somewhat wistful, though aged and etched by thirty-five additional years. "Marilyn?"

"Hi, Mom." The words contained a surprising note of confidence, momentary good cheer.

For a second they gazed at each other in the mirror. "Is everything all right, honey?"

"Oh, sure," she replied and almost managed to sound flippant. "But my left hand feels sort of naked right now." She held it up for inspection. It was a slender, graceful hand with long fingers now slightly tremulous. "I gave Lon his ring back tonight."

Two

Marilyn Cannon and her widowed mother Maria had talked until nearly five in the morning, and at last she had fallen asleep, exhausted and comforted there beside her mom in the king-sized bed. That same bed had always been her sanctuary as a child when nightmares or goblins attacked, when tooth or tummy aches came, lightning and thunder . . . whatever the need. It was there for her now even though she was a "grown woman" at age twenty-five.

Once just before sunrise she had begun to cry in her sleep, dry, heaving little sobs, crying in whispers, half awakening to hear murmurs of love and consolation, to feel her mother's arms about her. The birds of daylight were twittering, and through the open window came odors of new-mown hay from Lije Marriott's field nearby.

At noon she was "laying out" on the shores of Pine View, lissome in a teal green swimsuit, anointed with tanning oil, provocative in her blaze pink lipstick, intriguingly anonymous thanks to her sunglasses. For two hundred yards in either direction the shoreline was hers alone. Despite her solitude, however, it seemed vital that she look terrific, if only to the great mirror of water and endless blue gaze of the sky. If only to the seagulls in their rising and falling on the thermals, their plaintive calling and cackles of derision as they dipped and hovered in search of something for their craws. Her portable radio was playing almost inaudibly, but the sentiment was a bit too much—a gently impassioned man and woman alternately lamenting in the lovelorn sorrow of a breakup: "On my own . . . on my own . . ."

She switched to another station and didn't do much better—an oldie this time, one that had never lost complete currency: "You're too good to be true, can't take my eyes off of you . . . You're like heaven to touch, I want to hold you so much."

Sighing, she lay back, succumbing to the caress of the sun and temptations of nostalgia. Obviously—yes, obviously now—he had been too good to be true. For one thing it suddenly seemed pretty naive to expect that anyone as remarkable looking as Lon Yeager would escape vanity or commit himself uncompromisingly to a single woman, no matter what her qualifications might be. "I can't decide," an envious young friend once enthused, "whether he looks more like Tom Selleck or Robert Redford." Marilyn had laughed, relishing the moment, rolling her eyes with mock seductiveness. Then, with a kind of ho-hum sigh, milking it to the maximum, she had replied archly, "Ah yes, dahling—it *is* a difficult decision, isn't it?" They had both giggled like twelve-year-olds.

But even after the engagement had become well known, the wedding date set, Lon couldn't quite resist being all things to all women. The familiarity he accorded them, though light and bantering on the surface, never really diminished for long. The ever-constant, suggestive little innuendoes, the caressing quality of his eyes . . . even with her closest friends . . . the taking of both their hands in his as they conversed, as he admonished them in pseudo-brotherly fashion on some important aspect of life or other—decisions regarding school, job, boyfriends, even matters of Church doctrine in some cases. He was the supreme confidant, holding them all in his palm, all of them entranced in his gaze—often concluding his advice by stroking an enflamed cheek with the flat of his thumb, the tips of his fingers. Frequently also there was a little massage to the back of the neck which usually ended with that same neck entrapped in the crook of his arm—all seemingly very buddy-buddy but automatically creating plenty of body alignment. All these things with the apparent assumption on Lon Yeager's part that there was nothing wrong with "a little lovin' " among friends and that anybody with such terrific cool should not really be bound by the constraints of normal mortals.

Much of his talk was also sex oriented, even some of his comments about Marilyn's own mother—what a "terrific build" she must have had in her younger days, still had!—how she couldn't possibly be a woman of sixty. Once during a backyard picnic, in fact, when Maria had mentioned the need to watch her diet, Lon had favored her with an appraising glance and insisted that it didn't look that way to him at all. "Matter of fact," he had added admiringly, "I'll bet anything you'd still look great in a swimsuit—a French cut." Maria Cannon had always been a woman of poise, and it was the first time in years that Marilyn had seen her mother flustered.

That evening, parked with Lon beside her Ogden apartment,

Marilyn had decided it was time for an honest discussion. "Lon?" she had said a bit nervously, gently staving off his attempted embrace and turning her face away for a moment.

"What's the matter?" came the reply. "I got bad breath or something?"

"No, not that." She laughed, then became serious again. "It's just that . . . well, I think we need to talk—really communicate—about something."

"I'm communicating," he joked, "I'm communicating," and reached for her again. "Body language."

"No, Lon, seriously," she insisted, restraining him a second time. "It's something I really need to get out because I don't feel good about it."

There was a momentary pause, and when he looked at her, the sensitivity and apparent sincerity of his glance was almost enough to dissolve her. "Sure, babe, what is it?"

"Well . . ." She drew the word out and her stomach in, taking a deep breath. For a moment she averted his gaze, staring at the polished, moon-glossed hood of his handsome Jaguar. Lon Yeager had an apparent genius for business and selling. By age twenty-seven he had acquired an MBA, his realtor's license, and was involved in several lucrative marketing enterprises. He and two of his partners even had their own plane, a twin-engine Cessna, which they used for recreation and for importing merchandise from countries "south of the border." All very laudable in some respects, and she could not deny the appeal of potential affluence. Simultaneously, given Lon's temperament and general life-style, she feared where it might lead.

That, however, was not her concern at the moment. "Well," she continued slowly, "I don't really know how to say this without sounding like some jealous little prude, and I honestly don't think that I am."

"I don't think you are either," he replied quietly. "Go ahead, beautiful, what's the story?"

"Well . . ." A long pause followed, filled with tentative chirps from the season's first crickets and the sound of flowing traffic along Harrison two blocks below. Telling him was going to be tougher than she supposed. "Let me put it this way." Her voice sounded rather strained and childish. She swallowed and moistened her lips. "How—and I want you to really be honest now

—how would you feel if I was always, well, going around and putting my hands on guys like Bart and Jack, and . . . oh, practically all your other friends? Always sort of getting physical and cuddling up every time I talked to them?"

He laughed, sounded genuinely perplexed, then became teasing. "Well, heck, why not share the wealth? I mean, if that's really your thing, I mean why be a miser?"

There was a moment of silence, awkward because he was clearly expecting a laugh and didn't get it. "Don't pretend you don't know what I'm saying," she said.

"Like that's what *I'm* doing?"

"You know perfectly well it's what you're doing," she said quietly—firmly but lovingly—grateful to find herself in better control.

The silence was strained. "Okay," he said at last, "guess I do. But I don't mean anything by it, Lyn, honest." He had taken her bare and slender arms in both hands and was looking earnestly into her face with those remarkable yet disconcerting eyes, a deep uncanny blue, colored now with a sheen like mercury from the moon and distant streetlight.

"If you don't *mean* anything by it," she said cautiously, "then why do it? Most guys don't, right? At least not that much, even if they're *not* engaged. And if *I'm* not even sure where you're coming from, don't you think a lot of other people might wonder a little?"

"Yeah, well . . . okay." He glanced down momentarily in concession. "I guess it's just kind of ingrained. Sorry, I just didn't realize it bugged you all that much."

Marilyn gave a colorless little laugh. "I didn't either—for a while—and maybe I'm overreacting. But, *Lon*?" She peered into his face, knowing that her own at the moment was sweetly reasonable yet imploring—a look that few people could resist. "Hey, we're engaged. We're supposed to be getting married one of these days . . . *forever*."

"Okay, beautiful," he said, nodding and sounding fairly contrite even though his smile seemed faintly amused. Tolerant? But the love in his glance, the admiration, was real. "I hear you, and you're absolutely correct. Never again—okay?" His eyes were irresistibly searching, so invasive she felt a little ambivalent. "Forgiven?"

"Sure," she replied, "but it wasn't really a case of forgiveness exactly. It was just something I had to . . ." She had wanted to stress the importance of communication and of always being honest with each other, that such things were the bedrock of any good marriage, but he cut her off.

"I know, I understand—don't talk." And maybe he was right. Crucial though a given concept might be, it was sometimes possible to engage in overkill, and there was also the matter of timing. Even as they kissed, however, she was also thinking that no man had the right to be so winning, to make a simple phrase like the last so romantic, seductive, without half trying.

Three

"You can get skin cancer that way," the voice said.

Her eyelids fluttered open, squinting against the sun even under her dark glasses. "Kelly!" she exclaimed happily and, rising to one elbow, reached to squeeze her brother's outstretched hand.

Without further comment for the moment, he seated himself Indian style on the sand beside her and appraised the water. He was wearing loose-fitting white pants tied at the waist with a drawstring, the lower half of an old karate *gi*, actually, and a chlorine green T-shirt that revealed impressive biceps. "So how's the battle?"

"Mom told you?" she asked.

"Yeah, that's a tough one." He gave his head a slight shake. "Sure sorry, kid. I've been through that scene, and it ain't no fun."

It was actually too big a ring anyway," Marilyn said and tried to restrain the tears with partial levity. "Full carat—that's really too much show for a little old Valley girl."

Her brother nodded, trying to keep it light. "Well, you know what happens when people start dangling carats."

"Yes, I guess. But it really was, oh, sort of like I was trying to lord it over some of my friends who got smaller ones." She held up her left hand, inspecting the naked finger with its faint band of paleness, untanned as yet by the sun. For a few moments she remembered the scintillating rainbow tones that first morning as she had driven to her job at Weber State, each facet of the diamond capturing, refracting, and flashing the sun in countless dancing angles on the ceiling and dashboard of her car. She remembered the almost overwhelming sense of self-conscious joyousness.

"Yeah," he said, "a real doorknob, wasn't it?"

"To the wrong door." Her smile was fleeting and bitter.

A speedboat was circling their direction in a wide arc, and a water-skier behind swung even wider, pancaking momentarily from one swell to the next, tanned and flashing a white-toothed grin much like Lon Yeager's, a bit too dazzling.

"So you want to talk about it?" Kelly asked.

She sighed. "I don't really know. I sort of poured it all out on Mom last night."

"Okay," he replied, "whatever's fair. Just want you to know I'm around and love ya."

"I love you too—bunches."

"And . . . ," he added casually, obviously wanting to avoid sentimentality, "you're in my prayers."

"Thanks." She sniffed a little. "I need 'em." Waves from the boat lapped the shore near their feet. A seagull hovered, tilting, then drifted up and off. "For a while there I actually thought he'd adopted a hands-off policy. Then I started hearing rumors—well, more than rumors—from some pretty reliable sources. The only hands off was for my eyes only."

"To borrow from a great old Bond thriller."

Marilyn laughed, knowing it was good medicine. "Right, and I'm beginning to think that's his whole problem—too much Bonding. But anyway . . ." She sighed and sat up beside him, clasping her knees in both arms. "Kel, he's actually been *dating* other girls ever since our engagement!"

"No kidding?" He squinted disbelievingly. "You know that for an absolute fact?"

"For an absolute fact, yes."

"What a crumb."

"Remember how I told you about all those times he was down visiting his folks in Springville, and I wondered why he never took me along?"

"Yah?" He glanced at her searchingly.

"So, now I know why he didn't."

Kelly's eyes narrowed and his head turned slightly to the side in disgust. "What a jerk! Guy's a real loser—glad you chucked him."

He had always been highly protective of his kid sister, and his anger was consoling. Nevertheless, her emotions were still contradictory. For a moment she closed her eyes again, knowing that she hadn't quite poured it all out the previous night after all. "Anyway, after we went out to dinner last night, I told him we'd better have another talk and confronted him with the whole miserable mess."

"What did he say?"

"Oh, he tried to tell me he wasn't actually 'dating' anybody, just trying to help a few poor little BYU girls with some problems. But there's lots more to it than that. I know for a fact that at least a couple of them haven't the slightest idea Lon's even engaged and think he's madly in love with them." She gave a morose little laugh, arched one eyebrow. "Who knows? Maybe he is!"

"What a prize chump!"

"Right, give him a gold medal." She paused, reflecting. A sailboat had materialized about four hundred yards away, sporting broad stripes of red, white, and blue. "But he has this fantastic ability to look you right in the eye, sort of hypnotically, and swear something is true when it definitely isn't. A lot of things that—once you can stand back and analyze a little bit objectively—are, well, pretty bizarre sometimes."

Kelly was shaking his head slowly and scowling. She saw the cleft, slightly jutting chin, the strong cheekbones. One of them contained a fading scar that curved upward across the bridge of his nose partway along his brow on the opposite side. The scar, however, detracted very little from his appearance, in some ways almost enhanced it, and the hazel eyes were sensitive, highly perceptive. "What makes guys like that tick?" he asked quietly. "Seriously, what's going on in there?"

"You tell me," she said. "But, Kel, he acts so sincere! I almost think he *believes* himself, right while he's saying it at least."

"Yes, maybe," he replied after a moment, "but just because somebody's such a con artist he can sometimes con himself . . . that's no excuse."

Marilyn nodded morosely. "That's for sure, but anyway—last night it didn't work. I was pretty relentless even though it practically killed me, and after a while the guilt just kind of oozed all the way out. I mean, I'd really done my research, and he couldn't deny it." The reservoir was gradually acquiring more boats and skiers. A big outboard vroomed by, trailing a water weenie, yellow and sharklike, straddled by four jubilant riders. For a few moments she smiled, forgetting her problems. Then she closed in again. "Funny thing is, though, I actually think he loves me. He kept saying none of the other girls *meant* anything, and maybe they don't, who knows? But, of course, I kept saying if they didn't mean anything then why was he messing around with them? And wasn't it pretty darned cruel—for them as well as me—to make them *think* he cared?" Her voice was becoming dry.

"But when I gave him"—she swallowed, struggling for composure—"gave him his ring, he got all choked up with tears in his eyes." The power of suggestion was too much. She removed the sunglasses, trying to wipe her own eyes with the back of her hand, and blurred them instead with tanning oil.

"Want to borrow my shirttail?" her brother said.

She sniffed, forcing a smile. "I'll probably need this whole beach towel before I'm through."

"Well," Kelly said and clucked his tongue, "maybe I should feel sorry for him, losing such a neat girl, but I can't. He cooked his own goose and burned it bad. Got what was coming to him." They could hear the distant sounds of Lije Marriott's tractor. The ancient patriarch was harvesting more hay. "But I know it wasn't exactly easy—for you I mean, having to bag it all."

Again she closed her eyes, the thick dark lashes contrasting dramatically with the blond of her hair. "It was the toughest thing I've ever done in my whole life; only hope I don't chicken out. After he left last night I hopped in my little car without even realizing it and took off. I didn't even know where I was going, just headed for Weber Canyon driving like a madwoman, and finally found myself clear up between Heber and Park City at about two A.M. It was really stupid because halfway there I was bawling so bad I could hardly . . . Once, and it's kind of funny now, everything was so blurry I got confused and turned on the windshield wipers!" By now they were both laughing. "Not a cloud in the sky."

Four

"Well," Kelly reflected eventually, "like the song says, 'Breakin' up is hard to do.' But, even at that, it's a heck of a lot better before you're spliced than after. You'll probably hear that from everybody in town the next little while, but it's true."

"I'm sure," she said pensively. Thirty feet offshore a carp broke the surface, landing with a plop and leaving concentric rings.

"Used to spear those things with pitchforks," Kelly mused. "Over in all those willows by Cottonwood Campground." Laugh wrinkles formed at the corners of his eyes. "Once I got this great big one on the end of my fork and gave it a humongous old heave with everything I had. Fish must of weighed six, seven pounds . . . flies off the pitchfork and comes down and clobbers Gordo Yates right in the back of the neck."

"Oh, that's awful!" Marilyn exclaimed. "It's a wonder you didn't *break* his neck!"

"True," he admitted but began to chuckle. "I didn't really plan it that way, though—just wanted to scare him. Luckily he was only shook up a little, and it really was kind of funny."

"Poor Gordie. Things are always happening to him."

Her brother was still grinning a little, shaking his head. "Yeah, always something. Really a good-hearted guy, but he's the only person I've ever known who has perfect strangers walk up for no apparent reason and slug him!"

"It's not funny," she protested. "Why are we laughing?" She knew the answer, however, why at least the laughter. Her brother had an instinctive wisdom for situations like the present one and wanted to provide a little relief.

"Well, kid, wish I knew what to tell you," he said at last. The carp swirled and splashed again farther out.

She was gazing off across the reservoir now, two miles or so to the spot where it entered the canyon. "And it's not just the playing around," she murmured, "it's something even more basic about the whole big plan. I mean, here he is—returned missionary, always goes to church, teaches a Sunday School class and everything." She paused. "Sixteen- and seventeen-year-olds, and you should see how many girls attend!" For a moment she felt an added surge of jealousy, eliminated it by a concerted act of will. "Lives the Word of Wisdom, pays a full tithe." A slight shrug. "I guess he does, anyway. But it's like going to the temple—" Her eyes narrowed, and she glanced to the side. "Kel, I dunno, it's like getting married in the temple's just sort of a social thing, something to do because it's expected. Know what I mean?"

He nodded. "Back there five, six years ago I was a lot that way myself. That was the main reason Liz decided to call it off. Once I got out there on my mission and really started to tune in on the temple, what it could really mean, it was too late. Got my Dear John with all the trimmings." His tone was one of complete equanimity, faint amusement, and she wondered how long it had taken him to get there. "Lucky for me, I found Shan and lived happily ever after."

Yes, Shannon—her best friend, her brother's wife. Their marriage had truly been idyllic. Thus far, more than two years, it had indeed been happily ever after, and for a moment she felt a slight surge of envy like an actual chemical release. That too she willed away. "But you couldn't see marrying in the temple back in the Liz Parker days because you were wondering about the whole gospel," Marilyn said. "Losing Dad . . . and some of those classes in college that I guess kind of shook your faith. You'd pretty well lost your testimony—right?"

"About lost my marbles." He gave a dry little laugh full of self-derision.

"But Lon still has a testimony—that's the weird part. At least he claims to. It's just that being a one-woman man isn't in his plans, maybe his personality. Especially when you're talking about forever." Her gaze dissolved in recollection. "One time, only a week or so after we'd gotten engaged, we were coming home from this absolutely gorgeous day up at Bear Lake. The trees were just starting to change color, but everything else was about the greenest it's ever been that time of year from all the rain."

"Yah, I remember," he said.

"Anyway, we were coming down by Sardine Pass, and I showed Lon that place on the mountain by Sherwood Hills where Mom and Dad always used to talk about building their castle." Kelly nodded, smiling. "So anyway, I told Lon about it, and he said maybe we'd just do that sometime—actually build a castle up there."

"Well, he'll probably have the bucks for it one of these days the way he's going," Kelly said.

"Probably. But then I started thinking about something you told me Uncle LaMar had said when he performed the marriage ceremony for you and Shannon." Another nod, another smile. They had always been on the same wavelength, even back in the gloomy days when her brother was floundering, beset by his own trials. "Remember what you said? How he told about asking that question to Aunt Ina one time?"

Kelly grinned, repeating the words verbatim. " 'Honey, I wonder what we'll be doing a million years from now.' " They pondered the thought for some time, fondly, captivated by all it portended. "That's what I remember most about the whole ceremony, except for the last part of course. That and the mirrors on both sides of the room so we could see ourselves and everybody there just going on and on." He held out his hands, palms up. "To infinity—forever."

For a minute or two Marilyn could not reply. "Wow, I'm such a wimp. Seems like all I can do is bawl every two seconds."

She felt his arm encircle her shoulder, the powerful, protective squeeze. "So?" he said gently. "Why do you think the Lord gave us tear glands?"

"But not to create the second flood," she laughed. "Anyway, that's what I said to Lon that evening last fall—'I wonder what we'll be doing a million years from now.' The whole idea was just so fun and romantic and everything. Something you could kid about, but so great, too. And I literally meant it."

"Sure."

"But ya know what?" Her face lost color. "Lon just looked at me and laughed. Not a warm, loving laugh . . . but as if I'd, well, said something sort of dumb that really made him nervous."

"Hmmm." That was the extent of Kelly's reply, but his tone was curious, perplexed, concerned—all in one.

"Remember that time you showed me how to break a choke hold with one of your karate moves?" Her brother was always showing her techniques in self-defense, coaching her in ways of protecting herself. "You told me to start choking you. Then all you did was poke your finger right here into the base of my throat where it joins the collarbone." She probed at the spot cautiously, blinked, smiled wincingly, and swallowed.

Kelly nodded, amused but obviously pleased. "Good move—couldn't be simpler, but it really works." He shrugged. "Something equally simple, if you really need to lay a guy low—that's the good old knee to the groin. It's really important for women to know that stuff. Every so often pretend somebody's got hold of you and practice till it's instinctive."

She nodded. Maybe I should, "but when you pushed there, right here in my throat, with your finger, I let go in a hurry. You didn't do it very hard, but it felt as if my windpipe was closing off and stayed that way for quite a while afterward." She hesitated, trying to keep her voice steady. "Well, that was a lot the way I felt when Lon laughed." A breeze had picked up in the cottonwoods south of their yard, wafting their cotton like light, dry snow there on the very brink of summer. "I really knew clear back then that something was wrong. I just didn't dare admit it." Kelly nodded. "But isn't that what it's all about? Actually thinking in terms of a million years from now?"

"That's what it's all about," he said.

Five

Two weeks later Marilyn was swimming along the same shoreline with her roommate Janie Johnson from Ogden. "You've got to fill the void with something," Janie had insisted earlier, "and there's nothing like some big, ferocious physical challenge." Anything exciting was ferocious in Janie's lexicon. Through constant repetition and the sheer force of her personality, she was on the verge of popularizing it as one of the great catchall words of modern time along with such gems as "gross" and "awesome."

"Believe me, Lyn Baby"—her own special nickname for Marilyn along with Lyn-Lyn and several others—"Believe me, I know; haven't I been there?" It was a rhetorical question in Janie's case, always referring to matters of experience rather than mere geography. "Anyway, I've signed us both up for the big Golden Spike Triathlon at the end of July."

"You've *what*?" Marilyn had been slightly aghast. "Triathlon!"

"Hey, it's not that bad an entree." *Not that bad an entree*—that too was Janie along with a whole gaggle of other expressions. "Besides, it's only a mile swim across the corner of Willard Bay, a bike race of some thirty miles out to Promontory, then a little five-mile run to the Golden Spike Monument."

"Oh, is *that* all?" Marilyn had laughed. "And here I was expecting to work up a sweat." Not that she was averse to exercise. Marilyn Cannon had taken up jogging in her early teens as part of the national craze. She was also "into" aerobic dance, had even worked out at one of Ogden's health clubs, partly because she believed all such activities were good for her, partly because they were the "in thing." Even so, Marilyn had never been serious about athletic competition and actually feared it in some ways.

"It'll take your mind off Rover," Janie had continued, using her special name for Lon Yeager ever since hearing of their breakup, "and it'll show you what you're made of."

"That's what scares me, that last part," Marilyn had said, but the desire to ease her mind, to soothe her seething innards, had made the challenge tempting. In addition, she was hoping that it would fortify her against the temptation to see him again.

"Besides . . ." Janie's arguments were unrelenting when it came to causes, all of which admittedly were good ones in her case. "It helps fight depression, actually increases the endorphins in your bloodstream. Seriously, Lyn Baby, it's an established fact!"

Now, swimming side by side with her friend, a girl sturdy of both mind and limb, Marilyn had an idea that the Golden Spike Triathlon might become a reality even though she had consented reluctantly under condition that it wouldn't hurt to work her way into the training regimen and "see how it goes."

At the moment they were going for a mile in the water, north to the peninsula called Cemetery Point and back—and after that, a three-mile jog that would return them to their starting place at her home in Huntsville just in time for supper. Each time her right arm stroked, her right ear plunged beneath the surface and heard the high-pitched reaming and simmering of boat motors coming through the water. Simultaneously, her left eye partook blurrily of the liquid expanse of Pine View to the south, the shoreline beyond, then the highway, ascending grain and hay fields blending with the hills beneath Mount Ogden. The mountain itself terminated in a series of lofty, serrated peaks still garbed in snow. It had been an intense winter, and the June runoff was still strong. The reservoir had rarely been as full or clear, and the spillway was disgorging white water with an awesome exuberance. The Ogden River exploding below was wild and dangerous.

Even though it had been two weeks since the ring episode, her finger felt unnatural. At times, at the very moment, in fact, it seemed as if the diamond were still there like the "ghost limb" that lingers following an amputation. Each time her left hand rose from the water and arched forward the ring seemed to materialize, shimmering and melting, flowing away like a giant tear.

No, it had not been an easy severance. He had called twice, insistently yet in tones of great humility, highly apologetic, asking for another chance. And both times, after an hour or more of repetitious discussion, she had hung up full of sorrow and gloom, in for another sleepless night. At present she was flitting impulsively between the Ogden apartment she shared with Janie and another friend named Carla Bonner and her home in Huntsville fifteen miles away, badly stressed, unable to concentrate on anything but her job for more than a few minutes at a time.

Two years earlier she had graduated with high honors from Weber State, majoring in English and communications, and shortly afterward landed her job as assistant director of the college news bureau. Fortunately, she loved the work. It was something she relished and did very well among people she liked, there upon a verdant, rolling campus in the lap of Ogden's foothills. The bureau director, an affable young bishop with a serene and guileless countenance, had always treated her with utmost respect and consideration, never failing to praise her efforts. This despite tremendous pressures in his own life occasioned in larger part by the recent loss of his wife to cancer.

Her swim with Janie Johnson terminated where it had begun, and they left the water, staggering a little from temporary imbalance, joking about people who "couldn't hold their liquor." In the Cannon residence they changed to their jogging attire and headed down the quiet Huntsville back street, passing the home of her brother, Kelly, next door. Kelly and Shannon had built much of it themselves, Shan working alongside her husband even in the final days of her first pregnancy. One section, designed to enhance solar heating, was still under construction, but the house promised to become a handsome and spacious dwelling before long. The broad expanse of front lawn was landscaped with new aspen and spruce. Century-old cottonwoods guarded the backyard, and a large garden beyond ran down to the shoreline.

"I don't know if I'm up to this or not." Marilyn shook her head. "The swim itself about finished me."

"Aw, you'll be okay, Lyn-Lyn" her friend assured. "Just takes a little while to get your land legs back again. Besides, it's a great way to knock the insomnia."

"Maybe," Marilyn allowed. "Then, instead of thinking about the guy all night long, I'll just dream about him." It helped somehow to call him "the guy," made everything more casual, less sentimental.

"When I get through with you"—Janie tossed her head Marilyn's way—"you'll be too bushed to dream, do anything but stuff your supper and crash." She had a strangely infectious chortle with a series of little warbling hiccoughs that were always even funnier than what she said—a laugh that automatically caused others to laugh.

They made a marked physical contrast, the two of them, jogging together there in that pastoral land. Janie, a mere five feet four, was stocky and exceptionally muscular, but also shapely sans fat—no "pinching an inch." Her face was round without the faintest line, only the pronounced dimples on each side of a mouth that was almost always smiling with fondness and mischief. Her blue eyes were so alive they fairly twittered.

Marilyn, on the other hand, was five feet nine, sylphlike, fluid as a willow in the breeze. She worried occasionally that she was too tall but had long ago overcome a tendency to slouch, thanks to corrective ridicule from her brother, and now carried herself, usually, like a ballerina. She worried at times that her neck was too long, her mouth too wide and full, but family and friends had at least partially convinced her that all these elements combined appealingly—essential to the uniqueness that was Marilyn Richards Cannon.

At age twenty-five she was modestly pleased with who she was, not merely physically but also what she was becoming as a person. The smile she saw in the mirror seemed to be growing in empathy, and yet was also a little bewitching. She considered that a fairly objective appraisal without much narcissism. Her eyes were large, a fusion of green and amber like her brother's. Human? She hoped so, hoped that they were at least becoming that way with experience.

"But the thing is . . ." Janie was saying. Her breathing was regular, as inaudible as though she were walking. "You just gotta keep active . . . not only this kind of stuff but in lots of other ways. You gotta have a program—know what I mean? Most of all see other guys, even if they all aren't that big a thrill. Can't just lay around and mope, correct?"

Lie around, Marilyn thought, *not lay.* But she let it pass. "Oh, I know what you mean, all right," she said. They were headed eastward toward the Southfork road, and the mountain half a mile to their left was flat on top like an immense mesa, now crowned by a solitary thunderhead. Otherwise the sky was a vibrant blue. "It's just that the thought of going out with anybody else right now appeals to me about as much as a cardboard sandwich."

Janie gave her turkey call of a laugh. "Right on! Cardboard and plaster. Haven't I been there?" A flock of blackbirds, several of them redwings, scattered from a bog of cattails nearby. A fawn-colored Jersey cow watched them, stolidly chewing its cud. "The only difference is, in my case *I* was the one who got dumped."

"I *told* you to quit beating him at arm wrestling," Marilyn said.

Another chortle. "Aw, I couldn't really beat him—not when he tried very hard. But say what you want . . . no matter how tough it is, it makes a big difference who gets to do the dumping. Who's calling the shots." They were catching their second wind, breathing more comfortably. "You think it's tough now, Lyn, and it is, but at least you're in charge of the program."

"Sometimes I wonder." Marilyn was staring a bit vacantly into the distance, along the broad valley eastward with its stream glancing the light of late afternoon, mirroring in places the fields of baled hay that gradually narrowed into the mouth of Southfork Canyon. "If he calls even one more time," she thought, "I wonder if I can—"

"Take my word, hon—it's ego. Remember how Dawson kept saying the same thing about Misti Taylor? How much easier it would have been breaking up a month or so earlier—even a couple of weeks—when she couldn't stay away from him? Then Misti starts going out with that Duane what's-his-face, turning the tables, and poor old Daws can't handle it. All of a sudden he's the one who comes begging, starts getting this big obsession that she's 'It' after all—definitely the only one for time and all eternity."

"Weird!"

"Not weird at all—human nature."

Six

She had remained at her Huntsville home that night to visit with her mother, and the call had come just before midnight, awakening her from a fairly tranquil sleep. "Hi," the voice said. Merely that single word, deep and vibrant. It excited and vexed her at the same time.

"Hi," Marilyn replied. Her own voice was slightly thick with grogginess.

There was an uncomfortable pause. "Sorry I woke you up," he said, "but . . . well, there's this incredible moon out there that shouldn't be going to waste." He paused and laughed nervously. That nervous laughter when he obviously felt embarrassed or uncomfortable was the only time his voice became a bit high. He even *sounded* like Selleck at such times, simply didn't seem as trustworthy. "Fact is, I'm going to be driving up that way, heading for Snow King to sort of get a better view of things. And . . . oh, I was half hoping I could maybe twist your arm into coming along."

"Lon . . . ," she said, partly in warning, struggling with herself, yet also determined. "I'm in bed, and I've got to be down to work at seven in the morning."

"Yeah, I know," he replied. "I know, and I apologize. It's just that—"

"Lon," she interrupted, "I'd really—"

"Look," he said, "I know it's stupid to be calling like this, and I know you need your sleep, but I promise it won't be for long. It's just that, well, I'm all hung up on some family problems and gotta have a friend."

"Family problems?"

"Yah." He heaved a sigh. "It's Mom—she's gotten a lot worse lately. I've been going down there nights after work. Just got back, in fact."

"Aw, Lon," she said and felt the flow of compassion. "I thought she was improving!" Lon Yeager's mother Emily was a saintly woman quietly stoical, despite the ravages of severe emphysema and certain other complications which Marilyn had never quite understood.

"She was for a while," he replied, "but the past month or so she's been going downhill again. I mean, she can hardly make it out of bed and has to cart around that little oxygen tank everywhere she goes."

The picture focused pitiably in her mind's eye, very sharply. "Lon, I'm *so* sorry—that's awful. Is there anything—?" She knew before ever finishing the sentence that she was committing herself to something, yet under the circumstances she felt that she had no option without forfeiting some of her humanity.

"They're doing everything they can," he said, "and Dad and I . . . we've administered to her, but . . ." He sighed even more heavily. "I shouldn't be bothering you because I know how you feel, and I definitely can't blame you. I've been a real crumb, I admit. Don't even deserve the time of day." He gave another of his little laughs. "Guess that's why I'm calling at night." Marilyn laughed too, thinking fleetingly that they both needed something to ease the strain and that despite the suaveness—all his cool—there was another personality that was surprisingly childlike and vulnerable. That, in fact, was part of his appeal.

"Anyway," he said after a moment, "I'm sorry I bothered you. I just needed somebody to talk to for a minute. Everything's a lot better now, just"—he hesitated—"well, hearing your voice. It's really one beautiful voice, no kidding."

"Flatterer," she chided, but it was getting to her a little even so.

"Not true, not true," he insisted, "just telling it like it is."

More silence. "But how come you're headed up to Snow King at this wild hour?" Marilyn asked.

"Well," he said, "we've been getting some vandalism up there lately, and our night security guy's just had heart surgery. So—the sales boys are standing in. I'm on like every tenth night, and this is it." Selling condo time-shares at Snow King Ski Resort was another of his money-making enterprises, some of which she still knew little about, if anything.

"So *anyway* . . ." He groaned slightly as if stretching or perhaps trying to cast off a real burden. "I'll be thinking about you when I'm up there, Lyn-Lyn. Looking right down on your rooftop and thinking, 'That's where she lies sleeping, the only girl I ever—' "

"Lon, don't," she warned. It sounded like some oldie, maybe a song by Gordon Lightfoot, but she felt vibrations inside like the wings of a giant dragonfly.

"Okay, tell you what," he said. "I'll be heading up there right now. Takes about forty minutes from down here in Ogden to reach the top. If by any remote chance you're still awake around that time, take a look out your window, and if you can spot anything different up there on the mountain—sort of special—just say a little prayer. Okay? Fair?"

"Sure," she said. "But . . ."

"Hey," he said mysteriously, "don't ask, might ruin the magic. Just say a prayer, okay? If you see anything different—pray, for you and for me, and especially for my mom."

"Okay, of course I will," she said and hung up rather abruptly, not wanting to cry into the phone.

A little over forty minutes later—she had watched the clock almost obsessively—she was crying in earnest, all her fragile reserves disintegrated. A new star had appeared atop the mountain, a bright red one casting its glow against the summit and the northern sky. It was only one of the railroad flares he carried in the back of his car. But he had lit one in that very spot once before. They had been up there together. The night he had given her the ring, the "red star" too had been a symbol of their engagement.

Seven

The late-night drive from her home in Huntsville around the eastern end of Pine View and on past the Wolf Creek Resort above Eden took only five minutes. It was another twenty up the steep, winding grade ribbed along the center with a continuous pile of new asphalt awaiting the next day's road grader. Yellow flasher lights marked its presence every hundred feet or so all the way, and she could smell the pungent odor of tar and creosote in the darkness, see mountain slopes painted a frail, shifting white by her headlights.

At times the grade became so steep she dropped her Mazda into low and felt it grumbling smoothly, uniformly along at only fifteen miles an hour or less. Then she was bearing right on an even narrower road of mere sand and crunching gravel past a parking lot with rain puddles from the previous night's brief thunderstorm, past a slow-ambling porcupine seeking shadow, making the final climb in a hundred yard question mark to the top. At one o'clock in the morning she parked in the darkness beyond the half-finished condo. Her lights bathed an immense pile of firewood, pale chunks of aspen sectioned by a chain saw and split into large wedges. Beyond to the left of a winding boardwalk was the swimming pool that had been completed and filled only a few days earlier.

Its waters, reflecting a luminous rind of moon, beckoned faintly as she climbed from her car. Red-pink flames from their special star fluttered on the little rise just beyond. For a moment she saw no one, then the ruddy glow on his arms, brow, and cheekbones as he arose from his seat on the fallen log to greet her.

She definitely hadn't intended to, specifically planned not to, but for a moment they embraced with utter spontaneity as though it were the most natural, inevitable thing in creation. "I really didn't think you'd come," he said.

Several seconds elapsed before she could reply; her vocal cords were completely untrustworthy. Then she drew back and appraised his face, looking him directly in the eyes and hoping to read whatever might be there. During their separation he had acquired a thick, slightly bristling mustache, but it certainly did not detract from his appeal. If anything it added even greater masculinity, a touch of fierceness, that attracted her unreasonably. "It's hard to resist a man who puts a new star in the sky for you," she said and almost kept her voice level. "And, after all, how could I just sort of huddle there in my little room peering out the open window when we were actually looking right at each other from only a few miles apart?" she paused. "And maybe the only people around who are still awake?"

He closed his eyes for an instant and gave that special half smile, half wince she knew so well, a kind of touché acquiescence, an unspoken apology. "I'm sorry," he confessed, "it was a dirty trick to wake you."

"No it wasn't," she insisted. "Not with all your worries about your mother." That, in fact, was what had led to the break in her resolve, the thought that his mother was in precarious straits and that he was truly alone at that hour, deeply concerned and suffering. All the way up there she had thought about it and simultaneously, reluctantly, questioned the integrity of her motives. Wasn't it also an easy excuse, one she had seized upon too effortlessly? The whole thing, her alter ego had kept whispering, could be a clever setup, yet almost indignantly she had also kept telling it to keep quiet. What really constituted cold calculation as opposed to a genuine expression of concern? Did a romantic, creative form of appeal necessarily make it ulterior?

"Tell me about your mom," she said. "I'm really worried about her."

"Thanks," he replied. "I knew you would be." He sighed and shook his head, looking genuinely downcast. "Guess there's not much more to tell. She's such a terrific, courageous little character, but she's definitely on the decline. And . . ." He gave another of his embarrassed little laughs. "Well, I guess my situation hasn't helped. She keeps fretting about it."

Marilyn felt a twinge of guilt and sorrow but also a sense of victimization, as if she were being compromised. She had wondered more than once, in fact, whether Lon's mother, his whole family, truly understood the cause of his broken engagement. This was not the time, however to wrestle with such matters. No, not now, but what was the proper response? She truly didn't know. "I'm so sorry," she said after a moment. "Please tell her she's in my prayers."

He nodded, still looking down. "Thanks, that will mean a lot." It was the logical moment, she realized, to tell him that he too was in her prayers, but for some reason she couldn't quite do it. Besides, it was hardly true, at least hadn't been. Her anger and self-pity had excluded the very thought.

Twenty miles northward the lights of a city twinkled faintly. "I still can't believe that's Logan out there," she said. "It looks so close."

"Yeah—seems like we're practically on top of it." The flare had gradually dwindled, its redness becoming a mere candle flame that sputtered in the shifting air, nearly expired, yet clung to its wick with strange tenacity.

"Doesn't want to give up the ghost, does it?" she said.

He offered no reply, merely put his arm around her shoulder, and for a long time they watched the flame. At last it was snuffed by a sudden breeze that drifted through the nearby aspen leaves with a soft and mounting frill. "Gone now," he mused. They remained in silence for some time. "By the way," he said at last, "we finally got that pool heating unit installed. The water's about perfect—want to give it a try?"

Marilyn laughed. "Wearing what? Our birthday suits?"

"Why sure," he replied, "it's a dark night."

She glanced at him suspiciously. "You've *got* to be kidding!"

His laughter was wholehearted, infectious. It was the kind that said he had almost fooled her. "Yeah, I'm kidding, but I've got a pair of cutoffs in the back of my Suzuki, and there's a woman's swimsuit—ah, probably just about your size—over in our demo unit."

"There is?" She was both amused and curious, somewhat suspicious. "And how, if I'm not too nosey, did a woman's suit happen to get there?"

Lon shrugged elaborately. "Search me. It's been hanging there in the closet for about a month. Guess somebody came up here and thought maybe the pool was ready to go back in May." He shrugged again. "Brought the suit along and forgot it—*I* dunno."

"Hmmmm." She was watching him from the corners of her eyes. The pool was a large one, kidney shaped to blend with the landscape, and its water had a subtle, phosphorescent sheen. The surface purled faintly under a warm and mellow breeze, making the reflected stars and crescent moon dance and shatter like slow-motion fireworks. Fascinated, she stooped toward it, resting one knee on the brink, and tested the water with her hand, sensing that by now she had practically committed herself unless the water was definitely too cold.

"How about it?" he prodded. "Perfect temp—right? Almost like bathwater."

"Not quite *that* warm!" But she had to admit that it was just about ideal. Besides, what was there to lose but more sleep? And . . . well, why not live a little, lay hold of the moment? "Okay," she said, suddenly almost jubilant. "You're on!"

They headed toward the empty condo unit hand in hand, sauntering, almost sashaying like a couple of teenage extroverts, laughing and kidding as if they'd never been separated. Then, in the middle of a happy little warble, she clapped her free hand to her mouth. Windows of the two-story condo just ahead stared at them blankly, but she realized that some of the units contained people who were asleep, or who had been until that moment. "Hey," she whispered, "we'd better cool it or we'll wake up the whole place."

"Yeah, right." His arm snugged her about the shoulders, pulling her slightly off balance.

"Lon, maybe we shouldn't be doing this. I wouldn't want to get you in—"

"Hey, no problem," he insisted, "none whatever, long as we tone it down a little."

Minutes later she was appraising herself in the mirror of what temporarily had become her own private bathroom. The suit was two-piece, ripe apricot color, a perfect fit. The mirror itself contained a faint gold tint, and temporarily, at least, she really liked what she saw. In that light and at that special moment everything, especially the spontaneous, faintly seductive smile, fell together very nicely.

"Hey-hey," he said as she left the bedroom, "you look terrif!" The thick, dark eyebrows arched, waggled playfully. "Perfect fit too—how *about* that!" Then they had entered the night. She could feel the wooden walkway beneath her bare feet, and the half-inch spaces between the two-by-fours made her feel more alive than ever. So did everything—the slightly illicit hour, the tang of damp earth from a recent excavation, the odor of new lumber, and the omnipresent chanting of the crickets.

As they stood on the brink of the pool, the aspens sighed with a sudden, growing exhalation, making the warm and waiting water more inviting than ever. "Well?" Lon slipped the white towel from his shoulders, and looked at her with a grin. Again he waggled his brows with playful seductiveness, a caricature of the real thing that ironically made him all the more attractive. He really did have remarkable charisma and a rare sense of humor. That as much as his appearance had drawn her to him in the first place. "Here we go to give the pool its baptism!"

She giggled. "Isn't it the other way around?"

"Shhh!" He raised a finger to his lips, then pressed his lips to her own, little more than a peck with an exaggerated pucker. "We dive with the grace of otters!" It was a line from an ancient, C-grade western titled "The Noble Redman" which they had once watched on video out of sheer craziness.

"Of course, by all means!" She stifled another giggle. The entire night, the whole "scene" was intoxicating. An instant later he delivered a firm thrust directly between her shoulder blades, and the dive of otterlike grace became the sprawl of a slaughtered ostrich.

He surfaced beside her, laughing. "Oh!" she spluttered, full of delighted outrage, struggling to tone down the results and failing badly. "You absolute brute! You *chump*!"

Still chuckling, he extended a long, sinewy arm like a water polo player and palmed her entire cranium, giving her an added dunk for good measure. "There, now," he said as she surfaced, gasping, "ladies first—bapto-baptizo."

"You're *insane*," she spluttered, "an absolute kook!"

"That's from the ancient Greek," he said, "—means completely submerge."

"Oh, really! All right, we'll see who gets submerged this time." She seized his wrists, making a wild grab for his shoulders, his head, climbing, trying to force him under with the weight of her entire body. "I'll bapto-baptizo you!"

"You can't," he laughed, "you don't have the authority." They struggled momentarily, but he was far too strong. "Feisty little customer, aren't you?"

"Darned right!" By now he had broken free, and she pursued him to the opposite end of the pool where they staged an undeclared truce, sitting together up to their necks in the shallows and lightly treading with their hands to maintain balance. The stars in the watery surface were shooting and exploding jubilantly.

Marilyn slicked the hair back from her eyes, ran one hand over her face. "Wow, this is grand!"

"*Si—magnifico*!" His expression was fondly indulgent. "And just think, you were the first one to grace these waters, with your own lovely form."

"Oh, yes—sure, aha." He hadn't lost any of his talent for flattery; that was obvious. For the next half hour they paddled about, enjoying the right to be childlike, and once she dived, this time truly with otterlike grace, gliding along the floor of the pool to its deepest point, feeling the pressure in her ears and sinuses. Momentarily, she traced the metal drain with her fingertips, not knowing why, almost as though trying to tempt fate. The water there, ten feet down, was black like dye, and despite its slightly foreboding quality also seemed to possess a strange drawing power. Then, arching her back, she pivoted upward and shot to the surface with a single stroke.

The night had become colder as they left the pool, even more aromatic, the breeze cascading across her wet skin strongly enough to make her teeth click. In consequence, they topped off their swim back at the condos in the fizzing warmth of a Jacuzzi. Then they went inside, dried and changed, sank back into a wonderfully soft and cushiony couch, gazing across an open balcony into the night. A few miles to the south a tiny scattering of lights flickered like fireflies caught in a net, erratically marking the streets of Huntsville. Beyond, very rarely, the headlights of a car traced the fringes of Pine View Reservoir.

For a time they talked of Lon's mother again, and the more they talked the more her compassion welled, the more convinced she became that her decision to join him there at that remote hour had not simply been an impulsive breaching of her resolve. At last they fell asleep, heads resting upon each other's shoulders, innocent as children.

When she awakened it was six o'clock, and the first rays of sunlight were caressing the valley below.

Eight

"Mom," she said a bit irritably, "nothing bad *happened*, believe me. Nothing the least bit sinister—okay?"

They were sitting at the breakfast table, and Marilyn had phoned work telling them she'd be a couple of hours late. They owed her some extra anyway for time beyond the call of duty, strictly because she loved her job and wanted to justify the growing esteem of her employers and colleagues. She was in their eyes indeed the golden-haired girl. And perhaps, ironically, for that same reason she was becoming all the more defensive regarding any criticism from her family.

"All I said, sweetheart," Maria replied rather pointedly, "was that you arrived home at a pretty late hour. Isn't that a reasonable observation?"

"The hour was so obvious a *fact*," Marilyn countered, "that it's really not necessary to mention it."

"All right," her mother said calmly. "Let's pretend I never did and just go on from there. Oatmeal, Wheaties, or cornflakes?"

"I'm sorry, Mom," she said after a few moments. "I didn't mean to sound so defensive. It's just that I'm twenty-five years old now and . . ."

"I understand," her mother replied gently. "It's your own business." She set a plate of buttered toast on the table and a newly opened jar of grape jelly, her daughter's favorite kind. "If you ever want to talk about anything, I'm always here—okay? If you don't, that's definitely your business."

Herman, one of their cats, blinked at them contentedly from his morning-sun spot on the outside windowsill. Black with white chest and paws, a nick and slight bare spot on one ear. Moments later, he was joined by Munster, a tabby-Angora cross, fur standing on end like a cartoon version of Garfield with his tail in a light socket. He was, in fact, as wild as he looked, never allowing anyone within twenty feet.

Marilyn watched the cats without quite seeing them. "Mom?"

she said and angled her mother a glance that was slightly haunted. "Maybe I'm not so grown-up after all. And, well . . . guess I do want to talk because right now I'm a pretty mixed-up kid."

Maria's hand caressed her shoulder. "All right, hon, tell me about it."

Moments later the whole story of her memorable night before was spilling out. "And I really wouldn't have gone in the first place," she concluded, "if it hadn't been for his mom and how worried he is about her. It just, oh, seemed pretty cruel for him to be up there all alone under the circumstances."

Maria was sitting across from her now, watching with her searching emerald-colored eyes. "That's one of your finest qualities," she said, "your empathy and compassion. It's just that sometimes I worry about people who might exploit it."

Their oatmeal was getting cold, but it didn't matter. "You think maybe that's what was happening last night?"

For a moment her mother's gaze drifted through the window and wandered off into the distance. "I don't know," she said eventually. "Not that I think he got you to do anything, well, bad; you know I believe you. It's just that we're *all* pretty vulnerable under such circumstances. Believe it or not, I'd be myself. But right now . . ." She shifted, frowning. "I'm even more concerned about the way an experience like that can play havoc with a person's morale."

"Right now," Marilyn said, "my morale's higher than it's been for about three weeks." Her expression, however, was a little uncertain.

Maria nodded. "I can see that, darling, and in a way I'm happy. But frankly, I'm fearful as to where it's all leading. I mean, what's your expectation?" The frown returned. "It's just that the whole thing was *so* idyllic, everything sort of falling into . . " She shrugged. "And *so* romantic—the red star on the mountain!"

"Maybe he's a Russian agent in disguise." Marilyn laughed.

"What?" Her mother looked bemused.

"Oh, I'm just being dumb," Marilyn replied. "*Red star*—get it?"

Maria laughed, wincing. "I'm just not with it, am I? You're way ahead of me."

"Actually, we got the red star idea from Kelly and Shannon," Marilyn reminded her. "Remember how they used to say Mars was their love star, even if Mars *is* the god of war?" Maria nodded, smiling a mother's smile.

"But, Mom, he was just so real and fun. I know we shouldn't have been alone in the condo like that, but it . . . Anyway, we didn't do a single thing we shouldn't have. And he didn't try to commit me to anything. He was just really neat. Great, in fact!"

"I'm sure he can be," her mother acknowledged. One eyebrow arched very faintly.

"What really got to me, though, was the last thing he said when we left this morning."

"What was that?"

"He just said," she began and struggled with her voice for a moment. " 'I know I don't deserve you, not right now—but just remember, repentance is possible, even for worse sinners than I am.' "

"It's hard to argue with something like that, isn't it?" her mother said after a moment.

Marilyn nodded, eyes glistening. The cats had left their lair in the window, attracted by a lilac bush full of sparrows beside the garage. "So what should I do? Just tell him, 'That's tough'? 'You've had your big chance, sonny, and you blew it'?"

"I honestly don't know," Maria said cautiously. "That's something we'd better pray hard about." She sighed. "It's just that I don't want to see you get caught up in it all again. At least, without really *knowing* he's definitely made a permanent change. After all, that's what he already assured you once before, right?"

"Well, he didn't actually say, 'I've repented,' not in so many words."

"But didn't he say—didn't he promise you solemnly—that he was going to change, that there'd be no more playing around? And in reality, he didn't have the slightest intention of doing it."

"I guess that's right." The words came grudgingly.

"You know it's right," her mother insisted.

Marilyn sighed. "Maybe he did try, I don't know," she said, realizing that it was a feeble argument.

"But if he did, and it hardly looks likely from all you've told me, it was certainly pretty halfhearted at best. Practically overnight he was back to his old tricks again."

For that she had no reply. Instead, she merely sat there feeling increasingly hostile toward her mother for being so irrefutable. "Looks like a kind of catch-22," she murmured at last. "I really can't become involved with him unless he changes, and yet I can't know if he does change unless I become involved with him."

Maria reached for a slender glass of orange juice, barely sipped, her lowered lids exposing thick, dark lashes exactly like her daughter's. Her hair, once gold, was now ash and silver. "I'm not so sure about that," she said. "You have contacts—people here and there who have a fairly good idea where Lon is and what he's up to."

"You mean have a spy system?" she asked a bit cynically.

"If you want to call it that, but that's not exactly how I'd characterize it. Seems to me there's a difference in people sneaking around, eavesdropping, peering through windows and so on, and . . . oh, just those who by the very nature of their association with Lon are willing to honestly tell you what's happening."

"But how many will honestly tell me?"

"I don't know," Maria admitted, "but there are ways of finding out."

"And you don't think I should see him at all until I can collect enough witnesses that tell me he's being a good boy now?"

Her mother sighed. Clearly, the challenges of parenthood were sometimes heavy. "Look, hon," she said, "I'm not trying to engage you in an argument—or even tell you what to do. You're twenty-five years old, and—"

"Don't I know it," Marilyn said.

"And I just want to help, to be your mom and your friend too, okay?"

Marilyn looked contrite. "I know, Mom. You're so great. It's just that the whole thing is sort of coming back on me, and last night I started to see what it might really be like, if only I knew . . ."

"Maybe . . . ," her mother began and hesitated.

"Maybe, what?"

"Well, I don't know—if I felt there was some way you could just date him, say once every week or two, but also see lots of other nice young men. Really circulate, even if all of them aren't that thrilling."

Somehow with each sentence her mother spoke Marilyn found herself vacillating between appreciation and irritation. Again she felt the latter, knowing that it was irrational, a conditioned younger-generation reaction to phrases like "nice young men." Make it read "nerds" instead. Marilyn closed her eyes. "Mom," she replied, "that's what everybody says—even Kelly and Shannon, back before I ever started dating Lon, in fact. Get out and circulate—and I do, but it just isn't that easy a lot of the time. The minute you start going out with one guy to any extent . . ." She took a gulp of her juice, accidentally got a bit into her windpipe, and had an attack of dry, wheezing little coughs that made her eyes water. "The minute you do, it's as if he's staked his claim. Everybody starts thinking you're private territory even when you're not all that excited about it."

"I know," her mother commiserated, "and I really think it's a kind of stupid straitjacket kids have inflicted upon themselves these days." She paused, frowning. "How did it all begin?"

"Search me," Marilyn replied, feeling and sounding downright petulant. "*I* sure didn't invent it. But I'll tell you something even stupider, and it's been around forever."

"What's that?"

"It's the old tradition that the man gets to do all the asking—for dating, marriage—the whole thing. The guy has all the options, all the mobility. The girl sits around like Little Miss Muffet or somebody, tends to her knitting, and hopes. Who invented that? Where's the logic in it? The *justice*?"

"I think maybe I can relate to that one," Maria said, and the strength of her understatement suddenly made Marilyn feel guilty. Her mother had been a widow for nearly ten years, and she was still a highly attractive, vibrant kind of woman. It was just possible that she too might enjoy some male company from time to time.

"Maybe you should come down and live in Ogden, Mom, or go to Salt Lake with Aunt Donna; she's sure asked you enough times. You're a beautiful lady, but you ought to have more visibility, not be hidden away up here in the Valley teaching at some isolated little middle school the rest of your days."

Maria's smile was both poignant and mischievous. "*Circulate*?"

Her daughter laughed, tossed her head in acknowledgement. "Very good, Mom, touché!" Then, after a second or two, becoming more serious: "*Nevertheless*, I still think maybe . . ."

"No," Maria said mildly and shook her head. "I belong here." The rest remained unstated, but it was all there very clearly, especially in the resigned, somewhat dreamy quality of her gaze. The people, the Valley, their home on the shore, the sense of closeness to her husband—gone, yet somehow present—Kelly and Shannon next door, her grandson, friends and neighbors like the patriarch Elijah "Lije" Marriott, Bishop Alma Belnap and his wife Vorn . . . her teaching, even though retirement was not so far away.

"I wonder where it all began," Marilyn murmured. "The man having all the options, I mean. But I doubt very much that it was a woman's idea." She finished her juice without further mishap. A few boats were droning out on the water, and the wake from one of them was spilling out like an immense white horse tail in the wind. "Maybe it began with Adam and Eve."

"As I recall," her mother replied and smiled, "that was what you'd call an arranged marriage. And even though they had their trials, it seems to have been a pretty nice arrangement."

Marilyn laughed. "Too bad all of us can't have it that good."

Nine

"Just hang loose," Janie said. "All your neck cords are standing out like piano wires. You're practically gritting your teeth." Janie was running easily beside her, muscles fluid and nicely synchronized. She talked effortlessly as if they were merely walking.

"I'm trying," Marilyn replied, "but I just don't feel right."

"Well, hang in for a while," her friend advised. "Just sort of sprawl along, read the old bod, and see what happens."

"Yeah, I'll do that, see what happens . . . you go ahead and win this thing." She was trying hard to keep from panting. "Don't hamstring yourself on account of me." The asphalt road leading toward Nordic Valley along the northern arm of Pine View Reservoir was blue-black like the feathers of a magpie except for a bright new yellow line running down the center. Heat waves simmered two hundred yards ahead where the road dipped and faded into tantalizing little mirages as if small lakes had arisen from the surrounding pastures and brimmed over.

Several runners were winnowing their way through those mirages, stringing out a little, and there were others farther still, now beyond the range of vision, even though Marilyn knew they were less than halfway into their seven-mile Valley Loop Run. A so-called "mini-marathon," although it didn't feel so mini at the time.

"No, let's stick together," Janie was telling her. "After all, this is only our practice run for the Big Tri, anyway." Obviously, she considered her final words a clever double entendre, in view of the number of times she had repeated them the past week—*Tri* for triathlon blending with *Try* as an important attempt or endeavor. At the moment, though, Marilyn found it a bit irritating and depressing. It also filled her with foreboding. She wasn't at all sure she wanted such a challenge in light of everything else she was facing.

"Jan . . . ," Marilyn said. She was definitely panting now, hadn't ever found her second wind, and the yellow sweatband around her brow was already soaked. At the moment she was also envious of her friend's condition and talent, her eternal nonchalance and ebullience. Enough so that she almost added at that point, "Please, just don't do me any more favors." But she restrained herself. "Just go on ahead. I'll feel lots better if . . . if you're really in the running." That was what she actually said.

"But it really doesn't—"

"Jan, *please*! Just do your own thing—run your own race. I'll be *okay*!"

At last her friend got the message, and for a rare moment looked hurt. Then, just as promptly, she rebounded. "Okay, Lyn-Lyn. Just pace yourself so it feels right and don't overextend."

"Oh no, never!" Marilyn tried to strike a lighter tone, to be a better sport, despite a distinct sinking feeling. Her legs simply didn't have their normal resilience. They had felt shaky from the onset, and she had begun to perspire, more a cold sweat initially, before even completing her warmups and stretches preceding the race. Maybe, she decided, she was catching the flu, or possibly just the nervous upset of a first race. Who knew?

"Don't worry!" Jan called cheerily. She was easing ahead gradually, trying not to make it appear too obvious. "It's probably just premenstrual syndrome!" The thought failed to enthrall her. "Probably just need more vitamin B!" Jan's voice trailed off into the simmering distance.

Marilyn rolled her eyes in a dubious plea for deliverance. She could hear someone coming up behind, rapidly gaining ground, and it was bad enough to have people continually passing her without treating them to a diagnosis of her alleged female problems. PMS—Janie had attributed Marilyn's periodic feelings of depression to that condition on a number of occasions—long before her problems had begun with Lon Yeager.

Anyway, someone else was now passing her—a surprisingly hefty girl, in fact, dimpled and cratered with "cellulite." It was humiliating, to say the least. Then came a tall, bronzed girl, rawboned and angular, with a beaked nose—modified Mayan—moving with incredibly long, pneumatic strides.

Seconds later, still another runner, and for a moment Marilyn had the strange sensation that perhaps she was moving backwards. "Well, hi, Lyn!" the voice quacked. "How's the *girl*?" It gave her quite a start, partly because it was a male voice of sorts, and also because she had concluded a mile or so earlier that all the male runners had left her behind from the onset. Furthermore, one of the last persons she had wanted to encounter under such circumstances was Cuddles Eskelson. His real name was Bernard, but Gordie Yates, Don Dawson, and others of her pals had afflicted him with the name Cuddles because of his puppy-dog lovability and even more, perhaps, because of his tendency to constantly invade people's space. The name, corrupted at times to Curdles when he became a bit obnoxious, had stuck like all-purpose glue, but he didn't appear to mind, actually seemed to enjoy it.

Gawky, with a spray of carrot-colored hair that nearly covered his yellow-gray eyes, Cuddles was all knees and elbows—"the only guy I know," Kelly had once noted, "who can step on your foot and bloody your nose with his head just shaking hands."

"Well, Lyn Baby!" He had adopted Jan's special pet name for her, as had several other acquaintances by now. His voice was so loud and nasal it might have attracted wild ducks. "I didn't know *you* were in this race."

"I'm not so sure I am," she managed. It wasn't something that she had advertised, in any case, fearing from the onset that her entire performance would be less than spectacular.

"So how come I didn't see you in the starting lineup?" Cuddles demanded.

"Well . . . ," she panted, "thought maybe you did . . . guess I was sort of keeping a low profile." Partly, she failed to add, because she had fervently hoped to avoid just such a dialog, and because Cuddles for all his lovability was also gauche in the nth degree. Among other things, he invariably blurted the first thought that entered his mind no matter what the occasion. Worse still, he always did so as though shouting through a megaphone.

"Hear you've told lover boy to take a running jump."

"News travels fast," she said. It had been a month now.

"How long ago d'it happen?"

"Oh . . ." Marilyn sighed. She definitely did not want a visit with Cuddles at the moment, any of his inevitable prying, especially regarding her lovelorn love life. "Just a couple of minutes ago actually."

"What? *Minutes*!" Cuddles was twenty-two years old, but his voice frequently broke like that of a beginning adolescent, especially when he was taken by surprise.

"Right—Lon just drove by on his way to Snow King. And I . . ." She paused, out of breath. "And, well, I just tossed my ring at him through the open window."

"You gotta be kidding!" It was a squawk of amazement, so great it sounded more like abject terror. He was pacing along beside her, so close his wide-winging right elbow occasionally grazed her own, once almost caught her in the ribs. At any moment he would probably be tripping both of them, or at least treading upon her heel and pulling her shoe half off. It had happened before when he was trailing her down a hallway at Weber State, leaving a smudge on the heel of a new Easter pink pump and nearly crippling her for life.

Periodically he regarded her from beneath the wilting spray of orange hair, trying to capture a glance. "Lyn-Lyn . . . hey, I mean, that's incredible!"

Yes, truly, she thought, and Cuddles Eskelson had to be the most naive soul ever to enter this mortal probation.

"I mean you've *got* to be kidding!"

"Yes, Bernard," she said contritely, "I'm kidding." She waited to regulate her breathing. Any talk whatever was difficult under the circumstances. "I'm also about ready to bag this whole race. I really don't feel too great."

Cuddles glanced at her, alarmed. "Hey, you don't look too hot either. Sorta gray and blotchy like maybe you're gonna pass out."

Oh, thanks, Cuddles, she thought, thanks a whole bunch.

"Hey," he quacked, "maybe you'd better just walk. I'll try to flag down a car and—"

"No, it's okay, Cuddles," she insisted. "I've just . . . gotta stop talking and catch my breath." For a moment they paced together in what for Marilyn was relatively blissful silence. The slopes of Nordic Valley were looming ahead to the left, shading from light to piney green. "You just go ahead and run your own race. I'll walk if I have to." Despite her earlier comment about bagging it, she still wanted to finish the race, no matter how humbly.

"Well . . . ," he said dubiously, face full of concern. "If you're really sure."

"I'm sure—go for it."

"Well," he repeated. "Okay—you take care, Lyn Baby. I'll drop by after the race."

"Right," she managed, trying not to wince. "Thanks." All of Cuddles's visits lasted for about two hours and were largely monologues on his part regarding matters she had heard before. Then he too was moving ahead, ambling and slightly pigeon-toed, elbows akimbo, hands flopping double-jointedly. He was wearing a ragged yellow T-shirt with the "Road Runner" bird on the front shouting "Beep-beep!" and a pair of baby blue bermudas so large and baggy they extended past his knees and looked like rompers. For a moment she didn't know whether to laugh or cry.

The sun was growing hotter, and swallows were rising, dipping and wheeling on either side, occasionally emitting little chitters. At times they arched across her line of vision only two or three yards ahead, almost flauntingly, it seemed. The tiny mirages expanded, shimmering, beckoning her onward.

For an instant Marilyn closed her eyes and opened them, blinking rapidly like a driver who had almost gone to sleep at the wheel. Hard to believe she was actually unconditioned. She had been working out aerobically, swimming and jogging greater and greater distances, and she hadn't started out too fast, simply eased into it, feeling her way. No, something negative was at work—maybe the flu, maybe the recent sleepless nights fraught with worry and indecision.

Lon Yeager had phoned several times since the Snow King episode, been to her office, and actually talked her into a late-night stroll on the golf course across from her Oak Hills apartment. What occurred then had left her in worse turmoil than ever.

"Guess you might call this kind of an anniversary," he had said. A nearly full moon was rising in the canyon eastward along the Ogden River, and she looked at him uncomprehendingly for a moment. "Exactly one month since you gave it back." Marilyn had failed to reply, merely averted her eyes, glancing down at the dark turf.

They were standing beside a great cottonwood much like those at her home in Huntsville, its leaves and trunk transforming to silver as the moon ascended. "Look," he said quietly, "I'm not trying to play any games . . . but it just seems like maybe this is the right time to reconsider." Still, she offered no reply, actually fearful of saying anything. "Hey, I can understand why you're scared to get involved again, and I sure don't blame you. I know what a lousy—"

And that loosened her tongue. "Don't keep saying it," she interjected a bit angrily. "What's happened has happened, but it doesn't do any good to just keep putting yourself down."

"Yeah, I guess you're right," he replied. "All's I'm asking is that you, oh . . ." He took a deep breath. "Sort of take it back in secret for a while. I mean, you don't even have to *tell* anybody or even wear the thing. Except, maybe, just once in a while when nobody else knows. To, well, just think and pray about it."

"Lon," she said and felt the strain almost as if a hand were tugging at her insides. "You're really putting me—"

"Hey," he said with infinite gentleness and took her even more gently by the shoulders. "I don't want to make things tough for you, okay? I just want you to take a look at it for a second—just one little look, that's all you have to do." Her eyes were still downcast, but she was awash with conflicting emotions. Would that be so terrible? Just one quick look?

"But why?" she implored. "What are you trying to prove?"

He sighed, and for a moment she was engulfed in compassion. "I don't exactly know, to tell you the truth. It's just this feeling that maybe it can tell us something. A crystal ball." He laughed nervously, once more, for an instant, the teenage kid with his defenses down.

Slowly, unwillingly, her gaze lifted, and there was the ring, affixed to the center of his little finger. A full carat that captured the moonlight, scintillating with a tiny inner fire, reflecting a mercury-colored sheen like the leaves overhead and the glowing surface of a nearby pond.

"Would you do me one more little favor?" he asked. "Just for ten seconds, put it on?" She stared at the ring half mesmerized, struggling to protest, but her vocal cords were too taut.

As he slipped the ring on her finger she had never felt anything more compelling or felt more as if she had been compromised—except within the embrace that followed. It lasted for a long time, absorbing all her resolve, and when at last she had forced herself to break away, they were both gasping and in tears.

Remembering it all now, jogging painfully along the hot July road, she felt hypnotized again, caught up in a strange trance that would not release her. The road with its shouting yellow line wound on and on, interminably, and the pain gathering in her side seemed to be spreading upward. "Wouldn't it be weird if I had a heart attack?" she thought. But then, how many healthy young women ever had heart attacks?

Ahead the swallows continued their acrobatics. Two white cabbage moths danced in little whirligigs, cavorted almost mockingly around a fence post. The pastures and the sky gyrated also, very slowly in opposite directions. The mirage ahead beckoned irresistibly, expanded suddenly and rose to her ankles, her knees . . . waist, her neck and head.

Then nothing.

Ten

"I still say we should get you down to the doctor for a thorough checkup," Maria said. Marilyn was lying on the couch in the front room of her Huntsville home, propped on pillows with a glass of lemonade in one hand. A rotating fan wafted coolness over her face, bruised chin and cheekbone, her arms, scraped elbow and knee. All her wounds had been lovingly cleansed by her mother and anointed with Neosporin, the elbow wrapped in gauze.

"Maybe so," she said, "but I'm just about positive it's nothing but the flu and a slight case of sunstroke or something."

"I sure hope so!" The voice was loud and adenoidal. "Like, I mean, I was *terrified*!" The voice broke, sounding more excited than terrified, almost delighted over the enormity of it all. Bernard "Cuddles" Eskelson was sitting across the room regarding her with a kind of dazed fascination. "I mean, I was *worried* about her all along, so every once in a while I kept glancing back over my shoulder—even turning around sometimes and running along backwards. I'm really good at that, by the way. I've actually done it for variety on numerous occasions!" The final words ascended in a strident falsetto as though Cuddles were impressed beyond all comprehension at his own phenomenal ability.

"That's really something," Kelly said. Seated at the foot of the couch next to his mother, he looked relaxed and languorous, a bit like a mountain lion. Marilyn flicked him a glance and saw that he had barely managed to keep a straight face. Only a little deepening of the laugh wrinkles, a coppery glint in the eye. Kelly had been the good-humored, at times long-suffering recipient of Cuddles's visits, on "numerous occasions," having become in many ways the young man's confidant and mentor. It was a true case of hero worship on Cuddles's part.

"But, I mean, all of a sudden I looked back from about like two hundred yards away, and she just wasn't there anymore. She just wasn't there!" He made a kind of snuffling sound, half laugh, half gasp. Sinus trouble plus hay fever. "Then I looked again, and saw this—well, just this little splotch of red lying there like a rag doll by the side of the road. So I started sprinting back the way I'd come, of course, and I mean sprinting! I'd probably have given those Olympic champions a good run for their money!" Again the laugh crinkles at the corners of Kelly's eyes. "I honestly think I *would* have, Kel. But by the time I arrived the good doctor was already on hand."

The "good doctor" was none other than close neighbor and long-time patriarch of the Ogden Valley Stake, Elijah H. Marriott, better known as Lije. Though not a doctor of medicine, Lije held a Ph.D. in biology, one obtained at about the age of seventy when, as he put it, "I was just a youngster." A one-time wrestling champion, he was a dedicated—some people thought fanatical—advocate of physical fitness. Now in his nineties, he still jogged or did his "road work" as he called it, and even participated in some of the local races. The old man was indeed a phenomenon, well known to the local population as a kind of living miracle.

It was therefore not strange that Lije Marriott had entered the Valley Loop Run that July day, just as he had done for several years, even though age and a gimpy leg had kept him at the back of the pack. Not only natural but fortunate from Marilyn's standpoint. Gradually as she had fallen behind, the old man was closing in, keeping an eye on her, suspecting that all was not well.

Marilyn was sprawled face down on the hot asphalt as he arrived, and Lije had halted abruptly, panting, sweat beading from the tip of his nose. Dropping to one knee, he had checked her breathing before scuttling about to seize her arms and heft her into the bordering cheat grass. Turning her face up, he had elevated her knees, restoring blood to her head. By then the first cars were stopping, and Cuddles had also arrived, greatly agitated and verging on hysteria.

Now, an hour later, having delivered Marilyn to her home, Lije Marriott returned to check his patient. The old man had been much like a grandfather or perhaps great-grandfather to Marilyn and Kelly all their lives, and now he hastened across the room with a stiff little trot, gave her a solicitous pat on the arm, and felt her brow. "You okay now, Honey Girl?" That had been one of his names for her from earliest recollection.

"Sure, Gramps," she replied. "Thanks to you and Cuddles."

"No thanks to me," Cuddles brayed. "I was so shook up, I about flipped out!"

The ancient patriarch regarded him for a moment with kindly amusement, then focused upon his patient again. "Well," he allowed philosophically, "I reckon you'll make it." His left eye was gentle, with a slightly drooping lid, and his right, though sunken, the socket somewhat scarred, was remarkably knowing, penetrating. "Color looks a lot better anyhow."

"Sure, everything's going to be fine," Marilyn said. "It's just that I feel like such a wimp."

"Why?" her mother asked. "For getting sick and passing out?"

Marilyn shrugged. "I don't know—just thought I could handle it better. Maybe it really *is* the flu. All night long I was in kind of a cold sweat, especially my head and face. I kept waking up every few minutes, and a couple of times my pillow was practically soaked."

"Sure sign," the old man asserted, "that something's a-coming on." At Maria's invitation he took a seat and joined the gathering. "Might be, too, you've got yourself a vitamin deficiency—E in partic'lar." Elijah Marriott was a great advocate of vitamins which he pronounced with a short *i* as in "it," and herbs, which he pronounced with an *h*. Simply a part of his rural background, the Lije mystique. "But when that starts a-happening," he continued, "the cold sweats or anything else gets out of kilter—headaches, dizziness, feisty belly, the runs . . . you need to listen to your body extra careful." He paused. "Specially when it comes to pumping iron, rasslin', road work, and the like."

"I thought I *was* listening," Marilyn said, "but, well, for a while I just decided I was babying myself and needed to get my second wind. And besides, I hated to chicken out, especially on my first race ever."

Lije nodded thoughtfully. "That part's commendable, the guts to hang tough, but by and by, you'll start to learn which kinds of problems are only there for a little mischief and which ones you got to treat respectful."

"That's a fact," Kelly said, "and it seems like everybody has to learn the hard way. I remember one time trying to run the four hundred meter when I had a pretty high temperature. Do or die for the good old team and all that." He grinned, showing a set of strong white teeth. "Barely staggered over the finish line and really laid myself low for the next week."

"Maybe *I* should start running the four hundred," Cuddles said. "I think I'm probably built even more for speed than for distance."

"Maybe so, Bernard," Kelly said and coughed a little, pressing his fist to his mouth. "You'd probably tear up the track."

By now Janie Johnson had also arrived, having taken third place in the women's division despite the handicap of hanging back so long to help her friend. Shannon, Kelly's wife, was there as well with their two-year-old son Moroni, better known as Rone.

Upon hearing the story she hastened to the couch, brown eyes full of alarm, intent on a loving embrace. "Better not get too close," Marilyn warned. "Seems I've come down with the falling sickness or something. Wouldn't want you catching it."

"Especially when she's catching for two," Kelly said, referring to her rounded midsection. Another baby would be arriving within the next few weeks.

"Right!" Marilyn said. "You too, Tiger!" she added, trying to stave off her nephew, Rone, who, at the moment, was bent on making a trampoline of her own midsection. A handsome child with the face and prospective build of his father, the large dark eyes and almost Hawaiian tan of his mother, Rone was a constant explosion of curiosity and energy. Sometimes a bit too much of a good thing.

"Well," Marilyn half sighed. "I've really learned how to grab attention, haven't I? Just fall on my face." Everyone laughed. Then, still keeping it light and breezy, she added, "And I seem to be getting pretty good at it lately." The laughter was more subdued, the glances more sympathetic.

Momentarily, there was an uncertain silence. She wondered wryly what they would think if they knew she had taken the ring back. Under duress, true, unwilling to wear it, yet not quite capable at the time of flinging it back in his face. Maybe the best thing would be to return it through one of Lon's buddies. Possibly, on the other hand, just possibly, he truly was turning his life around, and . . . Her thoughts were decimated by a loud quacking from Cuddles who had begun to talk energetically about a forthcoming trip to Lake Powell with some of those present and certain other friends, members of El Groupo, as it was sometimes called. Cuddles was, in fact, quite the arranger—a desirable talent in many respects, although she also wondered whether without it he might be a loner, almost excluded.

But the ring was there in the back of her drawer in the Canyon Cove apartment—ready, it seemed, to burn a hole in something, more like radioactive cobalt than a diamond.

Eleven

Their little caravan had arrived at Bullfrog Marina on Lake Powell as darkness was settling, and by the time they had reached the secluded cove near Hole in the Rock it was impossible to see without flashlights. Weary after the lengthy ride from Ogden, they grabbed their sleeping bags and bedded down here and there, at the first convenient spot, throughout the houseboat.

It was well after midnight when Marilyn awakened on the boat's large, flat roof. A three-quarter moon was swelling above the steep face of the canyon, gradually brimming over and swatching the inky waters with quicksilver. The members of El Groupo were all on hand, thanks to Cuddles's arrangementship—her roommates Janie Johnson and Carla Bonner lying next to her along with another friend, Tami Oda, who lived in the little town of Sunset southwest of Ogden. Scattered about below were Cuddles, Gordie Yates, Don Dawson, Jake "The Turk" Broadhead, and Kelly and Shannon. The latter two occupied the boat's little sleeping cabin and were along, in part, as chaperones even though none of those present used the word or quite admitted it.

Lying there beside her friends, Marilyn heard snores ascending from below. She felt the warm exhalations of a mid-July night, sensed the reluctant languishing of temperatures that had welled during the afternoon to more than one hundred degrees. It was her first time at Powell, an immense meandering lake with its endless and erratically proliferating inlets there in the southeastern reaches of Utah. Fortunately she had recovered quickly from her earlier illness and was definitely ready for some fun and relaxation. Anything especially that would divert her thoughts from one Lon Yeager.

Gradually, there in the darkness, she began to distinguish one set of snores from another, the snuffling gasps of Cuddles Eskelson, the deep, bearlike rumbles of Turk Broadhead, the two ascending alternately in an enchanting duet. The Turk himself seemed as unlikely a member of their little gathering as might be found. Built like a buffalo, he was nearly bald. The scant rim of hair remaining, in fact, he had shaved with a kind of macho disdain, counterbalancing what he lacked on top with eyebrows that seemed to move like thick black caterpillars. In addition, he had a slightly crossed right eye and a bristling mustache that curled on the ends.

Like Cuddles, Turk Broadhead had been drawn to the group in part through his admiration for Kelly, who had once bested him during a fracas outside the Trapper's Rendezvous in Ogden Canyon. Brutelike power had succumbed to black belt–level science in the martial arts. Unlike others in the gathering, all active Mormons, The Turk was a reformed alcoholic despite being a rather outspoken atheist. Thirty-five years old, he had been divorced for several years, a situation he rarely discussed except in cynical jest. Despite all this, however, he had found in the group a certain kinship, a pleasant alternative to the boozing and brawling ways of his past. They were people who helped keep him on the wagon, especially on occasions like the present when the tendency to "celebrate" became rather tempting. And despite his apparent lack of religion, the members of El Groupo, had come to regard him as something of a Father Confessor who would listen to their problems without judgment, offering at times amusingly earthy but practical advice. Above all, perhaps, he was a colorful, entertaining figure who gave them quite a "kick."

Yes . . . Marilyn smiled faintly at the rising moon. An interesting collection of bedfellows, united most of all by their sense of matrimonial aloneness. Excepting, of course, Kelly and Shannon, and they too had been there. Nearly all of them except Cuddles dated with varying degrees of frequency, but all of them as well felt a bit adrift, bleakly comforted at times by the awareness that they were not alone in their aloneness, part of a growing throng that didn't quite know what to do with itself.

Such thoughts passed steadily, rather wistfully, through her mind as the moonlight flooded the water more brightly, ascended the nearby canyon walls and gradually illumined the quiet boat, the somnolent figures beside her. What, she wondered, were they dreaming? Wouldn't it be fascinating, she told herself, if one could tune in on the dreams of others, simply push a button with the dreamer's number like the switching of channels on TV. Or better still, simply blend dreams. She smiled very faintly, sadly. In a way, perhaps, that was what they were doing.

Gradually she drifted off, cheek pressed against her pillow, and was carried into strange dreams of her own. Somewhere along the way there was a fire in her apartment, one that seemed to have ignited in the drawer where the ring was . . . and suddenly she was unable to find her way out of the building despite the frantic shouts and cries of her friends. And the heat—the heat was becoming unbearable.

She awakened in the brilliant morning sunlight, a blast of brilliance that was already invading her nylon sleeping bag almost scorchingly. Smoke from burning grease and maybe a blackened pancake was wafting up through the kitchen vent, and voices were shouting, "Go ahead, jump!" At the same moment Carla Bonner—already clad in her strawberry-colored swimsuit and standing only ten feet away on the houseboat roof—gave a wild leap and landed with a loud splunge in the water below. Simultaneously, from the base of the cliffs, fifty yards above, Gordie, Dawson, and Kelly began racing downward through the deep white sand. The slope descended steeply, forty-five degrees or more, but they plunged and leaped mightily, whooping and laughing, to hit the water in wild dives.

The first of their three days at Powell was underway.

Twelve

That was how it began in one sense; in another, it began for Marilyn R. Cannon with the words "Hit it!"—her own voice shouting as though of its own volition. Balanced there in the shallows of their private cove on one foot, the other foot gripped securely in its rubber encasement on the water ski, she heard the motor launch rev with a burbling grumble. Then it was taking off, the tow rope whipping up taut from the water, the wooden handle in her clenched fists wrenching, tugging at her arm sockets and threatening to tear free of her fingertips. It began in full as she shot forward, deftly catching her balance when the ski slalomed for an instant, plowing a furrow in the turquoise liquid, then steadied on the surface as she took command.

It was her favorite outdoor sport, with the possible exception of snow skiing, and it was one she performed with grace and confidence, with definite pride. She had begun water skiing, in fact, at about age ten with the old family outboard on Pine View, knowing even in those first moments of knee-wobbling terror that few people were fortunate enough to launch on the water in such beautiful surroundings and from their own backyard. The boat towing her now, however, was an impressive one with a hold large enough to sleep four people, a brightly chromed rail, and seemingly limitless power. Its owner and captain Jake "The Turk" Broadhead cast a glance over his shoulder, grinning savagely, exposing the slot from a missing eyetooth. He wore a red bandanna for a headband, the classic pirate of old, sole to crown. That was another reason The Turk sought communion with El Groupo: clearly, he enjoyed an amused and admiring audience, a convivial crew to go with his ship.

Kelly and Shannon were seated opposite each other in the stern, Shannon's auburn hair billowing on the wind, Kelly sighting in with his new video camera and recording it all for decades to come. Automatically, Marilyn became even more graceful and versatile. As the boat swung in a huge fishhook she began an orbit of her own that gyrated her across the wake with sudden acceleration by the power of centrifugal force. She was now skimming the surface like a bird, and at one point as the speed reached its maximum she was sheening along almost parallel to the boat. For an instant she saw the face of Gordie Boy, his kinky, brindle-colored hair in a kind of modified Afro, dark shades a bit Hollywood. Somehow, especially with his wriggling, pencil-line mustache, he had never quite looked the part of a returned missionary, but he was essentially true to it.

Braking against the oncoming boat wash, she slowed abruptly, leaning back on the ski and raising the tip a foot or more above the surface. Then she headed boldly into the wake where the water frothed up white, weaving back and forth between the crests, dancing like a dragonfly. She could see the fluttering of a yellow flag in the wind, and the constant flowing of Shannon's hair, sometimes sweeping across her cheek and mouth, and the strong, white-toothed grin of her brother. "Way to go, Lyn Baby!" It was Cuddles, awkwardly giving her the raised victory fist. At the moment, life was euphoria in near crescendo, all her sorrows and frustrations obliterated. For a time, in fact, it was almost as if the boat and its inhabitants were in her control, responding to the slightest touch of a single long rein.

She relinquished her ski to others fifteen minutes later with reluctance despite the fact that there would be many more opportunities before their vacation was over. And, as it turned out, there were nice compensations—sitting beside her sister-in-law in the stern of the boat and feeling her love, aware of the life within her swelling abdomen, speculating on the age-old question—boy or girl. Shannon linking an arm with hers, leaning a head upon her shoulder and saying, "One of these days you're going to have babies of your own, Lyn—believe me, I *know* it!" The word *know* had been uttered with the kind of devotion and conviction that could hardly be disputed, no matter how faltering her own faith in that particular might be at that moment. "But until then . . . well, always, but especially till then, will you really make these kids of ours . . ." She caught herself and laughed. "I'm talking as if the second one's already born!"

Marilyn laughed too. "Just about is, from the looks of things. I think you're pretty brave coming on this trip under the circumstances."

Shannon rolled her eyes. "Dumb! That's probably a more accurate word. But you know what I'm saying? Will you make them *yours* too?" It was a beautiful face, heart-shaped, the brows like raven's wings, the eyes and pupils very large and dark. The spirit gazing out and the smile, highly empathic.

"Sure," Marilyn said. "And my brother's right—you really are quite an angel." It seemed an odd moment and place to be exchanging such intimacies, there in the roaring stern of the boat, buffeted by the wind, her brother cavorting intrepidly on the water behind them. She could see the blaze orange trunks, the muscles tanned and glistening. Yet somehow, the whole experience seemed right, almost inevitable. It was one of those times she would always remember even in the forgetfulness of old age.

It stayed with her throughout the remainder of that day and the one to follow, when it seemed that many of them, Marilyn and Jan especially, could never get enough of the water. The two of them had begun the following morning while the canyons and coves were slumbering in shadow, swimming half a mile along the shoreline and back. It was a part of their continued training for the "Big Tri," but also for the sheer joy of it, because the great lake, now dark and mysterious in tones of moss and ivy, would not be denied. Even at that early hour it had been a perfect temperature, and as they returned the final hundred yards or so the sun was barely appearing in a bright corona behind a rugged vault of cliffs near the houseboat, rimming up magical and fierce like a cauldron of molten steel on the verge of flowing over.

As they neared the boat, Cuddles—in another pair of rompers, pastel pink this time—dived from the upper deck—sprawled, actually—and landed with a terrible belly flopper. Even so, he seemed undaunted, swimming to meet them with remarkable vigor, flinging his arms forward mechanically and slapping the water loudly with each stroke. Meanwhile, his legs bent at the knees, thrashing a bit like the rotating wheel of an old-time paddleboat. Moments later, had they not been watchful, fully anticipating just such a possibility, Cuddles would likely have collided with them head-on. "Well, well, well! Lyn Baby and Janie Girl!" he rejoiced. "Why didn't you wake me? We could have all gone together?"

They had paused beside the hull of Turk's motor launch, and Marilyn felt a pang of guilt. Cuddles *had* said something the night before about wanting to join them since he too was training for the Big Tri, but they had replied evasively, not eager to have a threesome, not eager for that much wallowing and quacking.

"Sorry, Bernard," Marilyn said, feeling even more guilty now because she sensed that a little white lie was surfacing before the words were out. "It's just that you were sleeping so soundly we hated to disturb you."

"Right," Jan said. "You were snoring away so peacefully it would have been a real crime."

"Was I snoring?" Cuddles asked. His sinuses were so swollen the words emerged in bleats.

"Snoring?" Janie offered up one of her special turkey chortles. "We were all about ready to crowd inside the boat, thought a thunderstorm was coming."

"Aw, come off it!" Cuddles had also laughed, but his eyes were still credulous. "It wasn't *that* bad!"

But the lake had continued to beckon them—far out in the depths where even at the sun's zenith it remained navy blue and unfathomable . . . among the grottos and caverns darker still and ominous beneath the cliffs, and in shallow inlets with their clumps of willow, burning quarter-moon beaches of white sand where the water was pastel green, darting with fish, warm and benign like the enchantment of a dream.

"Hey, Marilyn!" The Turk bellowed. "Come get some of this grub before these chowhounds hog it all!" She glided up through the shallows in a swimsuit the color of dandelions, waded ashore glistening, fingering the dripping hair back from her brow.

"Wow!" she gasped, "I've never experienced anything like it. Can't get enough of this water!"

Gordie Boy Yates tossed a towel her way, yuk-yukking amusement, Adam's apple bobbling. "Girl's hooked for sure." They were all sitting or sprawled there in the sand in an exotic little bay, joking about how she'd gone water-crazy.

"Lyn-Lyn," Donald Dawson said admiringly. His thick-lensed glasses flashed prismatically. "You shoulda been a mermaid." He had just bitten hugely from a corned beef sandwich containing an entire dill pickle. The words were somewhat garbled.

"What?" Turk grumbled, "and sacrifice them laigs for a fish tail?" Laughing, she flung the towel in his face just as he was preparing to drain the last from a can of Mountain Dew—the nearest he ever came to satisfying his own addiction these days.

Thirteen

That same afternoon they journeyed southwest in The Turk's motor launch for more than an hour, all the way from their houseboat near Hole in the Rock to Glen Canyon Dam, a mighty concrete gate thrusting back the Colorado River to form the sprawling, eighty-mile lake. On their return they stopped at Rainbow Bridge to gaze in literal awe at one of the West's "greatest natural wonders"—a cliché perpetuated in numerous articles and travel folders, yet undeniably true.

Standing there beneath that monstrous stone archway, Marilyn felt as well as saw the ribs of deep purple, the browns, the muted, faintly burning spans of red blending to orange. And she could hear from somewhere, perhaps only the universe of her own mind, the windblown sands that had formed and crafted it throughout the hisses and whispers of untold millennia. She shook her head incredulously and glanced at the others—Gordie Yates, who had removed his amber-colored shades and was squinting with one eye nearly closed, almost painfully it seemed; Cuddles Eskelson, his plain and slightly pulpy face vacant with wonderment or stupefaction; Kelly, squatting beside a mound of rock, grimacing with concentration, trying to focus the wide-angle lens of his camera and capture as much as possible. Moments later, in a somewhat lighter mood, he backed off to a different angle and with little coaxing induced Turk Broadhead to stand upon the same rock and raise his hands skyward like Atlas supporting the world—in this case, the Rainbow Bridge—thanks to photographic illusion. Then Gordie, Dawson, and Cuddles were getting into the same act.

Pausing there alone for a time after all the horseplay, Marilyn reflected upon history, wondering what the explorer John Wesley Powell must have thought upon first sighting that mighty arch, and also the first savages long, long before. In those days, until fairly recently in fact, only dry land had lain beneath. Now the bridge spanned a narrow estuary formed by the expanding lake. She returned to the present with a slight start, realizing that her brother and some of the others were engaged in lively conversation.

''I always wanted to do this,'' Kelly said, looking both thoughtful and mischievous. ''Swim beneath the big horseshoe.'' He bent over to remove a pair of frazzled, holey joggers, his only attire except for the orange swim trunks he had been wearing all day. His shoulders and neck, despite their tan, were becoming sunburned. Straightening up, he appraised the water, then lowered himself between two boulders to the brink and dived. Moments later he was followed by his pals Gordie and Dawson. ''Come on, ladies,'' Daws yelled. His face looked a bit denuded without its yellow-tinted aviator-goggle glasses, his nose larger and more curved, somewhat jointed in the center.

''Hey, you're on!'' Janie shrilled. ''Come on Lyn-Lyn!''

''We dive with the grace of otters,'' Marilyn laughed and entered the water just behind her friend. Simultaneously, she felt a momentary pang, remembering where she had last heard those words. Then they were all swimming, and only seconds later had begun their passage beneath the arch.

''Swim on your back,'' Kelly gargled, ''gotta see it as we go.'' Marilyn pivoted, following her brother's lead, face up, rotating her arms and shoulders in a graceful backstroke. Glancing upward, she saw the immense band of rock against a sky of stunning blue with mounting clouds of white that sprawled and enlarged even as she gazed.

Already Kelly and Janie had passed beneath, followed a short distance behind by Gordie Boy. ''Where y'all headed?'' Daws bellowed. Swimming was not his forte, and he trailed the others by several yards. For a moment there was no answer.

Kelly had emerged from the water, pulling himself up over a ledge of rock on the narrow shore across the inlet. ''Just a little old cliff dive!'' he shouted. ''For the sake of history and the viewing audience.'' A slender, precarious-looking trail snaked upward along a span of lichen-blackened cliffs beside the arch, and shortly he was making his way along it with remarkable agility. After only a moment of appraisal Janie followed, a bit more slowly but almost as effortlessly.

''Come on,'' she called cheerily, glancing back. ''Everybody dives!''

''Not on your life, girl!'' Dawson trumpeted. He was treading water, blinking and peering about myopically. ''Not from where Kelly boy's headed. I know that dude too well.''

"Well, I'm not really diving either," Jan confessed, "just a little old jump. Come on, guys, don't wimp out on us."

"I never wimped in!" Gordie countered and offered a nervous laugh like the snickering of a hyena. Even so, he was pulling himself up on the ledge, dripping, feeling for handholds and footholds. Dawson meanwhile was carrying on about being allergic to heights, explaining that he couldn't even see the water from up that high.

"Kel?" Across the waterway Shannon was half-poised with the video. She was wearing a white terry cloth cover-up, and her lips were parted in distress. "You're not going to dive from that high, hon!"

"Why not?" he answered. "I've dived from higher up at Causey." Marilyn had been there with him before—a reservoir several miles above Pine View toward Monte Cristo—and had seen him in action, but she questioned his assertion. None of his diving cliffs at Causey had ever seemed that high, possibly because she had never been so close. At Causey she had always been a hundred yards or more away across the narrow arm of reservoir. Like Dawson, she was "allergic to heights," and now she suffered a touch of vertigo. She was clinging to the rocky shore somewhat anxiously, and the expanding clouds above the canyon's rim made her slightly dizzy.

"But how do you know it's deep enough?" Shannon pleaded.

"That's right, Kel," Marilyn shouted, "it might—"

"It's deep enough, don't worry." He sounded a trifle amused and condescending. "I can tell from the color." Jan was beside him now, agreeing less loudly but confident enough.

"Got 'er ready?" Kelly called, referring to the video camera. His young wife's reply was dubious, ambiguous at best. "Okay?" he persisted. His smile was confident. "Okay . . . ," he repeated, poised and gauging the distance, "start shooting—here comes Johnny!" With that, he launched from the ledge in a perfect swan, his orange trunks tracing a flame against the cliff face, and for an instant Marilyn was reminded of divers at Acapulco who descended from incredible heights nearly three times that great. Then he was angling vertically, entering the water spearlike with a deep plunging sound, casting a white geyser. For several ominous seconds nothing else was visible. Then he surfaced halfway across the inlet, wearing the same grin, mischievous and triumphant, snorting like an otter.

Moments later Janie followed, leaping outward with a shrill squeal, holding her nose with one hand, the other thrust aloft, waving. Then she too had vanished beneath the surface, emerging a few seconds afterward with a gasp. Her face was glistening, never prettier, Marilyn thought, and like Kelly's it radiated triumph. "Oh, Lyn Baby!" she rejoiced. "You've just *got* to give it one try. You'll love it."

"Love it I won't," Marilyn protested, but her reply was drowned by further urgings and commands, from Gordie Yates along with certain traitors on the far side. Yates had now reached the ledge himself. He was wearing neon green bermudas, and his body looked wiry and simian almost as though made for clinging to rocks and precarious little niches.

"What is it?" someone yelled.

"It's Gollum, it's Gollum!" Kelly chuckled. He was breaststroking his way effortlessly toward the cliff once more, and Gordie offered a series of yuks, hamming it up, eyes bulging with mock horror almost like boiled egg halves.

"One for the money!" Cuddles brayed, safely ashore in his rompers. "Two for the show . . ." Gordie flexed his knees, rocking back and forth, one foot planted ahead of the other like a distance runner preparing for the gun. "Three to get ready, and four to gooohhhh!" The word rose and fell in an attenuated parabola along with his body, hands clawing the air, legs flailing as though pedaling a giant tricycle.

He whooped wildly all the way down and offered up another short one as he surfaced. "Yeah, man!" he enthused. "Very *invigorating*!" Everything was "very invigorating" with Yates. Once he had even described a highly effective sneak punch to his own belly in those terms. "Come on, Lyn Girl," he urged, rolling into a sidestroke. "Try it—great training."

"Great training for what?" she demanded.

"Same thing next time!"

"Come on, Lyn-Lyn," Janie urged. "We'll go together—it'll be an experience."

"Don't push her," Shannon called. "Let her do what she wants." For some reason that Marilyn failed to comprehend, those words more than the cajolery impelled her up from the water and onto the narrow trail. And with that single act she knew that she was committed.

"Should I try it?" She was looking at Kelly, her tone timorous, half pleading for a reprieve. If brother Kelly said no, not necessary, that was all the authority she needed. By now he was climbing the cliff again, and for a moment he looked back, their gazes blending —same color, same eyes. "Only if you want to, babe," he said, "not because somebody hassles you into it." Then he continued his climb. Jan and Gordie followed, and without quite realizing it, she felt herself drawn along after them, clutching fearfully at the cliff face, feeling its harshness, the sharp and sometimes brittle edges. This was definitely no fun at all, not a bit like swimming or waterskiing. And yet—the thought flitted batlike—how much fun were they her first try? The inquiry brought scant comfort.

Somehow she made it to the landing without looking down, sans all sense of context, knowing for certain that was the only way she could have managed it, yet knowing even more that she was letting herself in for a grim surprise. Her knees and arms were trembling as she reached the ledge and felt Kelly's hand on her elbow. "Don't look down too quick," he said, "just sort of ease into it."

But there was no way she could look slowly; you either looked or you didn't, and vision moved with the speed of light. Now she saw, and what she saw was paralyzing. By some sinister, utterly sadistic quirk of fate, the height had suddenly doubled itself. "Oh, we can't be on the same ledge you were on before," she gasped, fully believing it. "You guys tricked me."

Her brother, the fiend, laughed heartily. "No, Lyn Girl, no trick."

"Same one, Lyn Baby," Janie chortled—eternally the extrovert —and laughter had never sounded more inappropriate. For an instant Marilyn hated her. Jan was the one who had dragged her into this in the first place, pushed her into that stupid race earlier where she had fallen and . . . Her stomach knotted.

"There he goes!" She saw her brother's body arching outward in another swan dive, his flaring back and shoulders, the muscles starkly articulated, the blaze orange trunks like a warning flag, and she felt the sense of dissertion . . . then heard the splash a hundred miles below. Seconds later Janie was leaping again, followed by Yates, both clowning it up outrageously in the face of imminent disaster. It was simply too high, too awful, absolutely irrational. She definitely could not, would not do it.

Voices were calling from below, cajoling, encouraging, and from the opposite shore in another world, Shannon, her dearest friend, insisting that they "stop bugging her," that she shouldn't be forced into something like that. The cliff face below seemed to have acquired a bulge and grown darker. *Lichens,* she thought irrelevantly, *why all the lichens?* A shadow was passing across the sun. Suddenly her body seemed numb with cold. Her teeth were chattering.

"Go on, Honey Girl," Gordie quipped, "go for the gold! Do it!"

And then, legs become milk toast, in a near swoon, on the verge of retching and complete collapse, knowing that total ignominy was her sole alternative now, Marilyn R. Cannon made her suicidal leap. Her eyes were clenched, and there were no antics—merely the incredible, awesome unreality of her descent, drawn and quartered, an invisible grappling hook trailing her innards behind.

The water which had waited so placidly suddenly rose to meet her with a great ripping wallop, stinging the soles of her feet, crashing into her groin, armpits, the undersides of her arms, wrenching one elbow, surging into her sinuses. Only then did her eyes open to take in the swirling cone of light green, the froth and bubbles, white like tumbling snow that suddenly darkened and nearly vanished as she submerged more deeply. Then they were returning, welling and transforming again to blue-green as she surfaced in the sunlight, only a few feet beyond the shadow of the great stone arch.

Cheers were rising from the circle of friends there in the water around her and from across the little estuary. "Way to go, kid!" Gordie was treading the surface nearby, waggling his eyebrows wildly in a kind of maniacal approbation. "Very *invigorating*!" She could also see The Turk seated on a rocky outcropping, hands on both knees, furry as a bumble bee, looking like some pagan ruler, grinning and gap-toothed. And Cuddles. "You did it, girl," he quacked, "ya *did* it!"

"I'm alive," she gasped, "I'm actually alive!"

Fourteen

They built a large bonfire on the beach that night, roasted hot dogs, and sat in a semicircle along the sandy slope just above, laughing and reminiscing about the activities of the day. The fire cast its reflection into the quiet lagoon, steadily flickering snakes' tongues of yellow-orange within water the color of molasses.

At one point there was an unexpected lull in the conversation, the kidding and laughter. It persisted for some time until Cuddles at last exclaimed, apparently for want of anything better, "Well, here we all are!"

"Right on," Gordie said, "too bad we aren't all there."

"Speak for yourself, son," Tami Oda giggled. She was in many ways a Japanese version of Janie Johnson, slighter in build, face a bit more pixielike, but with the same lively cheeriness. Tami was a convert to the Church from Buddhism, but her parents, though staunch in their own religion, didn't seem to mind. Her father, in fact, often introduced her rather proudly as "my Mormon daughter" to friends and patrons of his flourishing Ogden noodle parlor.

"Yeah, here we are," Dawson affirmed. He had a talent for mimicry, and at the moment it was W. C. Fields. "The Matchless and Multifarious Society of Marvelous Mormon Misfits!"

"What, pray tell, brought that on?" Marilyn laughed.

"Who knows?" Kelly gave his special grin and lathered his hot dog with mustard and ketchup. "Who ever knows *what* will issue forth from the mouths of babes?" Kelly and Donald K. Dawson had been "close buds" from the time of their missionary days together in Japan several years earlier. It was an association that had been nurtured in part ever since by good-natured jibes.

Again the silence settled, and in the midst of it all Marilyn found herself reflecting on Dawson's observation. Despite their outlandishness, his words contained a measure of truth. Suddenly, in fact, it occurred to her that none of them except Kelly and Shannon quite seemed to belong anywhere. Cuddles, lovable like a stray puppy, but also gauche and klutzy beyond belief, accepted as a kind of mascot in the group yet without a truly intimate friend of his own anywhere. Somehow he was either too comical or too much the bore. Gordie, the eternal comedian but eternally, also, falling for girls slightly beyond his reach, those who refused to take him seriously even when he desperately wanted them to. Marilyn herself had been one of those girls, resisting Gordie's romantic overtures some years ago when he had first returned from his own mission a short time ahead of her brother. Reluctantly he had eventually accepted his only recourse, that of being her friend and confidant but nothing more.

The same had also held true for Dawson, who had also accepted the consolation prize of being her pal. Daws, however, had at one point been much closer to matrimony than Gordie ever had, though never with Marilyn. His affairs of the heart had taken the form of two girlfriends, each of whom had won his ardent devotion, had for a time appeared willing, and each of whom had gone her separate way hurt and slightly disgusted when he shilly-shallied too long. Now one of them was happily married and expecting, the other recently engaged.

For some reason the situation had struck Kelly and other of Dawson's buddies as amusing, and they had even given him a little ribbing. Fortunately, like Gordie, he had a sense of humor and considerable ability to laugh at himself. In this case, though, the laughter had been somewhat hollow. Keen-minded and even scholarly in some respects, especially concerning computers and related technology, Daws had nevertheless earned the reputation of being notoriously indecisive and something of a bungler.

Both Yates and Dawson had now reached the age, twenty-seven and twenty-eight respectively, at which they wanted greatly, even obsessively, to find the "right girl." Simultaneously they were both as Gordie sometimes put it, always "getting ready to commence to begin to make the big leap."

"Fat chance," Carla Bonner had once retorted. "You're just like all those other guys out there—a couple of devout cowards." Carla had been Marilyn's roommate at Canyon Cove in Ogden along with Janie Johnson for nearly a year now, and Marilyn knew only too well her penchant for sarcasm, one clearly augmented by the fact that she was divorced, bitter over it and over the nearly two dateless years that had followed. But it was true, Marilyn told herself. Daws and Gordie, like many others, had become increasingly leery of commitments, of disrupting the comfortable status quo to confront the obligations of marriage—especially one designed to last forever.

"Yeah, boys," Janie had chided, "when are you going to get it all together? There's a lot of great women out there just waiting and wondering."

"Right," The Turk had rumbled, "like little Janie J., for instance. Terrific catch for somebody with real smarts."

"Absolutely!" Janie chortled. "Just don't maim yourselves fighting over me."

That was also true, Marilyn had thought. Janie really *would* be a terrific catch—great little wife and mother.

At the very moment, in fact, there on the beach at Powell, Carla Bonner was quietly holding forth on the same general subject, more pointedly about her own marriage and divorce. Quietly, yes, though apparently not unwilling to be overheard by the others. "Ever since it happened," she was saying wryly, "I've felt like one of the outcasts of Poker Flat—like maybe I've come down with AIDS or something."

"It's not that way at the college ward, is it?" Tami asked.

Carla shrugged, looking bleak and slightly disdainful. "Oh, there's you guys—you're always great, but otherwise . . . well, I just don't feel like I belong anywhere, sometimes not even there. Ya *know*? People say, 'Hi, Carla—how ya doing?' " The *how ya doing* part contained a singsongy little inflection tinged with irony. "Or they say, 'What's happening?' and that's always a winner because it really doesn't mean a darned thing; a lot of them couldn't care less. I mean, they're about as sincere as store clerks and cashiers and people like that who say, 'Have a nice day,' and don't even look at you."

Kelly shifted, frowning. "But what do *you*—" he began.

Carla Bonner, however, didn't appear to hear him. "And so . . . ," she continued, "well, then I go back to my home ward once in a while. And the bishop—oh, he's a good man, and he tries to be friendly—but it always seems like he's got about a hundred other things to worry about."

"Probably does," Kelly said.

Carla frowned and looked slightly irritated. Her face was rather angular and narrow, a bit grayhoundish, Marilyn sometimes thought, with large, rather cold gray eyes. Her lips were thin and often petulant, but during the rare times that she truly smiled they could become very captivating, her whole countenance far more appealing. "He probably does," she agreed. "And it's not that anybody really wants to be mean, it's just that they all have their own little lives to lead, and that, well . . ." She shrugged. "It's sort of like the parting of the Red Sea, if you know what I mean."

Marilyn nodded. "*I* do," she said. "At least a little. It's not quite like a divorce, I realize. But just this past month since—"

Carla continued, however, scarcely seeming to hear her. "A couple of weeks ago I attended the Gospel Doctrine class in our home ward." She paused. "And the subject was eternal marriage, which is all right—great, in fact, if you could actually find somebody. But Brother—" She paused, apparently not wanting to implicate the man personally. "But the teacher just made it all sound so pat and simple—snap your fingers, one, two, three."

"And there's Mr. Right—*right*?" Janie interjected. "Riding straight your way out of the sunrise on his great white stallion."

"With a hearty 'Hi-yo, Silver,' " Gordie yukked.

"Well, just about. Just pray hard, be a good girl, and tend to your knitting, and pretty soon he'll come along—The One and Only."

"And you'll *know* without a shadow of a doubt—absolutely no question!" Marilyn said, catching more than she had expected of Carla's cynicism. Bitterness?

"But sometimes . . . ," Shannon said quietly, "it really happens. And just because . . ." She was low-keying it, fearful of sounding smug, Marilyn sensed immediately. "Well, just because it doesn't happen within a particular time frame, that doesn't prove it can't. That it never will happen, I mean."

"That's easy for you to say, Shan," Carla replied, "because you've got your man, and he's not only Mr. Right, he's Mr. Perfect."

"Hey now," Kelly laughed, "that's so true! That's what I keep telling her!" His face was suddenly a bit more red than it had been from the firelight, and for once, Marilyn realized, her brother's cool had been disrupted a little. Carla's tone, however, had not sounded as bitter in this case as honest. Honest envy.

"Yes," Shannon replied, "the person I'd literally been waiting for ever since I was about eight years old. But there were a couple of years . . ." She paused abruptly because of the catch in her voice. There was the faintest glistening in her eyes, and Marilyn wondered if anyone else had detected it aside from Kelly himself. She knew with near certainty, though, what the remainder of Shannon's sentence would have been—"a couple of years when I'd about given up all hope—when I thought for sure I'd blown it, ruined everything." A time, indeed, when she was in abject despair, literally determined to end it all.

"But that wasn't the only problem," Carla continued. "With that class, I mean. On top of everything else, he kept talking over and over about how terrible divorce is, and I walked out of there feeling like I was the world's worst sinner, like maybe I should have a big letter *A* stamped in the middle of my forehead or something."

There was a ripple of laughter; even Carla herself laughed and immediately looked prettier.

"But on the other hand, divorce *is* a problem," Jan said, "and—"

"Tell me about it." Carla's smile withered.

Jan refused to be deflected, however. "And how can we, well, ever really deal with it if we don't discuss—?"

"Right," Cuddles blurted, "but it's the way you deal with it. You can't make the people involved feel like they're bad news."

"At's a fact," The Turk grunted.

"Sometimes they got no choice," Cuddles continued, "like my older brother, for example—his wife just up and ran out on him one day without the slightest explanation." *Was it because he always talked like someone with a bullhorn?* Marilyn wondered. "I mean, he really treated her great and gave her a good allowance to run the home on, but for some crazy reason she just went ape."

"But the thing is . . ." Kelly shifted, frowning a little, tossed a paper plate into the fire. "Maybe your Sunday School teacher's a real nerd with the sensitivity of a road grader." The plate flared yellow, then blue, dying, curling in a blackened scroll. "Maybe, though, the guy's trying to do his very best and just needs a little friendly wising up like all the rest of us in a lot of things. Maybe, too, a lot of people wouldn't exactly take what he said as a personal put-down." He hesitated. "But, hey, don't get me wrong. *I'm* not putting you down either. I know it's not easy, and I can understand why you might have been feeling defensive."

"Oh, I was feeling defensive, all right. I *am* defensive." Without explanation, Carla Bonner rose abruptly. Her face was set, eyes glittering with tears as she turned and headed off down the darkened shoreline.

Fifteen

It was nearly two A.M. when the storm moved in, saturating the atmosphere with ozone and the lingering odor of campfire. Then came the first gusts of wind, bearing grains of sand, and after that the warm rain, forcing them all into the interior of the houseboat.

An hour or so later it cleared off, and Marilyn returned with her sleeping bag to the rooftop. Countless little cataracts and rivulets were descending along the cliff face above, and it was good to be alone for a while. It was good to hear the gurgle and splash of descending water, to breathe deeply of the cool night as little waves sloshed against the boat hull, washed, whispered, and fizzed along the shoreline. That and the fading mumble of distant thunder.

They would be leaving the next morning, and her mind was flowing with images, especially the ever-expanding panoramas of lake, rock, and sky during their long hours of boating and skiing. She saw again the sun-spangled water and frothing wakes, coves the color of turquoise and new moss, half-moon bays of white and burning sand. She saw tumbled talus slopes, occasional trails wisping precariously upward to the cliff dwellings of centuries past, some of which they had visited. Habitations arid and empty yet somehow permeated with a faint simmering from the long ago, a sense of spirit presence hovering there among the heat waves.

Again, she saw the endless canyons, caverns dark and forbidding, invaded by water of seemingly limitless depths, saw the shifting panoply of cliffs as though all had combined on some colossal treadmill powered by the rotation of the earth itself—temples and pagodas carved by the hand of time, expanses of granite, sandstone, limestone, shading from salmon and rust to yellow-grays, maroons blending in shadow to purple-black and lichen-colored deadness. Steadily, without volition, her mind expanded with sky and watery vastnesses, with the rocky expanses between—slabs, concavities, fissures, and fractures, all evolving in a menagerie of bizarre forms and faces: eagles and mastodons, cat heads, a school of deformed sharks, a benign pair of grandparents arm in arm, eternally waiting, tarantulas and segmented snakes, the leering profile of a devil with nose like a down-curved sickle, a band of sheep pursued forever by a coyote with only one front leg . . . on and on and on.

And then she was running upward once more with Jan and Kelly along stone hills that mounted above the water like gigantic, chaotically molded loaves of french bread. Running toward a vitally blue sky traced by a single, lonely raven. Drawn ever onward and higher, the water below filled with dancing sparklers, feeling the sun on her legs and shoulders, mildly burning in her scalp. The pull of nature had been exhilaratingly, almost frighteningly, magnetic, and for a time it seemed that she would never grow tired, her body resurrected and inexhaustible.

Everything simmered and vibrated, and the raven cawed. And from somewhere, the very atmosphere, she seemed to hear the bass notes of a great stringed instrument resonating in portentous affirmation. Only the distant cries of her friend and brother drew her back. "Lyn-Lyn!" Janie was calling like the last complaint of a gull. "Maarrrilyn!" the deeper tones from Kelly now, moving in concentric rings and echoing. "Where ya headed, girl?"

She had stopped with utmost reluctance, breathing deeply and rhythmically, glancing back over her shoulder. They were standing there together some three hundred yards down the rambling incline. Kelly was shading his eyes with one hand. "Who knows?" she called joyously. "Maybe to the moon!" *Moon . . . moonnn . . . mooonnnn . . .* The final word became attenuating echoes, continuing somewhere forever.

And at length another voice was calling her back, far away at first, or so it seemed. Then very close and gentle. "Lyn?" A moment of silence. "You okay?" The voice of her sister-in-law Shannon.

Marilyn stirred. "Yah." Her vocal cords were cloaked with sleep. "Great."

"I thought I heard you calling," Shannon said.

Marilyn struggled to one elbow, a bit disoriented. "Guess I was dreaming, just starting to. I was up there on top again, like the other day when I couldn't stop running." She yawned, blinking. "Hey, the storm's all gone—the moon's coming out."

"Right." Shannon began rolling out her bag. "I just had to come and be here in the open. I was getting claustrophobia." She laughed. "Half the people down there are snoring. Clear at the other end of the boat, but every time I begin to drift off it sounds like the motor's starting up."

"Ha!" Marilyn smiled. "I can practically feel the vibrations." Somewhere an owl called mutedly. "How's that, babe?" came the reply.

"It's getting claustrophobia too. Doing pushups or something right now, in fact." Shannon settled down on the sleeping bag beside her. "Just put your hand right here for a sec."

Marilyn reached out, and for a moment there was nothing but the roundness—that and a benign sense of life, a kind of radiation. Then from within, astonishingly near the surface, came a half tug, half flutter like the strike of a fish. Moments later, a pronounced thrust, as if to say, "I'm here—I exist!"

Marilyn gasped, barely suppressing a squeal. "Oh, hey—wow!"

"That's your next nephew or niece," Shannon laughed. "Just telling you hi."

"So magical," Marilyn said wonderingly, "so incredible. Where in this whole world is there a greater—" She was going to say *miracle,* but unexpectedly the word caught in her throat.

"Lyn?" For a time she could not trust herself to reply, only to breathe deeply and a bit quiveringly. "Did I say something wrong?" Shannon's voice contained its own fragility and a note of apprehension.

"No, no—not at all." Marilyn shook her head slowly, feeling her eyes moisten. "It's just that—"

Then Shannon was crying a little too. "I feel so happy, and yet . . . sometimes so guilty! Why should I have it so great, everything so ideal, when the rest of—" She gave a loud snuffle, half laughed half sobbed. They were both wiping their eyes and they bumped elbows in the process, offering up more of the same strange sounds. "But I do—I feel so guilty having it all so great. I mean, *you're* the one who should—"

"No, Shan, don't say it."

"But you've always led such a perfect—"

"No," Marilyn insisted, "don't even think it. You've got a brand new slate now. Everything's pure and new and clean." Reaching out, she gave Shannon's arm a squeeze and kind of little shake. "Everything." Then, sighing—"And besides, I'm a million light years from perfect."

For a while they lay there watching the moon rise, hearing the faint cannonading of thunder miles upon miles away along the cliffs and inlets. Marilyn was remembering now with sharp, electrical twinges of remorse a time in Shannon's life back in the days of Kelly's mission when she had made a bad mistake. Her closest friends, Marilyn included, had forsaken her, gossiping up a scandal. But Shannon had paid her debt in full, walked in a newness of life and forgiveness, and in the process Marilyn had done her own repenting, turned from betrayal to rescue. And yet, sometimes even now . . . "*No*, don't even think about it," she warned herself. "Don't envy her for having it so good; she deserves it, every single thing. *Don't envy anybody, ever.*"

The stars had emerged now in the storm's wake with great vividness and munificence, and the wavelets were gradually subsiding. "I keep thinking," Shannon said at last, "about Rainbow Bridge. About you and your giant leap."

"Me?" Marilyn laughed, partly in pain, mostly in relief. "First and last. I must have been crazy." She shook her head a little, smiling at the stars. "Guess I just had to prove I wasn't a complete chicken or something." The thunder offered a few last mumbles, leaving a glimmer of faint yellow-green against the horizon, little more than an optical illusion. "Which is actually pretty stupid when you think about it. I mean, if you do something because you're scared people might call you a wimp, that's exactly what you become. Right?"

"Yes, maybe so, but that's not why you did it," Shannon replied. "Not really."

"It isn't?"

"No, I don't think so." The words were slow and studious. "I think you wanted to find out something pretty important."

Marilyn laughed wryly. "Like just how far the water really is from forty-plus feet up—and how hard it is when you hit?"

"No," Shannon repeated. "I'm not sure what it was, but it was something important, and I was really praying for you." She gave an embarrassed little laugh. " 'Please, please, *please* . . . don't let anything bad happen!' " The silence itself seemed to be in delicate balance. " 'Please let it be a good experience.' "

Again Marilyn felt her eyes welling. The tear ducts seemed to be operating overtime these days, always primed. "You're an angel, Shan," she murmured, "a real angel."

"I'm a long way from that," Shannon said, "but I love ya, anyway." The streamlets and tiny waterfalls along the cliffs above had become mere trickles now, barely audible. "Have you ever thought," she mused, then paused for some time, "that things like that—your great big leap—are sort of like what happened when we came into this world?"

Marilyn felt herself smile again, warming with concurrence. "Maybe so. In fact, it must have been pretty scary, a mighty big leap." She paused. "Downright terrifying, the more you think about it."

"Really!" Shannon said. "Kel has this wild theory that maybe in order to get down here we had to go through one of those black holes out there in space, the ones astronomers are always talking about."

Marilyn laughed. "Wild." Her brother had quite an imagination, but often it was hard to tell whether he was kidding or serious. "No wonder a third of the host of heaven stayed behind!"

"Right! In fact, Kel has this idea that a lot of the scary things—the big challenges we force ourselves into down here—are probably symbolical, sort of a . . . well, what? a reenactment. Maybe reinforcement too."

Marilyn blinked. Sleep was beginning to absorb her. "Maybe so." Something to ponder, but the stars were melting now like part of a van Gogh painting.

"In fact, there's even more to it than that." The words were almost inaudible yet also compelling.

"Really?" Marilyn felt herself surfacing. "Like what?"

Shannon's laughter was gentle, empathic. "I'm not sure. Just something Lije told Kelly and me one time. He said to keep thinking about it and see if we could come up with an answer."

Sixteen

It was a Shogun eighteen-speed that normally sold for some six hundred dollars but which she had obtained for less than half that price, thanks to a special sale at Herman's and the fact that both Yates and Dawson worked there. Until recently she had done most of her cycling on a rather dilapidated ten-speed, a hand-me-down several years earlier from brother Kelly, but the new bike was a combined marvel of technological advancement and mechanical simplicity.

At the moment, in fact, she was taking her maiden voyage on the Shogun, continuing to train for the Golden Spike Triathlon coming up only a week hence. For a while, despite Janie Johnson's exhortations, she had almost abandoned the idea, mainly because of her traumatic downfall in the Ogden Valley race a short time earlier. Her experiences at Lake Powell, however, had changed things—the cliff jump, despite its terrors; her endless euphoria waterskiing and swimming; and certainly the running. Again she saw great stone hills mounding upward between the water and sky, and the afternoon when it seemed as if she could never stop running. What really would have happened if Kelly and Jan had not called her back? The thought was both enthralling and a little frightening.

In any event, all these things had changed her attitude, creating a different emotional response to the big challenge ahead, and it almost seemed that her athletic ability had improved. "Hey, girl," Jan had enthused, "you've really laid hold of something—you're a natural!" Now, at least, anticipation and positive attitude outweighed anxiety.

What she needed most at the moment was more experience with her new bike, and consequently she had taken the morning off from her job at Weber State. The Shogun was slightly psychedelic, deep green blending to purple-blue with a bright pink section near the pedals. It had durable, somewhat knobby tires for rugged trails and backcountry, a sturdy and reliable-looking frame, yet the entire machine was light enough to carry under her arm with one hand if necessary. The two of them had become simpatico immediately from the second she had first glimpsed it. Her only problem now was exactly how and when to apply the different gears.

She had left her apartment by the golf course in Canyon Cove at seven A.M. under a pearl gray overcast and was journeying the five miles or so to North Ogden Pass along Mountain Road, gliding steadily ahead beneath the narrow irrigation canal that wound along the base of Lewis Peak. Below were sloped orchards and pastures dotted with cattle, and westward far beyond lay the Great Salt Lake. The air had been purified by the night's rain, and there were narrow windows in the overcast through which came muted shafts of sunlight, tinting the water like pale gold foil.

It was a morning of reflection, nostalgia, and for a time she began thinking about the men in her life, some past and some present. At present she could see the face of her father, Frank L. Cannon—a successful and compassionate lawyer who had often failed to collect his legal fees or even present them to those suffering financial hardship. Former bishop of the Huntsville Ward, revered and loved by his congregation. Father and patriarch in the home—a sensitive, caring man who gave advice when it was needed but who listened even more. Tall, slightly gaunt and Lincolnesque, reminiscing eyes that emanated warmth, often a little mischief. Especially when she delighted or amused him. How healing his presence could have been the past few months! But he had been gone for a decade, life over at age fifty, thanks to a drunken driver who survived with only minor injuries.

She thought of Alma Belnap, bishop until recently of the Huntsville Ward, now stake president. Rangy and rawboned like her dad, but grizzled and thinning on top now, with a prominent nose that was hooked and slightly battered, Alma Belnap was truly a son of the soil. His eyes were rather small and close-set, reminding her of ripe chokecherries, amusingly mournful yet utterly guileless. A man with a rough exterior who had accepted his callings with a painful sense of inadequacy yet had succeeded beyond all expectation. Alma had come closer to being a second dad than anyone, both for Marilyn and Kelly.

A flock of starlings lofted across the road ahead, mingling wings, dipped in unison and rose again, sifting through a rank of poplars. A white cat half crouched, watching intently from the edge of a ditch bank, then turned back, vanishing into the weeds. She thought of the patriarch Elijah H. Marriott and wondered about his secret, the one of which Shannon had spoken only recently during their final night on Lake Powell. Why, why all the striving and challenge, anyway? The constant testing and question . . . when it would be so much more peaceful to relax and drift with the tide? And yet, she reminded herself, nothing living could simply drift with the tide forever.

Five minutes later she had left Mountain Road and was angling eastward toward the upper valley along North Ogden Pass. The sun had burned holes in the overcast and was dappling the road and rising slopes to her left with light and shadow. She could smell the faintly damp odor of sage, cheat grass, and of something Kelly called "horse-sweat plant." Something they had never been able to identify, but it was real and rather pleasant. It mingled with the other odors, calming her soul and for some reason inducing a growing sense of nostalgia.

Throughout much of the past week, thanks to the Powell adventure, all the fun and frivolity with El Groupo, she had managed to keep her thoughts of Lon Yeager at low ebb, actually feeling at times that perhaps she could erase his image and banish their entire experience together permanently. Now, though, she was less certain, and it was tempting to indulge the imagination much as it was tempting for the alcoholic to "take just one little drink." She recognized the danger clearly and simultaneously felt herself rationalizing its seriousness.

Half a dozen magpies were crisscrossing the road ahead, issuing an erratic series of screeching cackles. With their long, graceful tails, they were a stark contrast of black and white against the landscape and occasionally their feathers refracted light, shimmering green—like the head of a mallard—or an equally startling blue. It was that latter color that reminded her of his eyes. Uncanny blue, so intense that people sometimes asked her whether he wore tinted contacts. The question always amused her and appealed to her vanity as well.

"If only," Carla Bonner had said on one occasion, "he wasn't so *gorgeous*!" Carla had made no attempt to disguise her envy, even though she was thinking of Marilyn's welfare at the time, the importance of helping her forget the man. Well, yes . . . appearance was a distinct factor. How much easier it would have been to break things off, to forget, if he were simply an average-looking male like . . . well, Daws or Gordie. The thought troubled her rather frequently, made her wonder about her values, her own vanity.

And yet . . . Another magpie lilted by, this time with a vivid flash of blue, its feathers reflecting the opening sky. And yet, she wondered, how was it possible to separate personality from appearance? Were people ever attracted to members of the opposite sex on a basis of personality alone? The whole matter was pretty complicated and perplexing, and for now it merely seemed that any further attempt to think about it, especially to think about Yeager, would breed trouble.

The incline was becoming steeper, and she geared down a bit for easier pedaling. It was eight A.M., and groves of aspen were beginning to appear ahead on her left, trembling and scintillating ethereally in the morning light. It had been a day much like this the first time she met him a year earlier, the same hour—almost the exact minute, in fact. *No, no, forget it,* she told herself. The hillside ahead was scrambled with rocks, big ones some of them, weighing a ton or more. "You'll never break free if you keep wallowing in memory—never, ever."

But it *had* been a morning almost like this one. Her former car, a VW beetle well beyond its prime, had thrown a rod in the middle of Harrison Boulevard on her way to work. The VW, to its credit, had gone out with a bang instead of a whimper, expiring with a hideous death rattle like the sound of a Gatling gun, belching clouds of black smoke. Struggling to guide and push the idiotic contraption simultaneously, she had promptly backed up traffic for two hundred yards. She was, in fact, swiftly becoming desperate when a masculine voice directly behind her commanded, "You hop in and steer—I'll push." The hand completely surrounded her upper arm, gently yet insistently drawing her back. "Easier that way—I'm bigger." The voice was deep and resonant, tolerantly amused, and she glanced over her shoulder, startled. He was indeed bigger—slender yet broad, built like a swimming champion—and the blue eyes were dazzling. For an instant she thought of sparks from an emery wheel.

"Thanks," she squeaked, badly flustered but very grateful. At almost the same instant her VW began to accelerate with astonishing speed for a vehicle that had just expired in such agony. With barely enough time to collect her wits and fling herself inside, she turned into the exit of a drive-in bank only to slam on her brakes in a panic at direct loggerheads with a vintage 1970 Dodge the size and shape of a gunboat. The driver was chomping savagely on a dilapidated cigar, his neck, face, and balding scalp all flaring an exotic rose shade. Extracting the stogie, he craned his head out the open window and oinked, "Wrong way, lady—wrong way! Back off!"

Immediately her confusion transformed to anger. "I can't back off—my car's broken down!" Besides, any idiot could see at a glance that she had barely escaped the onslaught of bumper-to-bumper traffic with little room to spare. The driver of the gunboat, however, was in a lather over something, possibly about having been held up a few minutes already by the same traffic.

"Don't matter," he blurted, "you shoulda pulled off to the side so's people can get on past!"

By now she was truly incensed, on the verge of tears, her gold-green eyes large and dangerous. "I didn't have *time*!" she retorted.

Meanwhile, the man who had been pushing her VW was circling it with long, purposeful strides. She glimpsed a sky blue western-style shirt, trim-hipped Wrangler jeans, cowboy boots . . . thick black hair, a bit wavy, a handsome masculine profile, frowning and vexed. "Look, friend," he said, keeping his voice controlled and even. "This young lady's in a bad situation." He was leaning over slightly now, a hand on the Dodge's upper windshield, staring into the swollen face below. His tone was civil, a bit as though talking to a child, but also uncompromising. "So be a nice guy and back up a ways so we can get this into the parking lot." He paused. "Okay? Got the picture?" Muttering but clearly deflated, the driver did as directed—his scowl, the way he gripped the wheel and laid rubber leaving the parking area by a nearby side exit, all of it depicting a very sour apple.

"And by the way," her rescuer called, "loosen your collar and chuck that cigar! Live lots longer!" His tone and expression were mirthful, belonging to someone, it appeared, for whom other people afforded considerable entertainment.

Marilyn, however, was still rather shaken, not only over the demise of her car and the trauma immediately following but also over the dirt streak on her white skirt and, worse still, the fact that she was almost late for an important interview with Weber State's academic vice president. Some important organizational changes were underway, various departments being combined to meet the demands of a shrunken budget, and Marilyn was writing a feature article for *Comment*, a faculty newsletter which she also edited.

"Don't go away," her benefactor called, "I'll be back in a jiff." He headed toward the highway at an agile lope, returning seconds later in a sports car black and gleaming as freshly chipped tar. She wasn't even sure of the make, maybe a Jaguar, but it was sleek and low and looked as if it had been driven from the dealer's showcase. The motor purred with power.

"Here . . ." He leaned across from the driver's side and opened the door. "Hop in."

She hesitated, glancing into his upturned face, wondered with a flutter whether he was a TV newscaster, movie actor, or big-time cattle rancher. Yes, the outfit was definitely western; he even wore an open vest and matching string tie, and he read her glance, laughing. "Yeah, I know—corny outfit—but we're all going wild, wild west up at Snow King where I work—Pioneer Days and all."

"Looks very nice," she said shyly, "but . . . I don't want to impose on—"

"No imposition," he insisted, "not the slightest. Come on, hop in. I'm completely safe, and you're already late for work, right?"

"Well, yes," Marilyn confessed, "but . . ." She glanced over her shoulder. "What about my car?"

"Leave it," he said. "There's plenty of parking space, and nobody's going to run off with it, I'll guarantee."

"That's for sure," she laughed. "I can get it towed later, and my insurance will even pay for it."

"So there ya go," he said. "Hop in."

"Well, okay, thanks," she replied and, almost without realizing it, slipped into the glovelike leather seat.

"By the way"—his grin was remarkably enveloping—"my credentials . . . driver's license." She peered, smiling, and realized that the man was so handsome he even looked great in a driver's license photo. By now she was laughing a little, protesting that official identification was hardly necessary. "See, name's Lon M. Yeager—even says so on my Visa card, and here's my Weber County library card . . . avid reader! Expired hunting and fishing license . . . great outdoorsman. And, how about that? Lifesaving and water safety certificate. See, you're even safe with me in the *water*!" She actually giggled, unable to suppress it, feeling a sudden excitement, slightly giddy. Incredulous. "And finally . . ." He hesitated. "You LDS? No, wait, don't tell me—let me tell you. Extending a hand, he barely touched her brow, tracing his finger along her hairline, and she felt her pulse rate increase ridiculously. "Yeah, definitely. I can still feel the vestigial bumps."

"Bumps?"

"Sure—where our ancestors used to grow horns. Didn't you know all the early-day Mormons had horns?" He shrugged, the mirth and mischief welling lambently.

Marilyn laughed, shaking her head. He was delightfully crazy, a bit like Kelly. "Oh—well, sure, of course." She was watching him from the corners of her eyes.

"And finally," he continued, pausing portentously, "here's my temple recommend! Returned missionary," he grinned, "at your service."

"Now I *know* I'm in danger!" she said, and by then they were both laughing, almost boisterously for the moment.

"So where's work?" he asked. "We'd better get you there fast—right?"

"Weber State," she said, "and you're a real lifesaver. I'm already fifteen minutes late for a meeting with the academic VP."

"Hey-hey, now," he said, "that's gotta be a high-level operation." By then, the eight o'clock traffic had thinned, and soon he was winnowing through what remained, right hand on the wheel, the elbow of his opposite arm resting in the open window frame. In the process, he was inquiring about her job, acting much impressed, and collecting data on her personal background just as deftly. Minutes later he had deposited her at the very door of the Administration Building, driving down the long tunnel reserved for official vehicles, all the way to the basement entrance. "Now," he said, "all you have to do is run like mad down the hall and hope the elevator's waiting, correct?"

"Exactly," Marilyn said, realizing that she had discovered virtually nothing about him, except of course for what his wallet contained. But there was no time for further conversation. "Hey, I really appreciate all this," she said fervently, "you're an absolute lifesaver."

"*De nada,*" he purred. "Any time."

"Don't know how I can ever repay you," she called, thrusting her way though the heavy metal doors, "but thanks millions."

"Oh, I'll think of something," his voice trailed.

The winding road along North Ogden Pass was becoming steeper, and she geared her Shogun down even more, felt the sunlight's growing intensity. Tiny beads of perspiration like spray from an atomizer were springing out along her hairline, "the vestigial horn area," as Lon had called it. For an instant her smile was far more fond and nostalgic than she realized.

Well . . . Marilyn shook her head sardonically. She had certainly succeeded marvelously in excluding Lon Yeager from her mind. As usual, he had insinuated himself into her thoughts with the same ease and élan that he had entered her life. He had, in fact, called her that afternoon a year ago, the same day as the Harrison Boulevard rescue operation, insisting in mock-authoritarian tones that he wanted a full report on her meeting with the Weber State VP. Then, the casually assured afterthought: "Why don't you tell me about it over a bite to eat tonight?" She had hesitated, feeling giddy, her mind a sudden blank regarding what might have been scheduled for the evening, and in that moment he had clinched his sale. "Lion's Den about seven—okay?"

"Well, ah . . . okay. Sounds—"

"Pick you up at a quarter to."

Later she realized with a start that Tami Oda had lined her up for a blind date with someone from Salt Lake City. Following a feeble struggle with her conscience, however, she had backed out, rationalizing that he hadn't sounded very enthusiastic during their phone conversation to confirm the arrangement, and rather vague as to what they'd be doing.

So that night over sirloin steaks in the Lion's Den with its atmosphere of shadow and muted amber-gold lighting, she learned more about one Lon Yeager. Native of Springville, Utah, missionary to Peru about eight years earlier, graduate from Brigham Young with an MBA from Thunderbird in Arizona. His career interests were definitely oriented toward the international scene. At present, however, he was selling condo time-shares at Snow King Ski Resort, was also a licensed pilot dealing in diamonds and other gems through connections in South America. And that, she had quickly begun to feel, was only the beginning of it.

The clouds had filled in again, leaving only a streak or two of blue above the pass ahead, and a cool breeze was drifting downward, frilling more aspen and tossing a few sparrows, evaporating the moisture on her skin with a pleasant tingling. The evening of that first meeting after their dinner at the Lion's Den they had driven to Snow King and afterward, back at her apartment in the mouth of Ogden Canyon, he had kissed her good night. It was their first date, yes, but she had offered no resistance. Why? Simply because he had been so attractive, unquestionably the most appealing male she had ever dated. And . . . Her gaze became distant, unfocused. Well . . . because it had just seemed so natural. "Too bad about your VW today," he'd said. The disabled beetle was now at a garage a short distance from where she had parked it, prognosis highly discouraging. "But I've got some pretty good connections—probably find you quite a deal if you're ever in the market."

"Sounds interesting," she said and felt her face warming, heard the unexpected little-girl lilt in her voice. "I just might have no choice."

"Well, it's something to think about . . . but anyway," he confided, "I'm sort of glad your car bombed out in the fast lane today."

"Oh?" Her glance was amused and curious. "How come?"

"Well—because!" He shrugged, the perfect parody of a man surrendering his very soul. "I'd never have gotten acquainted with the most gorgeous girl in merry old Ogden."

"Oh, for sure!" She blushed magnificently.

"Absolutely true, and . . . well, let's face it—I'd just have to keep on living a lonely, miserable, celibate existence!" They were parked in the velvet darkness of Canyon Cove directly behind her apartment, the hollow and hillside rising up almost junglelike behind, but she could still see the color of his eyes, or at least feel it. Ion blue.

"Liar," she laughed. "I'll never buy that in a million years."

"Believe what?" His eyebrows lofted. The words were wrapped in a laughing little protest of innocence—one she would come to know a lot better. "That I can get you a great deal on a new car?"

"No, not that," she chided. "The lonely, miserable, celibate bit."

"Absolutely true," he insisted. Even in the darkness she could see the faint laugh wrinkles at the sides of his eyes. "I'll swear on a stack of Elvis Presley records. Sweet twenty-seven and never been kissed.'' At that she burst into laughter. He really *was* crazy. One hand encircled her arm as it had when he took command in the rush hour traffic that morning. The other moved confidently from her shoulder to her neck, deftly flirting her hair back in the process.

''My heart bleeds,'' she said. And it literally did, pumping at far greater volume as the kiss took hold. Half embarrassed, she felt the pulsebeat surging in her neck artery, realizing that his fingertips felt it too. And then for a full minute or more she really didn't care, immersed willingly in the experience and in the deep, oriole-warbling darkness of the hollow.

She emerged into the bright rigor of North Ogden Pass, not far from the top. Sunlight had broken through the overcast again, and the incline was even steeper. Nostalgia binges of the kind she had just indulged in did not strengthen the legs or encourage endurance. Despite having shifted further down to minimize strain, she could feel the heavy pull of gravity and the surging of her heart, much as she had felt it without any exertion whatever that night nearly a year ago.

Seventeen

A few minutes later, pedaling at the rate of a slow jog, she reached the top and began the long sinuous coast downward toward the little town of Liberty. Occasionally, for no discernible reason, she could go for hours, even a day or two, scarcely thinking about him. At Lake Powell, for example, although she had sometimes seen his face in the heat waves or the sky. And once . . . well, yes, that one time at Powell it had been pretty bad for a while. They had stopped to gas up the boat at Waweap Marina just over the Arizona border, and she had spotted a traumatically familiar figure walking along the wooden dock a short distance ahead. He was wearing a white T-shirt and red trunks, a rakishly tilted golf cap the same color. Same long tan legs with long, well-defined calf muscles, same whorls of dark hair covering his body.

For a moment she had followed, half mesmerized, then felt a surge of panic and jealousy as he leaned down to a docked speedboat and extended his hand to assist a curvaceous little brunette in matching attire. It was, in fact, the matching attire that hit her the hardest. For an instant she had been determined to greet him, force out something friendly and offhand, but upon seeing the girl, she had stopped, feeling a wave of . . . what? Jealousy? Yes, to the point of nausea. On the verge of retracing her steps, she realized that he had turned and was looking at her. The countenance belonged to a different man, not bad looking but hardly handsome—a sunburned Karl Malden nose, a bit horse-faced. His glance was appraising as if he had felt her gaze right through his back, tuned in on her thoughts. She had felt it follow her as she glanced about, pretending to be in search of someone else, then casually made her retreat.

"I know what was going through your mind," Jan confided later. "I had the same impression for a minute there. And don't think Little Janie Girl hasn't been there." She had begun applying the latter appellation to herself quite often lately, sometimes fondly, sometimes in exasperation. "For the next few months you'll be seeing him practically everywhere you look—upstairs, downstairs, in my lady's chamber."

"Especially the latter," Marilyn had mused, "knowing Little Lonnie Boy."

Jan offered up her inimitable chortle. "Oh, cynical, Lyn-Lyn, *cynical!*"

Well, the jesting and laughter had helped. It always did, at least a little, and for the most part she had been in pretty good command of herself during the Powell adventure. At times Lon Yeager had almost ceased to exist. Now he was back with her, obsessively. It was one thing to tell herself that she had willpower, to insist on it, to berate herself mentally when it failed her. Yet at times, no amount of willpower could keep her mind in the right channel.

Suddenly a chipmunk darted into the road ahead, made it to the yellow line, then doubled back, nearly getting squashed in the process. Traveling at thirty miles an hour, she swerved, applying a little too much front brake with her left hand and narrowly avoiding a serious mishap. Any more pressure in front and she might have pitched over the handlebars. She was definitely taking the curves too fast.

Part of the problem with Lon, though . . . "Here we go again," the little voice in her mind sang. But part of the problem was that crazy ring—still burning away there in the back of her drawer. Maybe once she got rid of it permanently he would have less power over her, and yet . . . she couldn't quite bring herself to return the thing. Why? Was she still clinging to the fragile hope that he might change? He had practically pleaded for another chance on several occasions, calling late at night, at her office as well, asked how she could ever know whether he had changed if she never put him to the test. "So how do you test a thing like that?" she had demanded. "I could hardly be with you every second of the day and night."

Even in the process of trying to refute him, she was half hoping that he might provide her an answer, and in fact he had, even though it was a somewhat facetious one. "Easy," he had laughed. "*Be* with me every second of the day and night." Then, more earnestly: "Really simple—we go out together every single night. *Comprende, vida mia*? You never let me out of your lovely sight."

It almost sounded logical on the surface, but the more she reflected upon it the more untenable it became. You didn't ensure righteousness with a straitjacket, she had reminded him, only to be reminded in turn that there was an immense difference between a straitjacket and a loving embrace! She had closed her eyes, shaking her head, then glanced at the phone in her hand askance almost as though it were a part of him or at least privy to all his clever little ploys. It was only after their conversation, however, that she had recognized the flaw in his argument. There was a difference in a loving embrace and a jealous one. Enforced righteousness might sometimes be the lesser evil, but as a general policy, permanent requirement, it was almost Luciferian.

What, on the other hand, was the alternative? It was a dilemma, either way she turned, catch-22. Increasingly, she was learning that there were problems in life that were never clearly soluble, that right and wrong could not always be differentiated, even within the framework of the gospel to which she so strongly subscribed. At least answers were not that clear to the mortal mind. But that, of course, was where prayer came in, and related study of the scriptures. Practically anybody could tell her that, but all too often, she mused, practically anybody needed to. It was so *easy* to forget! Yet even then—trying her very best—answers weren't always forthcoming, at least not the kind she could recognize.

Below and to the southeast she could see the aquamarine tones of her lifetime friend and comforter Pine View Reservoir. Initially she had planned to bear right at the little town of Eden, passing across the dam and on down Ogden Canyon to her apartment at its mouth eight miles below. The narrow, winding canyon, however, was increasingly hazardous for cyclists. Better, she decided, to swing around the upper end of the reservoir eastward and stop at her home in Huntsville. Perhaps a visit with her family, and afterward one of them could probably drive her to the apartment.

Fifteen minutes later she had rounded the tip of Pine View and was headed down the road to her home. It was nine A.M., the sunlight now in full force, and to her surprise Kelly's tan Camaro was parked in the drive of his own place next door. Usually he was long gone by now attending classes and visiting hospitals for his final year of med school at the University of Utah. The thought that he might still be home, however, filled her with pleasure. Maybe a little visit: she needed his ear, his strong, understanding heart, probably more of his advice.

Her reflections ended as the front door to his house suddenly opened. Her mother was just leaving, holding grandson Moroni by the hand and calling something over her shoulder: "I'll just change these slacks—I'm all dirty from the garden—and follow you on down. Delpha says she'll come right over for Rone!" Turning, Maria caught sight of her daughter. "Marilyn!" Her expression was pleased and astonished. "We've been trying to phone you at work." Turning back toward the open door, she called, "Marilyn's *here*, Shan, right now—on her bike!"

By then Marilyn had coasted to a stop near the porch. "What's going on? Is everything—"

But even before her words were out, she knew the answer. "Shannon's going to have her baby. The contractions started before Kelly was supposed to leave, and the past few have been coming every five minutes!"

By now young Rone had tugged free from his grandmother's hand and was clambering up onto his aunt and her bicycle simultaneously. "Mommy have my baby," he announced. His eyes were dark and luminous with a faint ruddy tint—root beer-colored, his dad said. From the beginning of Shannon's pregnancy she had told him that it would also be *his* baby brother or sister. "At hothpital in Oggen," he explained. His two-year-old body was astonishingly firm and resilient, and for a moment they hugged each other almost fiercely. She could feel the smooth cheek against hers, the steady beating of his heart, and her eyes clenched shut in satisfaction. "Oh, what a little *chunk* you are!" she murmured.

By then Shannon and Kelly were exiting through the side door, and Shannon was indeed great with child. Her cheeks were flushed and glowing, her long auburn hair literally casting an aura in the morning light. She wore a loose vanilla-colored dress containing the faintest tint of lemon. An instant later they were having a quick embrace. "Shan," Marilyn exclaimed, "you look celestial! Everything okay?"

"If we just keep moving," Kelly laughed. He sounded like a nervous teenager yet somehow jubilant too.

"Yes, everything's fine," Shannon said. Her voice was calm, faintly breathy. "Last time I didn't quite know what to expect, thought it might be a false alarm, but not this—"

"Come on, kid," Kelly said, guiding her toward the car. "Let's go for it." He was carrying a red plaid overnight bag and his new video camera slung over one shoulder. "I'd hate to be playing O. B. halfway there." Seconds later they were backing out the drive amid calls about love and prayers, about how Maria and Marilyn would be leaving the instant they could change. Unnecessary women's explanations, obviously, from Kelly's standpoint, that had probably been made before. He was already backing swiftly out of the driveway.

Eighteen

Half an hour later Marilyn and her mother had reached the McKay-Dee Hospital in Ogden. Shannon's mother, Alice, now divorced for several years, had left her job nearby and arrived to join them in the birthing room. The room was large and pleasant with floral wallpaper and comfortable armchairs, in keeping with a hospital policy that encouraged homey atmosphere and permitted close family members to be present during the birth. Already Shannon was lying on the delivery table clad in a blue hospital gown. Her lips were parted and glistening, her angled glance welcoming with only the merest trace of apprehension.

"Welcome to 'This Is Your Life,' " Kelly said. He was also clad in a blue gown, the kind that tied with strings in the back, and he had on a disposable blue shower cap which, if possible, made his face appear even more masculine. Already Marilyn could see the doctor her brother would become—strong, alert, always blending the proper amount of humor with concern and assurance. The vital bedside manner. The video camera was slung over his shoulder, and he gestured at it with his thumb. "Still sure you want this documented for posterity?"

The expectant mother closed her eyes and gave a quick nod, half smiled in the midst of a contraction. "Just use discreet camera angles."

"Yeah," he replied, "sure." A cord attached to Shannon's abdomen beneath the covering led to the fetal monitor machine, which graphed uterine contractions on one line and the unborn child's heart action on the other. If the heartbeats became too slow for too long, if the zigzag undulations of the lines suggested pronounced fetal distress, prompt action could be taken to expedite delivery. The lines were electric green, and momentarily everyone seemed to be watching as if the machine might actually impart revelations of an even more special nature.

"Quite a setup, isn't it?" Kelly observed. "Deus ex machina." Suddenly the uterine contraction line began to rise, peaking in a high, slender triangle. "Mrs. Cannon," he said, "you're having another contraction."

Shannon's eyes had closed, and she was hyperventilating slightly, her face turning pale for the moment. Her smile upon recovering was a trifle wincing. "Tell me about it," she said.

Marilyn saw the faint mischief in her brother's gaze melt to contrition, barely linger, and the others present chided him a bit. Who but an unfeeling male? "Hey, I'm sorry, beautiful," he said. The apology was filled with tenderness. Kelly had undergone an almost steady refinement ever since the early days of his mission, and it had accelerated markedly with marriage and the arrival of his son. At the very moment it seemed to expand visibly. "You okay?"

"Sure," Shannon said and managed to sound almost chipper, a courageous kind of rally. "I just want to get this show on the road."

"Still positive about doing it natural?" he said quietly. "You know you don't have to prove anything." She nodded, and he squeezed her hand. "Okay, doll, just remember it isn't like you've signed a contract. Let me know if you want an epidural or whatever."

"That's right," the nurse affirmed and began to check Shannon's heart with a stethoscope. She was a stocky woman with the face of a pleasant owl, highly professional, no wasted motions. "You just want the star to come on stage, right?"

"Maybe that's the problem—stage fright," Maria said. Then, more seriously: "Sure you wouldn't like a little more privacy, hon? We really are quite a multitude. Maybe just your mom and husband?"

Shannon shook her head, eyes closing. "No, exactly the right number. And the right people." For a moment, though, Marilyn thought of Shannon's father, divorced and living in California, of her teenage brother and sister staying there with him part of the summer. Perhaps the saying really was true—about separation through divorce being worse than separation through death. Surely so in the light of her own theology with its profound hope in a life to come and the chance for family continuity.

Now, however, the fetal monitor machine was graphing another strong contraction. Shannon's obstetrician had also just appeared, Dr. T. H. Grundel, a gnomelike little man in his mid-sixties with a buoyant, youthful demeanor. He seemed, in fact, to twinkle all over, partly because of thick silver-rimmed glasses that caught the light like tiny heliographs, and he was rubbing his hands together as though in great anticipation.

"Well, well, well," he said gleefully, "sorry to keep the little mother waiting, but I just finished delivering twins."

"Twins?" Kelly's brow lofted and he feigned a dazed expression.

"And big ones—two husky boys that wouldn't stop wrestling each other!" He cackled delightedly and again rubbed his hands like a moneylender.

"Well, it's good you broke up the match," the nurse said. "This girl's ready. Contractions every couple of minutes."

"Excellent," the good doctor replied. He was cleansing his hands at the nearby sink. Moments later they were clothed in the requisite rubber gloves, and having conducted his own examination, he announced that all was indeed in readiness, "any minute now."

Kelly turned to Marilyn. "Gotta hold this girl's hand. Want to record the blessed event for posterity?"

For a moment she felt a sense of panic as though the delivery itself suddenly depended upon her. She hesitated. "Yes, but I'm not sure if I know . . ."

"Aw, come on," he persisted, "you've used it before." Still, she hesitated, desirous of preserving the miracle yet apprehensive, concerned too about the intimacy of it all. "Just stand on the opposite side by her shoulder."

"Okay," Marilyn said dubiously. "I press down right here—correct?"

"Exactly," came the reply, and by now the doctor was at work, offering his patient words of encouragement, advising Shannon that with only a few more big pushes the baby would be there. She was breathing heavily, hyperventilating through rounded lips in the prescribed manner, like someone desperately trying to whistle who didn't quite know how. The effort culminated in a combination moan and sob.

"Here she comes," the good doctor announced, still jovial though totally absorbed in his work.

"He keeps insisting it's a she," the owlish nurse said.

"Well, my predictions are right," he replied, "about fifty percent of the time."

Shannon gasped and clutched at Kelly's hand more tightly. He was murmuring words of encouragement amid exhortations from a second nurse to push harder. Even in the vacant moments of exhaustion between each monumental effort the young mother's face recaptured a sheen of serenity, joy under ordeal. "Ah, yes, see here?" the doctor exclaimed. "See here? Look at that magnificent dark hair. Has to be a girl!"

Magically within the camera eye a new human being was materializing. Marilyn caught her breath, feeling some of the pressure within her own body, marvelling with the others at the abundance of dark hair. The baby's head had now emerged, and soon the tiny shoulders were being freed, one at a time, delicate and dimpled, covered with peach fuzz, and then the entire body, the bright, glistening umbilical cord attached. Marilyn could see it all through the viewer . . . now the face as it turned, pinkish with a tinge of silver gray, eyes squinched shut against the dazzling light of the world, the lids slightly puffy, lips rather wide and contorted. The new infant was emitting snuffles, sporadic little gagging sounds. For an instant she thought it might sneeze like a kitten.

"Aha!" Doctor Grundel rejoiced, "just what we ordered!" His glasses twinkled. Beneath the wizened exterior was a mischievous boy. "Did I say a girl or didn't I?"

"Wahoo!" Kelly's voice broke in a teenage falsetto of rejoicing and disbelief. "One of each!" By now they were suctioning fluid from the infant's nostrils with a syringe, and the gagging sounds suddenly transformed into wails against the world.

"Oh, she's beautiful!" Shannon sighed. It was the perfect combination of exhausted jubilation. "And all that marvelous hair!" Exclamations were coming from the onlookers—the many fond, trivial little things that mortal welcomers succumb to at such times. Meanwhile Marilyn continued to capture it all, sight and sound, through the magic of technology as the new infant continued her protest against the world. Her tiny chin and lower lip vibrated piteously with each wail, her eyes occasionally creeping open, then clenching again like those of someone emerging from a cave into the noonday sun.

Already the cord had been cut and tied, the newest Cannon wrapped in a cotton blanket and fitted with a tiny white cap to prevent loss of body heat. "Well, Momma," Dr. Grundel beamed, "do you want this little screamer or not? If not, we'll just ship her off parcel post to the gypsies."

"Oh no you won't," Shannon replied and reached out adoringly. Her voice was faint and parched, yet very fervent. The babe was also glowing more brightly, the faint silver-gray sheen fading along with a small red-orange patch on one cheek that looked like an abrasion on a fresh peach. Immediately, however, she ceased to squall and nestled down against her mother with a tiny, quivering sigh.

"Such an experience, such an experience!" Alice murmured. Her pale blue eyes were knowing, her round face mellow and benign. "Simply coming *into* this world!" For a moment Marilyn remembered her giant leap from the ledge near Rainbow Bridge, the engulfing water, the emergence into light. And then . . . for an instant . . . it seemed as if she were at least feeling, if not fully recalling, something beyond, something far greater. Inwardly, Marilyn herself uttered a similar kind of sigh.

It was not until sometime later, however, that she had a chance to hold the newborn herself, having continued to record the activities while the euphoric father and both grandmothers had their turn. Then suddenly the infant daughter was wafted away to the receiving room with half a dozen other recent arrivals. Returning that afternoon during a late lunch break, she found Shannon alone in her private room. The young mother was sleeping, her face bathed in a faint secret smile, her spirit drifting on the tides of serenity, and moments later a nurse entered carrying her child. "Time for a little practice at breast-feeding," she whispered.

Marilyn's mouth formed a silent "oh" of reply, and then on impulse so that the nurse could merely read her lips—"Could I hold her for a minute first if I put on a gown? I'm her aunt, and I haven't had a chance yet."

The nurse smiled, nodding, and seconds later Marilyn was sitting by the bedside, the sleeping infant nestled in her arms. The baby's thick, dark hair had already begun to acquire a touch of auburn, the barest hint, and was adorned with a tiny pink bow. Already the face had lost its squinched quality, and as Marilyn watched, the features seemed to be changing like part of a timed exposure, steadily becoming more exquisite. The nostrils breathed rapidly but without stress, minuscule traces of air that sometimes sang with the barest audibility and occasionally emitted a comical little bleat like the sound of a small rubber rabbit. The eyelids contained delicate blue capillaries and occasionally fluttered, partially opened, struggling to assert themselves against the sedation of dreams.

Marilyn glanced from the dreaming daughter to the dreaming mother, felt the growing sense of warmth in her arms, a change too ethereal perhaps to register on a thermometer yet undeniable in its magic and felicity. Undeniable in its power to sensitize and heal simultaneously. If only, Marilyn thought, if only it were possible every single day—even once a week—simply to *hold* such pure, new life, to absorb the celestial emanations . . . well, it wouldn't solve all the problems of the world, but it would definitely help. And where in all the world, maybe the entire universe, was there a more profound miracle? Oh yes, she had heard it all before and felt it before, but never like this, never with such poignant conviction.

"Father in Heaven," she prayed, then paused for some time, not knowing what might be best. "Please bless this baby." She felt the warmth expand, incredibly! "With every blessing *possible*."

When she glanced down once more the eyes had triumphed. They were wide open, the color of black pearls yet far more lucid. Endlessly so . . . and they watched her searchingly, with faint perplexity, immense curiosity, straining for recognition. Indeed, and for an instant Marilyn felt very certain, for recollection.

Suddenly the face blurred; her own eyes were brimming with tears.

Nineteen

"Well, Lyn-Lyn Baby?" Janie Johnson glanced at her knowingly. Janie was wearing a new blaze pink swimsuit in honor of the occasion, and her small, compact body was brown as a Maori's from the sun, curvaceously sturdy—more than ever.

"Well?" Marilyn's brow lofted, and she took a deep quivering breath. She too was well-tanned, though she had a naturally lighter complexion, honey colored; and she had purchased a dazzling blue swimsuit of her own. For both of them the new acquisitions were not only in celebration of the occasion but also special morale boosters. In addition, they were both wearing the required blaze orange bathing caps, as were a hundred others there clustering along the sandbar in Willard Bay.

"This is the big one," Janie said, keeping it light. "How's she feel?"

"Don't ask," Marilyn laughed. Her heart was already flip-flopping, her limbs enervated as if she had donated a pint of blood about five minutes earlier. "Let's just say it's not as bad as the cliff jump."

"That's right, don't ask!" It was the familiar megaphone-like quacking of their friend Cuddles, the kind of voice that invariably made everyone in his vicinity turn and gawk. It was, in fact, an unconscious means of drawing attention. Or maybe highly conscious, Marilyn decided. How he got his strokes. That and his outrageous attire, which at the moment was relatively conservative—white trunks, a bit baggy, sprinkled with colored polka dots that looked as though he might be advertising Wonder bread. His swimming cap was pulled low, almost to the bridge of his nose, and he stared at them bug-eyed through a pair of blue-green goggles. Despite all his dedicated training in the sun his skin remained somewhat dough colored. "Anyway, this is the biggie, Marilyn Girl," he said and patted her shoulder, stepping on her foot in the process. "But don't let it throw ya—just don't pass out the way you did that day up in the Valley."

"Oh thanks, Cuddles," Marilyn said. Her voice sounded frail. "I'll write that down." It seemed as if everyone along the beach was watching her.

"Good old Curdles," Jan muttered from the corner of her mouth, "wouldn't you just know?"

"Wha's that?" Cuddles barked.

"Nothing," Janie said. "Marilyn's in great shape now. All she has to do is run her own race, and everything will come out super."

"I sure hope so," Cuddles persisted. "Just do your own thing, Lyn; don't worry about keeping up with Jan and me. After all, we've been at it for years." Janie rolled her eyes. "Well, like, I mean . . . *practically.*"

The participants were lining up along the water's edge now, and the long sandbar was somewhat mucky with occasional rocks and bits of slime-slicked driftwood. It smelled brackish, mingling fish odors with a briny tang from the Great Salt Lake westward. Marilyn felt her skin tingle, the catch of excitement in her lungs, the murmur, shouts and laughter of the participants. Several motorboats with lifeguards and water-safety equipment idled a short distance beyond, and by now the starter was giving his final instructions. It was a mile swim across that portion of the bay to a spot near the dike where their bicycles would be waiting. Then would come about thirty-five miles of back road and highway leading north toward Brigham City and angling west past the rocket testing center at Morton Thiokol. Then on to the barren reaches of Promontory. There, God willing—if she was still among the living—the final portion of the triathlon would occur, a five-mile run to the Golden Spike National Historic Site where the intercontinental railroad had been completed in 1869.

It was eight A.M., and the sun had just risen above the Wasatch Mountains a short distance to the east, turning the morning monotones of the water to blue-green and colors of molten steel. Beautiful, yet somehow frightening. Suddenly the entire prospect seemed insanely impossible. "Why," Marilyn wondered aloud, "am I getting myself *into* these things?" She turned an accusing eye on her friend. "You! You're the culprit!" Janie chortled, casting a glance over her shoulder toward the distant Promontory range jutting deep and Florida-shaped into the Great Salt Lake. Then she offered a final bit of pep talk. By now it was too late for anything else.

A few feet away Marilyn could see the remains of a large carp, scales like mail, gaping mouth, empty eye socket, a swirl of sand flies. Her stomach contracted. The instructions were still coming, but they made little sense. Off on the shore a hundred yards or so to her right was a prolific grove of saplings—cottonwoods, bright green—and suddenly she wanted to hide in them.

"Okay . . . swimmers ready!" Marilyn could feel the cool silt squishing up between her toes as she waded in with the line of other contestants. The water was rising to their knees, then to their waists, drawing her along helplessly with them. "Take your marks!" The gun fired like the mere crack of a cap pistol, but it was real, and Marilyn felt the bay embrace her chillingly, then surfaced to glimpse dozens of red-orange bathing caps, all of them bobbing like giant tangerines.

"Good luck, Lyn Baby," Cuddles gargled. From just ahead the boats revved up mildly and began frothing forward. At least, she thought, there's someone to fish me out if I get a cramp or start to . . . start to what? She didn't know, but it was no way to think. "Think positive, girl—PMA," she told herself. "'Just relax, Lyn Baby, and do your own thing; you've trained pretty hard, and besides, you're only competing with yourself. Just take it free and easy."

Already the jitteriness and hollow feeling had faded, and the water suddenly felt less frigid, more refreshing. Once a thrashing foot grazed her shoulder but caused no damage. She knew without looking that friend Cuddles was pummeling his way forward. It was amazing that he did so well considering his terrible swimming form and all the unnecessary energy expended in consequence. But the boy did have determination; she had to hand him that, truly admired him for it, even though it sometimes meant an inadvertent foot in the face or elbow in the eye.

Two hundred yards from shore she rolled into a temporary sidestroke and decided that there were only a dozen or so stragglers while several of the group—no doubt, Janie Johnson included—were already far ahead. The bathing caps now looked more like brightly colored fishing bobbers for some reason, and momentarily her insides slumped. Already she was practically out of the race. Silly to think she could finish the whole thing anyway. The entire idea was absurd. For a minute or two craven thoughts slithered into her mind again, thoughts about backing out. Maybe she could feign a cramp or manage to get sick again. Then she shook them loose, berating herself for regressing so easily, remembering with strange spontaneity something from a movie she had once seen, a quick take of someone dumping snakes from a burlap bag. That was it . . . dump out the bad and fill the empty space with something good. Better still, get a new bag, a fresh clean one, and fill it with something highly nourishing—apples, maybe. Yes, beautiful golden apples, delicious and glowing, full of life.

And besides—again the reminder—she was only competing with herself. Her strokes became more relaxed again and in the process more effective. Maybe not even competing with herself in fact, simply sustaining herself—me, myself, and I—a friendly kind of support system. Better . . . yes, better. Then reach out to include God. How did it go? Something she'd read or heard about the Lord and one person making a majority.

Okay, now to just think about form a little in a nice, relaxed way. Remember, she told herself, to keep the fingers together. Not forks that strain, paddles that pull. "Not claws—webs!" That was what Kelly used to tell her long ago when he was teaching her how to swim. "You're not a chicken, you're a duck." And, her thoughts continued, don't kill the arms. Torque your body on its axis and use the rotary action to power them. Let the back muscles and lats along the sides in on it, to take strain off the biceps and shoulder muscles. Yeah, that was it, the arms sort of scarecrowing forward—languid and loose, almost floppy. Right, definitely better. Her confidence was returning, backs of her hands pivoting inward at the wrists and slicing into the water along the side of the thumb, not slapping it like her water puppy of a friend.

Sunlight danced on the water, sparkled over her shoulder now like a million silver flares, and swirled around her arms in pastel green and platinum, frothing whitely along the edges. The air smelled fresher, with a slightly oceanic quality that made her feel even more at ease. Already, for better or worse, she had covered about a fourth of the total distance. And after all, she had swum a mile or more many times now, along the Pine View shoreline with Janie. Sometimes in the Weber State pool after work as well. She remembered the exhilaration of Lake Powell, how it had absorbed her irresistibly into its element. So? So, why shouldn't she at least do all right here at Willard Bay? Water was water.

Maybe that first big fiasco on the mini-marathon had made her gun-shy in more ways than one. But again . . . She continued to stroke gracefully, tensing only a little. That was not the way to think either. Think about accomplishments, about the girl nearly her own age some years earlier who had swum . . . how far was it? *Ninety miles?* Yes, she was pretty certain. Ninety miles through the ocean—all the way from the Bahamas to the tip of Florida. What was her name? Dana? No—no, but something like that. *Diana,* yes—Diana Nyad, that was it. Actually made it ninety miles nonstop. Marilyn could remember the news photo now, of Diana Nyad there on the Florida shoreline, collapsed upon the sand. The tide was washing about her feet, and she had fallen backward upon her elbows, head flung back also, eyes filling with the sky. Her mouth was open, gasping, not only from exhaustion but in utter exultation. Triumph!

Despite its spectacular nature, that accomplishment had gone unrecognized by the public in general, but it had not escaped the notice of the old patriarch himself, Elijah Marriott. He had commented upon it more than once, most pointedly in one of his famous Sunday School classes. "That remarkable young lady," Lije had marvelled, "accomplished the impossible if anybody ever did." He had paused portentously, his ancient face with all its deep, erratic cross-hatching aglow from the youth within. "But what do you suppose it required to *do* a thing of that magnitude?"

"Insanity," someone had joked. And there had, of course, been the answers one might expect: great natural ability, rigorous training, courage, ambition, positive attitude, and so on.

To all these things the old man had agreed with alacrity, even the first. Everybody was crazy to some degree in some way, he maintained, needed at least one "magnificent obsession." But there was something else, even more important, that no one in the class had quite touched upon. Gliding along through the waters of Willard Bay, feeling her heart, lungs, and limbs all working in healthy unison, Marilyn recalled his words vividly. "One more thing," Lije had said, holding up an admonitory forefinger. His body wasn't very large, shriveled and tough, a bit twisted—like beef jerky—but he had a grand spirit and surprisingly large hands. "I think that young lady had to have a special attitude about the water, about the big old ocean itself."

He had paused, waiting for the idea to break from its shell. "Supposing she'd said to herself, 'Oh no, hold on now—this here's the *ocean*! It's full of giant waves and currents, all kinds of ferocious critters, and besides that . . . it's *six miles deep*!' At its deepest, anyhow." The old man had a great flair for the dramatic, frequently supplementing his words with an impressive, often amusing variety of gestures and facial expressions. At the moment his body seemed to shrink while his eyes bulged in mock terror. " 'Why, *nobody* can handle a thing like *this*! Too much, just downright, plain *impossible*!' " Then the pungent pause. "So, what then? How far would she have made it?"

For a moment now, Marilyn felt the anxiety, even there within the relative safety of the bay. As she recalled, in fact, the old man's gaze had fastened upon her alone. "Probably never have even set foot in the water," she had replied.

Lije had nodded, still appraising her. "And even if she had," he'd replied, "it wouldn't have bought her much. She'd have been lucky to get past the first mile, maybe first hundred yards." He pursed his lips, stroked his jaw. "Nope! Never made it in forty years. That girl had to tell herself that the water was her friend, that water's designed to float people, not drag them down. It's the people sink *themselves*! But with the right attitude, the kind I been talking about . . . all's she had to do was keep a-moving her arms and legs, nice and calm and relaxed. That young lady had to be a *part* of the ocean itself." A long pause, eyes searching and undeniable. "Hear me?" Then he had added a brief footnote: "And in the process, she had to have the kind-a relaxation she could swim in her sleep."

The patriarch had left it at that. "Anyway, think on the matter —just cogitate a little." *Cogitate* was one of his favorite words, in fact.

Marilyn was halfway across the bay now. The rocky dike ahead was becoming larger and more substantial. A great metal power pole just beyond, near the adjoining shore, was gradually taking shape, looming like some colossal four-armed robot assigned to guard the spot where their swim would end. Well, she definitely planned to ponder Lije Marriott's words further, but something good was at work, some indefinable affinity with the water. Her strength was increasing.

Twenty

When she reached the opposite shore twenty minutes later the swimmers had scattered widely. Many were apparently still ahead, but there were also a lot more behind than there had been back in the time of her panic. A single glance suggested that about two-thirds of the original hundred-plus entrants were still in the water, possibly even three-fourths. It was hard to tell, but some were so far back their caps looked like orange Ping-Pong balls. So maybe she wasn't doing so badly. But no time for any of that now. The last thing she needed was to begin patting herself on the back.

Gordie Yates and Don Dawson were waiting along with a number of others not far ahead on a dirt road where the dike ended. Gordie's battered red pickup was parked nearby, and they had her bike along with the needed attire. "Hey, Lyn-Lyn, all right!" Daws extended his hand palm up as though halting traffic. She saw the jointed-looking nose, the nutcracker chin and slight underbite, the friendly grin. "Gimme five!" Reaching out to clap the waiting palm with her own, she staggered and nearly missed.

"Girl's dead drunk!" Gordie yukked. Weaving giddily across the sand, she pounded the side of her head with the heel of one hand, trying to dislodge the water from her ears and regain equilibrium. Then she was struggling into her running shorts right over the wet swimsuit, having no other option. Next came the sox and jogging shoes, and she nearly lost her balance again and would have fallen a time or two but for the ready assistance of her pals.

"Where's Janie and Cuddles?" she gasped, pulled off her bathing cap and shook her hair free. "Lost track of 'em way back there."

"Jan's on down the road," Dawson told her. "No sign of Curdles yet."

"Probably sank after the first ten feet like a broken-down thrashing machine," Gordie cackled. Marilyn felt a moment of mean amusement herself in view of Cuddles's constant advice about not passing out. But no time for that either. Already she was mounting her bike and heading off down the dirt lane leading to the highway. For an instant she swerved to avoid a rut, overcorrected, and found herself momentarily in the off-road gravel.

"All right?" Dawson called.

"Yeah . . ." She was still breathing hard from her swim, hardly in a mood for the rigors ahead. "Just being clever. Thanks loads, you guys." A swift glance over her shoulder, a half wave. Little whitecaps were washing in upon the beach, other swimmers emerging.

"No sweat—see ya out there in the sticks!" This from Gordie. Simultaneously a biker shot past her—a lean, whiplike character clad in black. Everything about him, including bike, hair, and mustache, was black, and he was hunched low over the handlebars, legs intimidatingly hairy and muscular. Well, more power to him, literally. They'd probably reach the Golden Spike Monument centuries apart, but . . . so what? She would just do her best and let the world keep turning.

Several horses watched her passage from a field lined with purple-flowered thistle. A hawk with something in its talons took flight from atop a telephone pole as clouds passed over the sun, and a mild tail wind evaporated the remaining water from her skin. Suddenly she actually felt shivery, but she knew that it would change. Even if the clouds remained, before long she'd be sweating—she had learned that during weeks of arduous training.

Pedaling along now over the dips and rises, she breathed deeply and steadily, watching for rocks or chuckholes. Once a large dog scrambled onto the road ahead from a borrow pit clogged with cattails, and for a heart-startling moment seemed to be heading for a direct collision. Then he veered off and circled, loping along beside her. His paws and chest were black with muck, and despite his size he frolicked like a pup. A golden lab maybe; she wasn't sure. His tail wagged happily, and his tongue flopped like a slice of bologna. Four hundred yards later, he was still keeping her company, and Marilyn began to fret. Maybe the dog was some little kid's pet, and if it continued to follow her it would end up lost in the wilds of Promontory. Probably lost already.

Once he cut directly in front of her, and she braked hard, nearly taking a spill. The idiot! "Go home, boy!" she shouted without the slightest effect. Her voice sounded embarrassingly shrill. Despite periodic shouts and warnings, he was still with her several minutes later as she reached the highway heading north to Brigham City. By now she was becoming quite distraught; the stupid animal was a real distraction, definitely not a responsibility she wanted at the moment. "Go home!" she repeated, this time more resolutely, yet still to no avail.

A highway patrol officer was waiting by the roadside, the warning light band on his car roof a sectioned ruby red and sapphire blue in the morning sun. "Watch out for the traffic," he advised with a warmth that seemed to extend beyond the normal call of duty. "Especially crossing the road." She barely glimpsed his face —youthful and swarthy, maybe even handsome, but the one-way sunglasses and the mustache gave him a certain anonymity. "That your pooch?" he called.

"No," she replied. "He just came out of nowhere and started following me. I wish he'd go back where he belongs."

Seconds later the patrol car rumbled into action, swung in a left U-turn across the highway, and began to follow them, its colored roof lights flashing. "Yah boy—c'mere!" the officer shouted. "Come on now!" The dog whirled back suddenly, nearly running into her and causing another mishap. For a moment he reminded her strongly of someone else she knew. Well, at least it was over now—so long, Rover, and good riddance.

Automatically she picked up speed, breathing a distinct sigh. Thirty seconds later, she heard even more distinct panting sounds, and there was the darling pup, loping joyously along beside her as if it had all been arranged before the world began. The patrol car was closing in just behind. "You sure this isn't your hound? Can't get my hands on 'im."

"No, he's not mine!" It was almost a yowl, but she didn't care. "I've never laid eyes on him before."

The patrolman paused uncertainly. "Well . . . just keep toolin'. He's bound to poop out sooner or later—if he doesn't get himself run over first." That disconcerted her all the more; she was truly becoming angry at the animal. Literally coming out of nowhere at practically the worst time possible and becoming such a crazy pest. First, worry about having him get lost, but now he might even be killed, and if that happened . . . "Here, boy!" the officer shouted. His voice was appropriately gruff and authoritative, but the pup refused to be impressed. "Come on now!" he bellowed. "Back off, ya knucklehead. Go on home!"

The final threat was suddenly different in tone, more like that of an exasperated teenager. Laughable under different circumstances, but she was in no mood to be amused—even though she loved dogs, even though they'd been part of her family forever. Heaving another deep sigh, she kept pedaling. Maybe the trick was not to think about him, just in case he was operating on some kind of telepathy.

She was passing country homes now, set back well from the road, a wide drive flanked by huge white wagon wheels. Initially the first several miles of biking were to have been routed along the main freeway directly bordering the bay, but parts of it were undergoing repair and the only access along a narrow, circling ramp was dangerous. Hence the older, less travelled route a short distance to the east with its farms and orchards, its numerous fruit and vegetable stands. It was a pleasant diversion, actually, even though a bit circuitous. And, wonder of wonders, the crazy hound had faded into the background. The patrolman, bless him, clearly had things under control by now.

But what after that? Off to some so-called animal shelter? They never used the words *dog pound* anymore, but sooner or later they still had to "put the animals away" if they went unclaimed or adopted. What if it had to be impounded and never was adopted? Ended up in a box full of carbon monoxide or something? Was that the way they still did it? She recalled reading something about it in the newspaper one time, something about protests from the Humane Society. One way or another, though, the dog might have to die. He could have chosen to follow any of dozens of people, but for some reason he had selected her. And that, like it or not, made him her responsibility.

The further she went, the more it gnawed at her mind. The dog was so young, so cute and goofy and happy, such a complete innocent. So free and full of life. Suddenly Marilyn felt sick. No, she simply couldn't go on. By turning back she would probably forfeit any slight chance of placing near the top. People would even laugh and make a big joke of it if they ever found out. Nevertheless . . . She braked to a stop on a shoulder of road and glanced back. Yes, the officer actually had Rover in hand now, had him by the collar next to his car, and it looked as if he was talking over his radio. But she'd have to go back.

As Marilyn turned and began pedaling toward the patrol car, a cyclist powered on past her, heading the opposite direction—another "lean machine," built like a cheetah, who barely cast her a glance. Obviously swimming wasn't his real forte, but obviously also, cycling was. The patrol officer noted her return with surprise.

"Hey, could I give you my name and phone real quick?" she panted. His eyebrows raised. She hadn't realized how her words might sound without a preface, but there was no time to be analytical.

"Hold on a sec," he said into the mike. The dog strained, trying to break free, clearly delighted to see her again.

"If you can't find the owner . . ." She gulped for air. "I don't want to complicate things, but would you let me know if you can't? Or if he has to go to the animal shelter or something?"

The young officer appeared puzzled but eyed her with growing interest. "Well . . . yeah," he replied. "Sure, guess I could do that."

"Great!" Moments later he had recorded the information, and she was off, but not before several more bikers had gone by. "Thanks a lot," she called. "I'll be responsible, okay? See he gets a good home, whatever!" Rover the retriever made another lunge to free himself, twisting and whining, but the grip was strong.

"Yeah—right!" he shouted. His tone was increasingly affable. "Will do!"

Seconds later another call came from just behind, and this time it was all too familiar. Not merely a quack or a baa, but rather a combination of both, like the sound she had once heard from a small penguin in the Hogle Zoo. "Hey, Lyn-Lyn! What's happenin'? Was that cop giving you a bad time or something?"

She felt a sinking in the spleen, fairly cringed. A conversation with Cuddles or anything even resembling a visit under the circumstances was definitely among her last desires.

"No, no problem, Cuddles," she said. "Tell you about it later."

"Didn't start to pass out, did ya?"

"No, Cuddles." It seemed to be his grand obsession, and her tone was pained. "Will you please get off that kick? I don't exactly pass out every two or three minutes of the day . . . in case you haven't noticed."

He drew alongside her, literally too close for comfort, not to mention safety, almost locking pedals. "Hey, I'm sorry," he panted. "It's just that I saw that cop and the dog and everything. And I started getting—"

"Everything's fine," Marilyn insisted. "I'll tell you about it later, okay?" She swerved slightly to avoid a ragged piece of tire tread. "For now . . . gotta save our breath. Long way to go."

"Yeah," he replied, apparently oblivious to everything she had said. "For some reason I got pretty disoriented back there in the bay—angled off west toward the lake."

"Too bad," Marilyn said. Even that was too much encouragement, she knew, but it was inhuman not to show some little concern.

"Yeah!" Cuddles repeated. The word blended with his familiar little laugh—a snuffle-gasp of incredulity. "Weird! I mean, that's not *like* me." The allergic snuffling persisted with each breath. His eyes were red-rimmed and watery from the pollen-filled air. "Normally," puff, puff, "I have an almost uncanny sense of direction."

At that precise moment their handlebars clicked against each other and narrowly missed locking. "*Bernard*!" Marilyn yelped, reverting to his real name in vexation. "You're way too close!" She was truly becoming irked now, almost tearful. So goodhearted, but such a clutz. No sense whatever when it came to the invasion of privacy, or invasion of space—literally. He was worse than the roving retriever, and there was no hope for help from animal control! Unexpectedly, the thought struck her as hilarious and weakened her with inner laughter. It escaped in the form of a little sob, almost a hiccup.

"You all right, Lyn-Lyn?" Cuddles inquired.

"Yes," she smothered a titter and shook a little. "I just have this . . . *frog* in my throat. It's . . ." She shook her head, chewing her lips.

"Maybe you should drink some H_2O," he said, referring to the plastic water bottle beneath her crossbar, "some good old aqua pura."

"Right, in a while. Can't talk any more now." They pedaled for a while in truly blissful silence. "You just ride your own race, I'll be okay." A cyclist passed them, a young woman with a ski-jump nose, frizzy hair the color of a Rhode Island Red. Her face and arms were sprayed with freckles on a near-albino background.

"Wow!" Cuddles bellowed. "That girl's cruisin'! Maybe I'll just follow along in her slipstream for a while."

"Good idea," Marilyn said. "You do that, son." It was a sadistic trick to play on the Rhode Island Red, but who knows, she thought, maybe they'd strike it off big. In any case, her faithful companion Tonto was moving out, his bike chains rasping slightly as he shifted gears.

How to ever pass him again without becoming ensnared in more Cuddlemania, she didn't know. Maybe she should have brought along a mask. Maybe she should learn to disguise her features—a female Martin Short playing one of his ghastly imbeciles. The thought choked her, and she began to feel hysterical again. Her legs grew weak from sheer silliness. At that rate, she would never make it to the turnoff near Brigham City.

On the right was a big orchard—pie cherries, then apricots, bordered by a white running fence that seemed to continue endlessly. The sun was burning more brightly, and she removed the colored glasses from the leather carrying case beneath her seat and put them on. Mirror lenses, gleaming gold. Hardly an adequate disguise even for tricking Cuddles, but it lent a touch of the exotic, went well with her breeze-drifted flaxen hair, the blue swimsuit, the bright yellow biking shorts, and her smooth and glowing tan.

Then her reflections returned to the Big Tri. How much of the race, she wondered, was due to the ever-growing interest in jogging and cycling, in distance races of all kinds, in concern for good health; how much the need to compete; and how much sheer exhibitionism—a desire to "be seen of men," or women, as the case might be? Daily on her return to Canyon Cove from Weber State she saw joggers and cyclists, many of them girls in very scanty attire, coursing along Harrison Boulevard. Invariably a lot of them not only selected the busiest street but the busiest hour, with plenty of dangerous traffic and carbon monoxide.

Well, for now, Marilyn herself was compelled to admit that it boosted her morale to look good, even if she came in last or never even made it. She had entered the little town of Perry, was passing a dark orange fruit stand with black lettering that said "Sumida's." Then came a small brick tabernacle with white trim, now converted into a theater for local thespians. A white sign in front featured "The Mystery of Edwin Drood." For some reason the title delighted her . . . maybe something to take in one evening soon with her pals from El Groupo. She passed a swaybacked barn that had probably never seen paint and had turned gray from the seasons, a cafe that featured "Jessie's Home Made Pies" with a sun-faded "Closed" sign in the window.

Not far ahead on her left was the Maddox Restaurant, famed for its steak and fried chicken. Come noontime its parking lot would be filling with cars. Periodically she had also been passing signs with red arrows and the words "Golden Spike Triathlon." Well, at least she was headed in the right direction and feeling good, pedaling at what seemed a reasonable rate, with about three-fourths of her journey remaining. Not far ahead was an intersection with a turnoff leading northeast through the mountains to Logan, but she continued her present course, happily catching the green light and gliding on through. To her right was a conglomeration of buildings, huge tan barracks-type structures that had once housed the Intermountain Indian School. Now they lay deserted in the morning sun. Not far beyond that another red arrow indicated the back road angling northwest, detouring Brigham City and heading toward Corrine.

A second patrol car was parked nearby, the officer waiting to issue crossover warnings, but there was no traffic in sight as she swung left and started down the narrow country road. Oddly enough, there was no sign of Bernard "Cuddles" Eskelson or the Rhode Island Red either. Minutes earlier, it seemed, they were only a short distance ahead, but now, nothing—neither on the highway as she crossed over nor along the road beyond. Strange, yes, though she had to admit it was also a relief.

She was breezing along now at a nice, steady clip, feeling the exertion in her legs but comfortably, with no great stress. Glancing back once about two hundred yards from the highway, she spotted several more cyclists who had just made the turnoff, dipping now into a swale, rising again, the sunlight gleaming on their lacquered helmets. How many contestants were ahead she could only guess, but it was becoming more evident that she had done quite well in the swimming phase, and only a few bikers had passed her despite the dumb dog episode. So . . . maybe her performance wouldn't be *too* terrible, if she could just hang loose and hang in.

The winding road beyond was empty except for a few heat waves. Cuddles and his new heartthrob had simply vanished. One moment they were rolling along only two hundred yards ahead at most; the next they were gone, evaporated. No possibility of accident. She'd have chanced upon them right away in that event. Occasionally she passed small side roads, little more than country lanes leading to solitary farm homes or off, it seemed, into nowhere.

Well, it was quite a mystery, but probably nothing sinister, and she could not spend her time fretting over every incident and bit of happenstance along the way. Every stray dog and cat. The thought amused her. Now that Cuddles knew something about the Rover situation, so would the world. It would provide some laughs for her family and friends, especially the members of El Groupo.

The problem for now was to pace herself properly, and even though this was indeed her race of races, why not enjoy the journey? What was it Lije had said? Or was it Bishop Alma Belnap? They were men cast from much the same mold. "Learn from the past . . . plan for the future . . . but live for the present." She nodded to herself. The day, the hour, the very moment. It was one of Kelly's favorites also. So who really knew? Something that might have been passed on down for generations. A kind of slogan, and sometimes slogans could be misleading, trite and awfully simplistic. On the other hand, some of them also condensed vital truths very effectively. Certainly, Marilyn told herself, this was one of them.

She was passing bogs and borrow pits clogged with cattails, then dillweed, wonderful pickle odors. Blackbirds thronged, rose in clustered flights, and landed on telephone wires. A lone poplar beckoned in the distance, and as she approached, its trunk began to darken at the base, the grayness steadily climbing to encompass the entire tree in the shadow of a passing cloud. Just beyond that lay the road to Corinne.

Twenty-One

It was the blue jay that had betrayed her, flitting unexpectedly from the poplar into the returning sunlight and filling her mind once more with the ultra-blue eyes of Lon Yeager. Now, more than two months since the breakup, and still she wondered—sometimes hour to hour—how she'd be able to survive without him.

A vagrant whiff of "seashore" from the west took her back to a summer rendezvous, one that commenced with an early evening cruise on the Great Salt Lake aboard the Silver Sands Schooner. It had begun in the flames of a fantastic sunset, perhaps the most exotic she had ever seen, one that only the most perfect cloud cover could produce. First were the darkling hills, which now from her bicycle were melting and neuter in the distant haze, yet on that night were plum toned and velvet textured along their tops. Her eyes had photographed, her brain imprinted an almost perfect series of images: the irregular band of sky, mild and limpid green like part of a fairy's dream, the scattered clouds above like embers, somber and gray-blue on their surfaces but disintegrating in ever-greater expanses of gold and vermillion. Far off, white sails had been transformed to red, and moments later the schooner's loudspeaker system had begun to play "Red Sails in the Sunset."

They stood together holding hands near the ship's prow, and afterward she murmured with a little laugh, "This is almost too romantic for anything but 'Love Boat,' isn't it?"

"Oh . . . ," he said reflectively, his eyes still visible, full of fond mischief, "I don't know; it's really *happening*, right?" He continued to regard her dotingly, lids half lowered. "One of my old profs used to say it's up to us to create our own reality. It's not just a case of circumstances or the particular place, it's a case"—glancing toward the horizon reflectively—"well, of the eyes and, I guess, the heart."

"I believe it," she replied, and felt the vibes. "But this one doesn't even take any imagination."

His laughter was amused, loving, delighted, and it melted her. "So why fight it? Why not go all the way?"

Marilyn glanced up at him faintly dazed and quizzical, felt herself both tingling and frightened.

"Figuratively speaking," he laughed, yet his voice purred. "I just meant . . ." He shrugged. "Long as it's romance, why not—well, ya know, really do it up right, go whole hog?"

" 'Whole hog' doesn't exactly do it," she chided.

Lon laughed, wincing, wonderfully vulnerable. "Too true, too true." Then more seriously, "But *you* do, beautiful. Your *eyes* do." He looked into her so searchingly she felt herself dissolve. "And so does your voice." The boat throbbed steadily onward, purling its white and constant wake against the water. "Ever happen to read a poem," he said, "about a woman's voice? Something about golden bells—no, wait . . ." He squinted, pressed one palm against his forehead. " 'Bells of singing gold at twilight over silent waters'—that was it, I'm pretty sure." For a moment she had almost lost her own voice. "And that's Marilyn Cannon," he said. His arm encircled her shoulders, and her eyes filled with tears of joy and incredulity.

"It reminds me of another poem," she replied at last, "about another sunset, a lot like this one." She hesitated for some time, fearful about forgetting the words once memorized with such care, then—cautiously at first—quoted them perfectly:

" 'Dark hills at evening in the west
Where sunset hovers like a sound
Of golden horns that laid to rest
Old bones of warriors under ground
Far now from all the bannered ways
Where flash the legions of the sun,
You fade—as if the last of days
Were fading, and all wars were done.'

"It's by Edwin Arlington Robinson," she said a few moments later. "I memorized it a while back for a class in oral interpretation. Our teacher asked us to come up with some poems in which you couldn't change a word—wouldn't ever want to change a single thing."

"Yeah," he said quietly, "really great," and looked down into her. "Wouldn't change a single thing." The kiss lasted long enough for their silhouette to trace itself across quite an expanse of sunset. And afterward they stood very close watching the hills blend into night.

A short while later their boat docked at the Salt Water Pavilion, a resort and dance hall on the very edge of the lake. There they danced almost alone in the near darkness on a vast floor illuminated only by skeins of small colored lights, a floor that seemed to extend onward indefinitely to blend with the water and star-sprinkled night in the west. Dancing on and on to old-time favorites with a subtle jungle throb like "Quiet Village." It was one her parents had sometimes danced to in their living room on summer evenings. And there on the great briny lake, Utah's "inland sea" . . . Lon and Marilyn, euphorically drifting in each other's arms, pulses blending, and all the songs somehow ideal—Lionel Richie, Dan Fogelberg, Christopher Cross: "Sailing . . . sailing away . . ."

Suddenly something stung Marilyn's cheek, and she wrenched from her reverie with a start, nearly running off the roadside into a ditch. A deerfly the color of gunmetal streaked off, circling. For a moment she felt a twinge of panic, then irritation, followed by an intense bitterness she failed at first to understand.

Twenty-Two

The deerfly followed pestiferously for several minutes, and each time she panicked—victim, she knew, to a typically feminine fear of insects, especially the biting or stinging variety—but also because she couldn't use both hands to ward it off. Worse still, the deerfly reminded her of bees and hornets, to which she was quite allergic. Once as a child she had been stung on the ankle by a yellow jacket and her entire lower leg had swollen badly all the way to the knee. Even now, twenty years later, she was still a bit paranoid in that regard.

Eventually, after a third or fourth attack from the deerfly and another painful bite, she pulled to a stop, straddling the bike and holding her arms out as bait. It was something she had seen Kelly do. "A deerfly always takes about two seconds to bite after it lands," he had told her, "but they're pretty skittish, so you have to keep your cool and give them time to settle down. Then . . ." He had grinned slyly, actually demonstrating with a live one. Slap! The creature had bounced from his forearm, dead. His reflexes were so fast he rarely missed. In fact, he could sometimes snare normal houseflies on the wing.

The fly of the moment, however, refused to accommodate; it was as if the creature could read her mind, and meanwhile she was passed by another cyclist. Worse still, almost worse than the deerfly, from a short distance behind came an all-too-familiar voice. "Hey Lyn-Lyn! Thanks for holding up, girl!" Marilyn closed her eyes, wincing. "Wait'll ya hear what happened to *me*!" He drew up alongside her, puffing happily, ecstatic, it seemed, at being with her once more. "This is not a triathlon," she thought, "it's a carnival."

"Remember that redheaded girl I started following a while back?"

"Yes, I seem to recall," she replied and started off again. Now she'd have both Cuddles and the deerfly, but she was admittedly curious regarding his recent whereabouts.

"Well, this crazy girl . . ." Puff, puff. He added a gagging snort of disbelief. "I mean, she's gotta be some sort of kook!"

"Oh, really?"

"Yeah, really. I just started following along in her slipstream, which is pefectly legitimate when it comes to racing, as you may know, and, well"—he continued to huff and puff erratically—"she apparently . . . well, didn't *like* it."

"Probably didn't enjoy having your front tire go all the way up the back of her neck." It was a cruel thing to say but perhaps necessary.

"I wasn't!" he protested. "All's I did was try to strike up a friendly conversation."

"But Cuddles," Marilyn said long-sufferingly, "hasn't it ever . . ." She was breathing deeply and regularly, trying to keep from puffing herself. A magpie, exploring the flattened remains of a rodent just ahead, abandoned them and flapped off across a field of sugar beets. "Occurred to you that some stranger might not want your entire family history?"

"But Lyn-Lyn—"

"Especially in the middle of—"

"But I wasn't *doing* that!" It sounded like the grating cluck of an outraged mudhen. "I was just trying to be a Good Samaritan." By now his panting was becoming wheezy. A touch of asthma. "And give her a couple tips about racing . . . like not sitting up so straight and catching all the wind. But, as it turns out . . . she wasn't even *in* the race!"

"Oh, Cuddles—*no*!" Marilyn began to titter, felt the hilarity rising.

"Yes! I mean, no, she wasn't!"

"Didn't you ever look to see if she had a number?"

"How could I? I was riding along behind her. Couldn't exactly see what she was wearing up front." They passed a strip of high weeds flipping and fidgety with grasshoppers. "But anyway, after a while she turned off down this little side road and . . . well, I just figured it was a shortcut or something. But then she stopped at somebody's house and . . . and I just naturally stopped for a sec too—to see if there was anything wrong. I thought you saw us."

"Nope—thought maybe you'd been carried off by a UFO." They were curving along a slight rise where the asphalt had been worn away in large patches, leaving only dirt and gravel. "I was pretty worried."

"Well, I just wanted to make sure she was okay . . . but do you know what? She was all freaked out—looked like she was going to start bawling or something. She went up on the porch of this house and started punching the doorbell like mad." He swerved to avoid a chuckhole and nearly ran into her. "Told me if I didn't leave her alone she was going to call the cops!"

Marilyn gave a gasp of laughter. "Oh—Cuddles, Cuddles!"

"Cuddles, Cuddles, what?" His tone was one of bewilderment, betrayal. "That's the *thanks* I get for being a Good Samaritan!"

"So I've got him back again," she told herself. "Maybe I should call the cops too." The more she contemplated the whole scenario the more ludicrous it became.

Suddenly Cuddles cried out in dismay. "Go on, get out of here, you lousy—Hey, Lyn!" It was a squawk of near terror. "I'm being attacked by an insect—a deerfly or somethin'!"

"Too bad," she called and tried not to giggle. "Better not talk, though—they're attracted to noise."

"Seriously?"

"Definitely—especially the human voice."

They passed a cement grain silo, then a line of storage sheds, blue sheet metal with white garage doors. "Well," Cuddles called after a long silence, his tone strangely subdued. "At least he hasn't attacked again."

"That's 'cause you're keeping quiet." No doubt by now their friend Janie was far ahead, possibly miles, she decided, but at least they had finally reached the road to Corinne and soon were crossing several sets of tracks at the old Brigham City train station. Occasionally she had taken small swigs of water from the plastic bottle in its container beneath her crossbar, but for now she refrained, fairly certain that Cuddles had chugalugged all of his own long ago and would feel no compunction whatever about requesting some of hers.

It was steadily growing hotter. She could feel the sunlight dancing in her hair, beginning to burn her arms and shoulders a little despite the tan. Westward was a flotilla of small mackerel clouds like scattered cottage cheese, and they were slowly moving her direction, or she in theirs. It was hard to tell, but maybe, just maybe they'd provide a little more shade before long.

Fanning before them were immense fields of sugar beets, occasional alfalfa as well, its dark blue-green sprinkled with millions of tiny purple flowers. Once they passed a patch of giant sunflowers, centers the size and color of pancakes, petals like molten gold. "Wow, I'm burning up," Cuddles called, voice still a little restrained. He was lagging about twenty yards behind. "Probably going to get dehydrated." It was his trial balloon, his first hint, and she let it float on by. Silence, like the flowers, was golden.

Shortly thereafter they were passing the Corinne general store with its adjoining cafe and gas station. "Man, am I ever thirsty!" Cuddles exclaimed. "I'm about ready to stop and buy a couple root beers."

"Wouldn't recommend that," Marilyn called, "but if you're out of water they've probably got a tap by those gas pumps."

"Hey, yeah!" The thought seemed to please him. "I might just do that." It definitely pleased her. Hopefully she could put some real yardage between them during the interim. It was a malicious thought in a way, and in some respects she actually enjoyed Cuddles's company simply because he was so innocent and good-natured, and because he accepted people for what they were even if they often mystified, even insulted him. And, well, she was pretty fond of the character despite everything. On the other hand, he was often something of an albatross, and she wanted to run her own race, think her own thoughts. Make up if at all possible for precious time lost.

A biker—two of them, in fact—were materializing ahead, and a few minutes later she passed them with a small feeling of triumph. Two girls, probably in their late teens, the same ones, as she recalled, who had left her behind back during the distraction with her good canine friend Rover. Cars continued to speed by periodically. Two or three times, in fact, she received whistles, and once a barbaric wolf howl from a pickup hurtling in the same direction as the bikers. It passed so close that she glimpsed her own startled face in its right side mirror along with a tattooed forearm, the elbow projecting from the open window.

Occasionally the lenses of oncoming headlights caught and reflected the sun brilliantly, and that made her think of diamonds, her own still burning away in the back of her drawer. No, *not* her diamond! It had been palmed off, literally, on her, and she would definitely have to send it back. That's all there was to it. The thought was enough, however, to trigger an imagined scene, one wherein Lon Yeager was pleading with her, humble and beautifully penitent, exhorting her with tears in his eyes to wear it again for just twenty-four hours.

She shook her head. No! No more fantasizing, no more reminiscing. Maybe, simply as a matter of survival, she should force herself to think more about other men. She thought of Gordie Yates and Don Dawson, who would be faithfully awaiting her at the finish line. Such good-hearted characters, but she had never been able to consider them as dating possibilities, let alone the quintessence of romance. She thought of Art Tillotson, a boyfriend from seasons past, and regretted the fact that he was a bit too diminutive and, to be honest, not quite good-looking enough to excite her. The realization gave her a sense of guilt because he had nearly all the other requisites she longed for, and because it made her feel prejudiced and vain. She definitely was, Marilyn confessed, too strongly influenced by outward appearances. And yet . . . you couldn't simply alter your feelings toward someone by an act of will.

She was passing immense fields of corn now, some of it just coming into tassel, unfurling in robust green for hundreds of yards. A road sign read, "Morton Thiokol 12—Golden Spike Monument 21." Another sixteen miles of biking and then the toughest part of all, the five-mile run.

Too much still to fully believe, certainly to dwell on. Instead she thought again of the men she had dated, two or three of them tall and fairly handsome yet somehow nondescript, or at least lacking uniqueness, especially in personality. That too was a problem. Rather clonelike essentially. In a few instances friends who had arranged the dates to begin with had become rather vexed with her for not responding with greater enthusiasm. "But *why* don't you like him?" they sometimes demanded. Even Janie, who had tried playing cupid more than once despite heartaches of her own. Not long ago, in fact, she had arranged a date for Marilyn with one of Weber State's assistant basketball coaches, a young man generally considered to be quite a prize for almost any girl.

"So how was it?" Jan had inquired afterward, lilting the words seductively.

"Oh . . ." The shrug had barely been visible. "Okay, I guess."

"Okay? You guess?" Janie looked dumbfounded. "Lyn Baby, you've just been out with one of the most sought-after males in town, and that's all you can say? 'Okay, I guess'?"

"We had a good time," Marilyn said, "and he's pretty nice." She tried her best to seine out any slight tone of disillusionment, of world-weariness.

"But what's wrong with him? Name me one single thing that's *wrong* with him!"

"There's nothing wrong with him, except that maybe he's a little too taken with himself. But . . . it's not really that. I just didn't feel any chemistry."

Jan shook her head, and her tone for once was somewhat dire. "You know, Marilyn . . ." That was the clue. She only used her actual name when she was ticked off at her. "I honestly think you're getting too picky!"

"I'm not *too picky,* Jan." She could feel the exasperation welling. "It's just that I wasn't wild over the guy, and I seriously doubt that he was wild over me. So let's just leave it at that, okay?" Later she apologized, tried to assure Janie that she truly appreciated her loyal friendship and all she'd done in trying to line her up. Before long they were laughing and lighthearted again. "Hey, maybe *you* should go out with him," Marilyn suggested. "Really, Jan, why not?" For the moment she was serious.

"Ha!" her friend snorted. "I'm about two feet tall, and he's about twenty. A date between a giraffe and an armadillo! Wouldn't dare get near a basketball floor with him—he'd probably try to dribble me!" And that indeed had cracked them up.

Journeying westward on her bike, she considered again what Janie had said. Was she actually "too picky," and if so, were some of her friends suffering the same affliction? She had posed the question to Kelly and Shannon only a few days earlier, in fact, during an evening visit in their backyard. Kelly had shrugged. "Always possible." His Levi's and shirt were still white with sawdust, even some of his hair. He had been working on the extension to their home. Shannon sat next to him nursing her baby daughter beneath a pink shawl, and Rone was having a joyous time nearby in a plastic wading pool. "But I'm not so sure that's true in your case. You just haven't found the right one yet. Thought you had for a while, and he turned out to be an eight ball." He removed his work shoes and socks, groaning with satisfaction. "Ah!" He wriggled his toes. "Such liberation!"

"Are you talking about Marilyn or your feet?" Shannon laughed.

"Both, I guess." Kelly laughed, then returned to the question at hand. "But, after all, you've gotta be selective—especially . . ." He glanced at his wife with obvious satisfaction. "Especially if you plan to make it forever. You'd better be sure."

Shannon's smile was knowing. "I was sure from about the age of eight," she said quietly. Her face was softly radiant there in the gathering evening, and the infant nursed steadily, emitting occasional little gurgles and sighs. "It just took Kel about ten years longer to get the message."

Kelly grinned and stretched, laid his hand on her shoulder, eyes fairly exuding devotion. "Well, I've got it now, Angel." It was one of his many little pet names for her, and Marilyn had felt a slight prick of envy, partly because all her life she had cherished the hope of finding a husband much like her brother and because by now her faith in that possibility had become a mere reed in the wind. Shannon had literally known from childhood who the man would be, had her own personal revelation on the subject, and it hardly seemed fair. Why should some people be handed such a gift with scarcely a word of request when others were left groping, *endlessly* it seemed in some cases? No matter how earnestly they tried, how hard they wept, or how long they prayed. It made no sense. It made God seem very arbitrary.

She was cycling doggedly now, almost angrily, on and on, lost in her own thoughts, gliding past fields of ripening wheat, past great rolls of harvested hay, tracing along a fence line with occasional "No Trespassing" signs. And again she was tempted by the reminder that she, Marilyn Richards Cannon, had gone all her life—twenty-five years—never breaking the moral laws of God, the laws of chastity, whereas her sister-in-law had once gotten into serious trouble. It simply wasn't fair! Simultaneously, she felt riddled with guilt at the very thought. Maybe Shannon had been subjected to even greater temptations, had been afflicted too directly at the time of her greatest disillusionment and vulnerability. Furthermore, how could anyone who knew the girl ever forget how she had suffered or what a regeneration she had undergone well before her marriage?

"No, Lyn-Lyn," she thought a bit caustically, "judge not that ye be not judged." Such impulses would simply have to be eliminated. Cast out. Annihilated!

Even then, however, she began to feel resentment again over the fact that certain well-meaning people—various good sisters in her home ward, mainly—had assured her that some fine day the right one would materialize. "Good old Mr. Right!" as Carla Bonner had so bitterly phrased it at Lake Powell. Maybe not quite the Snow White prince, but unquestionably The One and Only. Someday he would be there, and when it happened every girl would absolutely *know* if she just had enough faith and lived the right kind of life.

Her thoughts reverted once more to the evening with Kelly and Shannon. "It isn't always easy," Kelly had admitted. Understatement of the year. "It's a case of finding the right combination, and that doesn't happen like clockwork for everybody."

"You can say that again," Marilyn had replied.

"I know plenty of great girls, some real dolls, that are just waiting and wondering, that for some reason hardly ever get a date. I mean, it's really weird; I can't figure out why."

"That's because so many guys are wimps," Shannon said. What was it Carla Bonner had called them? "Devout cowards?" Marilyn found herself smiling a bit cynically. "They want marriage," Shannon continued, "and yet, they don't want it. They're afraid of the challenge."

Kelly nodded. "Already getting set in their ways, a lot of them. Once they hit, say, their upper twenties—even earlier in some cases—a lot of 'em start feeling ambivalent. They want to be married like mad on the one hand, but on the other they're in love with their freedom, leery of upsetting the status quo. Besides, they really enjoy having only one person to spend their bucks on—new car, plenty of fancy clothes, a chance to eat out whenever they feel like it . . . the whole bit."

Marilyn nodded, her smile faint and morose, still reminiscing. A field of rust-colored Indian tobacco drifted into view, a pond fringed with cattails and dotted with several teal, a bright yellow road sign with a curving black arrow. Not far ahead to her left was a little wayside bathhouse made of cinder block. The place was called "Stinkin' Springs," and she could smell its sulfurous fumes, the pungent, rotten-egg gas odor, before it ever became visible.

Well, inadvertently or otherwise, Kelly had described her own situation in some respects. The dichotomy of feeling was not always restricted to men. It truly seemed at times, in fact, as though she herself were two personalities. She recalled now the bridal shower a week earlier for a college acquaintance named Sally Thompson, one attended by various of her other friends as well—most of them now married, two conspicuously pregnant. One of the latter was suffering from mild toxemia, her skin splotched and puffy. She appeared to have acquired an extra forty pounds or more.

Marilyn had arrived in her new Mazda, a snazzy little job the color of melted butter, brilliantly waxed and polished for the occasion. She was wearing a silver-gray sheath with black pendant earrings, dark cat-eye sunglasses, her golden hair gathered in a silver clasp and long enough to reach her waist, draped over the front of one shoulder.

Oh, it was definitely a form of compensation, a transparent attempt to lord it over the rest of them. Something she had calculated from the onset, and it had worked. Afterward one of her friends—a girl named Connie Linford whose marriage had hit the rapids—drew her aside for a little advice. "Marilyn," she said with a slight quaver, "I know life's not easy for you after all that's happened the past while, but—" She struggled momentarily for control. Her face, though still quite pretty, seemed to have shrunken and become somewhat monkeylike. "Marriage isn't always sunshine and meadowlarks, believe me."

"I'm sure—" Marilyn began, only to have her friend continue impetuously.

"Practically everybody who was here today just about envies you to death!" No doubt that reaction represented a bit of projection on Connie's part, Marilyn later decided, but it probably contained a lot of truth too. "So enjoy the freedom and glamour while you can, Lyn. Don't wish it away too fast—know what I mean?"

Well, she had certainly achieved her objective. Her empty little goal.

Twenty-Three

So, yes, she had gained her hollow little triumph, but in reality it was just another case of "all dressed up and no place to go." At the moment, however, she did have a place to go—the Golden Spike National Monument—and she was on the final leg of her journey. She had entered the five-mile run, having left her bike behind in the hands of the race assistants.

Where, after the Golden Spike, she would go in life itself was one of the mysteries of the gospel, but for now it was enough simply to run her own race and do it rationally to the very best of her ability. That was her challenge. For some time she had been biking northwest but now she was jogging due west toward the upper tip of the lake. The clouds had thickened, closing out much of the sun and stretching ahead like an immense, gradually narrowing carpet—an illusion which lent the wild and barren terrain before her a tremendous sense of depth.

The farm fields had evolved to rolling hills festooned with sage and rabbit brush, juniper, and dry bunchgrass along the roadside. Occasionally, here and there, a dust devil sprang to life briefly, then expired, but there was a sense of change in the atmosphere. What had become of Cuddles she didn't know; she could only hope that he was still chugging along to the beat of his own drummer. Maybe he had succumbed to his natural lust for root beer—one glass too many, a thousand not enough. She shook her head, bemused, then thought with an unexpected pang how difficult his race in life was and might become. Would Cuddles Eskelson ever find his own special someone? It would require a different sort of girl for certain. Undoubtedly one who would be rather eccentric herself, a bit of a misfit. But maybe she was out there somewhere, a person who would even consider him quite wonderful, and together they could achieve the right symbiosis.

For now it was not quite the thing to worry about, but maybe in time she could help, help Cuddles to find someone even if she could never do the same for herself. Again she thought of Elijah Marriott. He had spent his entire life helping people, often in material ways, but also helping them become self-sufficient, helping them above all to acquire an upbeat attitude, to think and aspire BIG with capital letters.

The old man had been a competitor from the beginning, a professional wrestling champion in the days of weight divisions when "rasslin' was rasslin'." He was an inveterate outdoorsman, a jogger when such activity automatically labeled one "an exercise fanatic" or even a suspicious character. "Up until twenty years or so back," he had recently confided, "when I was a mere youngster in my seventies, everybody stared like I was one of them what-ya-callims. A streaker, yeah. Why, you'd have thought I was an outright menace to society." Stroking his wrinkled jowls, he continued, "Come to think of it, maybe I was. Some of 'em would about drive off the road into the nearest telephone pole. 'Anything wrong?' 'Need a ride somewhere?' Well, I'd just laugh and give 'em the hi sign plus a 'thanks but no thanks.' Ride was exactly what I didn't need, what most of them didn't need either. What they needed was to get off their hind sides and move their bones around before rigor mortis took and set in. And the same holds true today. Oh, there's been a change for the better, but most of the nation's still a-going to flab." Then raising the admonitory forefinger, almost threateningly: "And that includes too many good folks right inside the church. Eighty-ninth section says they 'shall run and not be weary, and shall walk and not faint.' Doesn't say, '*sun* and *rock*.' You want to run and not be weary and walk and not faint, why—you'd just better start a-doin' it!"

But always, always, Marilyn was beginning to realize, there was more to it than that. Racing was symbolical of life itself, a fact the Preacher had pointed out thousands of years ago. How did it go? "The race is not to the swift nor the battle to the strong, but he that endureth to the end . . ." She closed her eyes for an instant in acquiescence. "The important thing," Lije had told her, was "to just keep putting one foot ahead of the next. You keep a-doing that long enough and you'll surely get there in time. Whatever it is you're headed for, you'll get there in time, and it doesn't really matter how many's ahead of you—not if you've got hold of the big picture. After all, there's always somebody out there ahead of us in reality, and that's what makes it so grand; it's all part of the plan. Only thing you and I are asked to do is our best." His remarkable ancient face had suddenly flowed with that familiar quality of eternal youth that was so inescapably a part of Elijah Marriot. At times it was almost as though a young and vital actor had been made up as an old man.

Well, at least I'm still in the race, she thought. I'm still putting one foot ahead of the other even if they're both getting blisters. She was, in fact, doing better than that, than had perhaps seemed possible in light of her earlier doubts and interruptions. She had even gained strength toward the end of the biking phase, passing several other cyclists in the final stretch. It was a mile-long, uphill pull that looked like a killer, but she had hung in and felt surprisingly good.

So now, she told herself, just keep thinking positive. No more reminiscing about Lonnie Boy, not even the happiest times. Such things invariably weakened her one way or another, and they had become a near obsession.

The only way to keep him out of her mind very long, it seemed, was to fill the space with other people—Lije, Bishop Belnap, her mom, her brother, Shannon . . . her dad, ten years on the other side but nonetheless very real. And friends like Janie, still somewhere ahead in the race. Maybe she had already crossed the finish line, taken a first. Well, if so, more power to her. She deserved it.

Once she thought of Mark Aldous, her "boss" at work who was, in reality, anything but bossy. Here she was, fretting over a broken engagement every hour of the day, and for several months now Mark had been suffering the loss of his wife from leukemia, wondering how to care for his three young children. Recently he had been released as bishop over one of the college wards to spend more time with his family. Quite a remarkable dad and person throughout it all, from everything she could tell. Occasionally she had lunched with him in the UB cafeteria or college Sky Room, tried to be a listening ear and heart, though not nearly as well as he had following her shattered engagement.

She thought of Mark's wife Karen, a radiant soul without the slightest ostentation who rarely lost her smile or graciousness even in the face of her greatest suffering. Even as the pallor of death had settled, leaving her emaciated with an almost x-ray–like transparency, she had still retained that spiritual lambency.

And Mark . . . once or twice during Marilyn's conversations with him, the serene blue of his gaze had clouded, but never had she detected any self-pity or trace of bitterness. Always, as well, the gentleman, though far from goody-goody—"the genuine article," as Alma Belnap, a very genuine article himself, sometimes said of certain people. It was one of his highest compliments. Who did Mark remind her of? she wondered. Pat Boone? Yes, a little, that same kind of clean-cut, boyish appearance and affable demeanor without ever being at all juvenile.

Well, one day Mark would probably remarry, but it would take an exceptional person to replace Karen. On the other hand, not really a replacement, simply an addition, because Karen continued in another realm, united to Mark and her children forever.

For several minutes Marilyn reflected on the matter with increasingly mixed feelings. Momentarily she could see the face of Karen Aldous quite vividly and wondered how even a woman of her stature would respond if some day Mark were to marry again—again in the temple, which would probably be the case if he married at all. A stranger, come in to share, take over all that had been hers—household, husband, and children . . . and, well, face it, her bed. That was where it really got tough. It was definitely perplexing, disturbing, and the "dear departed" having no say whatever in the matter.

She was actually becoming a bit angry at Mark Aldous, ached for the sake of Karen, felt almost as though she herself had been victimized. Simultaneously she began to feel a burning in her left side and a short while later developed a slight charley horse in her right calf. Even one in the arch of her foot. Suddenly she felt a pang of anxiety. What if now, after all her work, after hanging in all this time, what if only three miles or so from the end she fizzled out? Maybe even passed out? Stupid Cuddles, anyway! "Just don't pass out, Lyn-Lyn! Whatever you do, just don't pass out!"

The pain in her side was definitely increasing, and soon the cramps in her calf and arch became so bad she had to limp and hobble. Terrifying—going to blow it, blow the whole thing! "Think relaxed," she told herself tensely, "think relaxed!" For an instant the irony escaped her. Then it grabbed hold, and she actually began to laugh a little right through her misery. "Calm down, pal," she told herself. "Hang loose, girl, just hang loose . . . like a scarecrow." That helped a little. The burning in her side diminished slightly. The knots in her leg muscles began to relax.

The season's first wild sunflowers were beginning to blossom along the roadside, petals of resplendent gold, and they made her feel even better. She tried to relive her jogs with Kelly, remember his advice about not running on the balls of her feet. That more than anything else caused the calf muscles to tire and cramp. The balls of the feet were strictly for sprinting. Jogging and racing distance, you barely touched them to the ground as shock absorbers, then rolled onto the heel. Or, when the legs were very tired, cramping as hers were now, you could set the heel down first—but not hard like some runners, who seemed determined to ruin their knees and lower backs, jar all their fillings loose in the process. No, just smooth and relaxed, gently in this case, rolling forward.

"Hang loose, Golden Girl," a familiar voice seemed to say. Golden Girl! The name her dad had given her long ago. Her dad! It was as if she had literally heard him. For a moment her eyes glistened. Much like Lije's "Honey Girl," a name always applied with great fondness. But maybe her dad really *was* there, accompanying her, encouraging, trying to get through, with only a very thin kind of veil separating them, on the verge of evaporating. It might seem a childish thought to some people, mere wishful thinking. On the other hand, why not? Especially at such a crucial time. For a wondrous, growing moment, the tingling sense of love and concern, of actual presence, increased. Her gaze grew wistful, and the tears came. "I love you, Dad," she murmured, "miss you so *much*!"

Once two crows flew by, sawing against the breeze with their gleaming black wings, and croaking. For some reason that unnerved her a little. It seemed to be an ill omen, but what bothered her even more was the breeze itself, blowing almost directly into her face now. That and the marked incline ahead, the road snaking upward for a hundred yards or more to a rock-studded horizon, all ajumble like a fallen fortress, something hit by an earthquake. Beyond lay the gray sky with only the faintest intimation of blue. Pain in the side, cramps in the leg and foot, a wind in her face, the hill ahead. Too much. Again the panic began to swell. It was too much to expect. She simply couldn't hack it against odds like that.

Her legs were weakening, head swirling. Maybe she really *would* faint after all, maybe there was something basically wrong with her. Two of the runners who had once been some distance behind were now passing her, and suddenly she became angry—first at them. They had no right to pass her, to take advantage of a person with . . . even a pain in her side! Maybe appendicitis! Then she became angry with herself. What a hypochondriac, what a crummy little coward! "You're not wimping out on this one, girl," she told herself. "Not if it kills you."

"And it's not going to kill you, dum-dum," another voice seemed to say. "The fact is, you're in great shape. Remember Lake Powell, the water and the mountains? How nothing could stop you? How you could just keep going on and on forever?" It was just a little conversation with herself, her alter ego.

"But what about the pain in my side?" she asked. "I'm limping. I can barely hobble."

"Yes, but why?" came the reply. "What was the basic cause, your body or your mind? Think *relax* . . . think *relax, calm, peace.* The pain is going away, going away, going away." With every stride she repeated the words "going away," and it actually began to happen, the burning to subside, the cramps to diminish.

"But what about the wind? It's blowing right in my face. The hill? It's even longer and steeper than I thought."

"Okay, so you misjudged a little, so what? It's the same wind and hill for everybody." Again she recalled her brother's advice, things learned during his days running cross-country in college and as a jogger ever since. "You don't fight a hill," he had told her, "and you don't fight the wind—you just lean into them and swing those elbows to give you momentum. If the hill's steep or the wind's strong you actually . . . well, you just sort of *fall* forward and keep putting one foot out there ahead of the other to catch yourself. That way gravity itself is doing a lot of the work."

"So all right," the voice within her responded. "You haven't tried it that much before, but what's to lose? The worst you can do is fall on your face. And you've already done that plenty of times, figuratively speaking." Amazingly, she began to experience the benefits almost instantly. In the process of falling forward, she found herself relaxing, the pain in her side easing, the strain on her legs, the cramps, diminishing. "Pain's going away," she told herself, "going away . . . going away."

"Don't even use words like 'pain,' " her alter ego advised. "Just say, 'better and better . . . feelin' good.' " Yeah, that was it, the way to go. With every two strides she was repeating the words *feeling better*, and gradually as her condition improved, *feelin' good.* The positive attitude principle was real and, specifically in this case, it was biofeedback. Conscious thoughts could control the emotions, and emotions could affect the mind and the body.

At the brow of the hill, she was assaulted by a huge tumbleweed. It seemed to bound at her from nowhere, caught her full in the face for an instant, prickling and jabbing, but she cast it aside and continued, refusing to be upset or even distracted.

Just ahead on her right was a sign that said, "Finish line two miles." One way or another, she was going to make it now, even if she had to crawl. But there was no need for that. Everything was getting better and better. All she needed to add now to her positive attitude was something even greater, something called faith. "Heavenly Father," she prayed and hesitated. Prayer had always been a part of her life, but what particularly, at this time and place, was appropriate? That she could do better than others? No, absurd. They were all his children too. Maybe just that she might be able to do her best. "Help me," she breathed. She was running smoothly now, inhaling and exhaling evenly. Her strides were long and loose, flowing. She was also dangling her hands occasionally and shaking them loosely at the ends of her wrists, even flopping her head a little from side to side to relax the neck; that was important. "Help me . . . help us *all* to do our best . . . and to learn something valuable."

Twenty-Four

Far off to the north lay Howell Valley, Snowville, and the Idaho border. Ahead, westward, beyond the finish line was the Promontory Range and waterfowl area, beyond that Spring Bay, the northern tip of the Great Salt Lake. Shafts of widening sunlight were breaking through the clouds, and she could see azure blue. All about her were the undulating hills of sage and juniper stretching on and on, seemingly endless.

It was different country from that of Lake Powell, more barren, less exotic and fabulous, but there was that same exhilarating sense of immensity, and . . . of what? Of being caught up in the hands of creation. She was still praying from time to time, repeating her request about gaining something valuable from the experience. For everybody involved. A flight of dun-toned mourning doves streaked by, arching and darting with the breeze. Metal fence posts, dirty orange with white tips, marched over rises and into swales along the road, sometimes vanishing behind the sagebrush. "And, Heavenly Father . . ." She found herself glancing skyward a bit expectantly. "Bless Cuddles—I mean Bernard." Somehow it didn't quite seem right to use his nickname with God. "That he'll find his way and not get lost."

Gradually the breeze was abating, and occasional warm drops of rain were dimpling her brow and cheeks, her arms. There was the smell of ozone and sage, of warm asphalt, even the sand and gravel along its fringes, the hint of brine from Spring Bay, the indefinable quality of cleanliness from the clearing sky, bursts of light appearing along the road ahead. And somewhere over distant ranges, faint ruminations of thunder. All these things filled her with a strange hope and happiness, seemed wholesomely intoxicating.

She was listening to her body now, and it sounded pretty optimistic. Despite all the energy expended—the mile swim, the thirty-five of biking, and now the running—everything seemed to be in order. The pain had been temporary, mentally induced in the main, not the kind of persistent warning that says, "Caution, something is definitely wrong. Ease up, rest, monitor with care." Not what she had experienced some time ago with her mini-marathon in the Valley, her first disastrous race.

"And please also, Lord, bless sick people everywhere, and bless the dog that kept following me that he can be happy and safe, that he can find the right owner and not have to lose his life." It was hardly a sophisticated prayer, she realized; she felt like a child. But God didn't care about sophistication or fancy wording; she knew that much. He cared about sincerity and gratitude. "Thank you for life, for a healthy body that can just keep going and going like this." The words in her mind were coming with near amazement. "And for thine endless, magnificent creations. This vast, wild land, all around us . . . for everything!"

She was feeling euphoric and joyously incredulous over the change, steadily increasing her pace, passing once more the runners who had passed her, slightly embarrassed, not wanting to show off or make others feel unhappy, but also gratified about doing well. A short distance ahead were two sturdy football player types, linemen, both moving like workhorses and sweating heavily. Within minutes she had passed them too, feeling almost apologetic, but apparently they were not at all insulted. "Way to do it," one of them huffed and flashed her a boyish grin. "Let 'er rip."

No question, she was flowing on the wings of euphoria. It was almost frightening, immensely exciting. She could see only one other figure ahead at the moment, and upon drawing nearer realized with a start that it was Janie Johnson. The compact, darkly tanned figure in its blaze pink shorts, white joggers, and golf cap. As Marilyn drew nearer, Janie cast a glance over her shoulder and panted joyously, "Lyn-Lyn—way to *go*!" But there was a distinct hitch in Janie's stride.

"You okay?" Marilyn asked, now pacing along beside her.

Janie smiled ruefully. "Yeah . . . just twisted my knee a little." Both of them were breathing too hard for much talk. "Tripped over a rock." Her knee, in fact, was bruised and bleeding a little. It looked as if she had fallen.

"Looks bad . . . wanna walk?"

Janie shook her head. "No—s'okay."

"Sure? Let's walk the rest of the way together."

Janie half closed her eyes, continued to shake her head. "Not on your life, girl. Go for it—don't hang back." Another flight of doves tilted by. A jackrabbit bounded across the road, ears forking, zigzagging wildly into the sage. "Win this thing . . . for both of us." Marilyn felt a little spasm in the pit of her stomach, a flare of excitement in the lungs. Was it possible? Actually *win*?

"You'll be okay? I don't want to leave—"

"I'll be just fine," Jan insisted. "Go on, look alive . . . here comes a buzzard!" It was a saying she had picked up from some long-gone boyfriend.

"Okay!" A mere gasp. "I'll try."

As she moved ahead there was no sign of buzzards, but a hawk was riding the thermals above the nearby hillside, and it seemed to be urging her onward. The sun was more constant now, striking the wing feathers with bronze, which faded to buff and white as it banked, exposing its pale breast.

Gazing enraptured at the hawk, she almost overlooked a final sign reading, "Finish line—one mile!" There the road turned left. Nearby a much larger sign, garish and multicolored, obviously rendered by someone with a sense of humor, pointed the opposite direction, reading: "Game Birds Unlimited—13 Mi." Well, not thirteen more for her, thank heaven—only one. It was hard to assimilate. On the one hand, she could feel the immense stress of the entire ordeal upon her body, the great investment of energy. On the other, she was still not exhausted. Reserves of strength were welling that she had never anticipated. "Father in Heaven, I thank thee so much for seeing me through this, for buoying me up. Please help me . . . help me now to endure to the end. And please, especially be with Janie." Two hundred yards ahead were several more runners—a boy in the lead and five girls gradually stringing out behind.

"Float," she told herself, "relax and float on the air like a butterfly. Breathe deep and easy . . . hang loose . . . enjoy the journey." A short while later she was passing them, hearing their labored breathing, passing everyone but the boy, striding beside him but unable to pull ahead. He was a long, ungainly specimen with a nervous but friendly smile, beaver teeth and a protruding Adam's apple. He also had amazingly long legs.

"Hi," he huffed, "you're lookin' real good."

"Thanks." She didn't know what else to say and wanted to conserve oxygen anyway.

"Buncha guys up there," he continued. "Prob'ly crossed the line."

She cast him a glance. "How many women?"

"Dunno . . . only a couple maybe." She could hear his lungs pumping steadily, but there was no wheezing. Both runners were slick with sweat. Her headband was so saturated she yanked it off and wadded it in her fist, squeezing out huge drops of water. There was nothing after that but the rhythm of their feet contacting the road, the alternations of their exhalations. That and the endless sound of cicadas, heard yet unheard, stinging out across the land like the hum of high voltage wires.

If that's true, though, she thought—only a couple more girls ahead—then I could actually come in third in the women's division. It boggled her mind a little. She had not expected to place at all, especially after all the distractions. But of course maybe there were lots of girls still ahead. How could this guy make more than an educated guess? Still, she felt the excitement rising. It surged very strongly as the road took another jog to the left, as a sign appeared indicating only half a mile remaining.

Her vision was blurring somewhat, sweat dripping into her eyes, but a figure was materializing ahead, and she could discern feminine contours even within the watery looking mirage that seemed to dissolve them. She saw the shimmer of long blond hair much like her own. Marilyn shook her head unconsciously. There was no way of overcoming a lead that great in the eight hundred yards or so remaining. As the figure became more substantial, however, it seemed to waver and wobble, almost as though running on a treadmill. Probably nothing but an optical illusion. Maybe the figure itself was merely a hallucination or freak energy reaction.

But no, it was steadily becoming clearer—another contestant who was undergoing a real struggle, driving herself to the limit. Gradually Marilyn was closing in, but by now the soles of her feet were burning, and her left knee was aching. Maybe it was merely in sympathy with Janie Johnson's, maybe strictly too much stress now. No time, though, even for reflection now, only for determination—to keep placing one foot ahead of the other, to relax, relax, relax.

Her long-legged male friend was pulling ahead now, almost as if to challenge her, to make her exert her utmost, and it seemed to help. Gradually she was drawing abreast of the girl who had previously never existed, and soon they were running side by side bound in an unspoken kinship. That even more than competition, even though the Golden Spike Historical Site with its rock-faced Park Service building was now within view across the sage- and juniper-dotted terrain ahead. The building itself! The actual finish line! She felt the flare of excitement, surges of disbelief and anxiety.

Once two yellow cabbage moths fluttered by, suddenly joined by several white ones in an endless and erratic little game of ring-around-the-rosy, just as they had during the Valley Run when she suddenly passed—She closed her eyes, nearly stumbled, opened them, trying to focus on the road ahead yet tempted by the dizzying swirl of the moths. Others were joining them. "So?" a voice seemed to say. "So don't look at them, *dummerkinder.*" It was the word her dad had sometimes used long ago when she had managed to make a mess or do something foolish. Offered chidingly but mostly with amusement and love.

"Okay, Dad," she thought—"I get the message." Her eyes were glistening again behind the gold-tinted glasses. "I sure do love ya. I'll try my best not to let you down."

Somewhere off to her left a brush fire was underway, sending up a mushroom cloud of pale tan smoke that drifted languidly skyward, its top billowing out white. She could smell the aroma of burning sage and beyond through a parting in the hills lay a patch of muffled blue from the lake.

A good finish . . . all that was required. That was everything, no matter where she placed, how many were ahead or behind. To give it her best shot. At last the whole long ordeal was taking its inevitable toll on her body—lungs, heart, brain, every cell demanding more oxygen, crying out for surcease. And yet, even now . . . not the same type of stress she had sometimes known in the early phases of her training, the kind of sick pain, the misery that overwhelmed with nausea, that made her want to shrivel up and—*Dummerkinder!* She could remind herself now. Don't *think* about it—just run the good race, fight the good fight.

Twinges of sorrow for Janie. Jan was the one who should be winning this race. But no, don't think about that either. It wouldn't do her friend or anybody else the slightest good. Scarcely realizing it, she was passing a white sign with a black steam engine painted on it, crossing some railroad tracks without quite comprehending what they signified. Then the road turned right. The Park Service building was only two hundred yards away. She saw the roof with its heavy cedar shingles, the facade with its gemstone facing, warm rock tones with shades of sea green and copper. Cars were in the parking lot, quite a crowd assembled along each side of the finish line. Voices? Someone calling her name. Yes, sounded like Yates.

Her daddy-long-legs friend with the Adam's apple had pulled too far ahead to overtake. Within moments he'd be crossing the line, but no matter. She was still running shoulder to shoulder with her only competitor; it was as if they were united by some magnetic force, almost fused, momentarily grazing elbows a time or two. Marilyn drifted slightly to the left, and realized that she was striving rather than flowing, tightening up, lurching her shoulders from side to side.

"Relax, girl," she told herself, "float . . . float, everything straight ahead, hands and arms loose." Her face was becoming contorted, the neck cords taut. She rotated her neck, dangled her arms, shook her hands loosely as though they were barely attached to her wrists. Loose, loose . . . flow. Jan and Kelly had both been drumming that into her for weeks now. Flow like a river. She could see the faces ahead clearly now, some of them familiar, it seemed, even the Golden Spike Monument, a squat white obelisk containing a bronze plaque with a message . . . something she vaguely recalled about the great union of the intercontinental rails from east to west, driving of the final spike to bind the east with the west.

The hawk was still circling and lofting above as if to mark the spot, as if in commemoration, and her lungs were torching. Her tongue tasted coppery, and she could feel the pull of tendons against muscles. And now, miraculously, with only fifty yards remaining, she was slowly, agonizingly leaving the other girl behind.

"Go for it, go for it, Lyn Baby!" She heard the shouts, but everything was a kind of grand blur. "Go, girl . . . *go!*" Then she was over the finish line, three or four strides ahead of her competition, knees beginning to buckle as the arms reached out to rescue her and keep her walking. She saw Dawson's thick-lensed glasses twinkling merrily, felt her arm draped around his neck. "Way to *go*, kid! *First place women's!*"

"Really?" she gasped. "Oh, no—no way!" Incredible—impossible!

Gordie Boy Yates was supporting her from the opposite side, and she glimpsed his face—the white, grinning teeth, mustache curling wickedly at the ends, the amber Hollywood shades. "Hey, hey, *hey*! Lyn Girl!" She was gasping for air, half laughing, half crying. "You did it, no joke! *Very invigorating!*"

Twenty-Five

One moment she was typing, immersed in the compact little world of her word processor—writing an article on a retiring technology prof who had patented many inventions. The next, she was sensing a familiar presence as if all the cells in her back were tiny vestigial eyes. The door to her office had been only a few inches ajar, and now it was wide open.

He was standing there, leaning against the frame. Tan sport coat, cream-colored slacks, creases pressed to a cutting edge, brown loafers. In one hand was a box of chocolates. That fact was obvious despite the fancy wrapping and blue ribbon. "I know you're in training, champ," he said, "but at least you can keep the ribbon."

There was no denying it, the catch in her lungs and the little thrill like peppermint in her skin, all the tiny vesicles throughout her arms and neck. "Oh, Lon," she gasped, "you shouldn't have!" and promptly flushed pink through her tan, realizing how trite and phony the response had sounded. Simultaneously there was the distinct impression that he really *shouldn't* have. Already, only the day before, there had been the vase of white carnations delivered from Jimmie's Flower shop to her apartment, the accompanying card in his strong, flamboyant hand reading, "Much love to a *real* winner."

And now this. She didn't know how to respond at all and felt like a girl in junior high. As long as you're taking in strays," he laughed, "I thought you'd at least say hi to an old friend."

The reference to strays suddenly relaxed everything and made her laugh too. "Wasn't that crazy?" she said. "I still don't know how that part about the dog ever got into the write-up." Then, as a quick afterthought, feeling inhospitable, "Sit down."

"Well, okay." He took the chair next to her desk. "That was quite a story in the *Standard,*" he said. "And here I didn't even know you were a runner." Yet somehow, his tone and expression said that he understood why in part, that it was some kind of compensation.

"I didn't either," Marilyn laughed. "Jan got me started, but I'm still not sure. Sometimes, it still seems like—" She shook her head, gazing inside herself. "Sort of like a dream, and Jan really should have won if she hadn't fouled up her knee."

"Don't be too sure about that," Lon said and slid the chocolates casually onto the edge of her desk. "You've got the legs for it." He grinned. "Great shot of you coming over the finish line."

"It was terrible!" she protested. "I looked like I was choking on a chicken bone or something. Like my eyes were going to pop out."

"Not in my book," he insisted. "In fact, you looked pretty darned . . ." He waggled his brows in the old, playful manner. "Tantalizing."

"Oh, come on!" She felt irked with herself at the way her stomach fluttered, the way he could simply push a button without half trying. "Tantalizing was the *last* thing I looked like." Certainly, too, the last thing she had felt or thought about.

He shrugged, appraising her with the mischievous blue glint. "Guess it all depends on the perspective." The gaze absorbed her. "Male or female." The old hypnotic vibes, there in superabundance as always.

"I still don't know how they found out about that crazy dog." She felt a nervous need to change the subject.

" 'Marilyn R. Cannon celebrated her beginning triathlon by posting a first-place win in the women's division, despite having taken time out along the way to look after a stray dog.' " Lon had quoted the *Standard Examiner* account verbatim with a twinkle of amusement and no little fondness. Then more seriously, absorbing her gaze in his own, "You're some girl, Marilyn R. Cannon."

"Some idiot," she laughed. "Cuddles and Janie both swear they never said a word about it; so do Gordie and Daws. Maybe it was that highway patrol guy." Then, in answer to his questions, she was explaining exactly what had happened, telling about the whole big race.

"Well, quite an experience," Lon said afterward, "and pretty terrific—dusting 'em all like that first go around, and even after time out for that silly pooch. I mean, I'm really *impressed*, really *proud* of you." He paused, bathing her with his gaze. "Who but our girl Lyn-Lyn could do something like that?"

"Oh," she smiled and refused to be flustered—almost. "Plenty of people probably, and besides, it only took a couple of minutes. With the dog, I mean."

"Yeah, but a couple of minutes in a race," he persisted, "that could mean all the difference, even in a triathlon. He held out his hands. "I used to run cross-country in college, same as Kelly, and that two minutes or whatever could have put you so far ahead you'd have taken it in a breeze."

She shrugged, keeping it light. "There *was* a breeze, in fact. Once this big humongous tumbleweed hit me right in the face, practically devoured me. But maybe . . . ," she mused, "maybe falling behind like that made me try harder." It was the noon hour, and outside her window students were drifting in all directions across the campus greensward. "But anyway, I'm sort of glad now that I had to struggle."

He nodded, smiling, but for a moment his eyes were more serious. "Guess that's part of the program, isn't it? No pain, no gain."

"I guess that's right," she replied quietly. For a few seconds it seemed there was nothing more to say. "I really want to thank you for those flowers. They're beautiful."

Lon grinned, flipped up his thumbs. "*De nada.*"

"Oh yes it was," she insisted. "You're always so thoughtful. And for"—she angled a glance at the box on her desk, eyebrows raised—"the chocolates?" He smiled blandly, watching her face. "Have to watch out that I don't get fat."

"Fat chance," he said, and she realized more than ever how much all the little compliments and innuendos were a part of his appeal. Even blatant flattery, the kind that was clearly manipulative, and every woman seemed to feel her woman-ness more the instant he glanced at her.

"Well!" he suddenly exclaimed and clapped his knees. "It looks like you've got a deadline to meet or something." He rose and moved a step or two toward the door.

"Not really," she replied, "just a little article I'm trying to pound out in the next day or two for *Comment.*"

He nodded, eyes searching yet boyishly vulnerable. That was probably his most devastating combination. "Well, hey, look—I'll bet anything you're going to be heading out for lunch pretty quick—right?"

"Well . . . ," she answered uncertainly. He was, in fact, correct. "Pretty soon, I guess." Even before the words were out Marilyn knew that she had overcommitted, compromised herself. And yet the only alternative would have been an outright lie.

"So?" His brow lofted beseechingly with irresistible logic. "Long as I'm here, how's about grabbing a bite in the Sky Room? Have you right back at your handy-dandy little machine in half an hour—fair enough?" She hesitated, full of turmoil. "Come on, Lyn Girl, live dangerously. We can be up there in a couple minutes—nice buffet all ready and waiting. True?"

Marilyn took a deep breath, closed her eyes fleetingly, opened them, glanced at him obliquely, as if to say, "I'm on to you, Lon Yeager—this has all been orchestrated very craftily, hasn't it?" Or had it been? Weren't such things simply a basic part of his mental metabolism? In any event, her lips said something quite different. "Okay," they replied casually, "but we'll go Dutch, understood?"

He shrugged elaborately in abject surrender, grinning total triumph. The utmost indulgence. "Sure—whatever it takes."

The Weber State Sky Room was appropriately named. Located atop the Student Union Building, it was virtually enveloped by glass, furnishing a panoramic view of the city, surrounding campus, and hills. From their table with its white linen cloth, they could see the stadium eastward, nestled in the lap of the mountains. Westward lay the Administration Building where she worked, heavily panelled with dark one-way glass, and nearby the artificial, acre-sized duck pond with its high, spouting fountain and waterfowl, and the rolling greensward, all classically landscaped and contoured.

"Beautiful campus," Lon said.

She nodded. "It really is. And all those spruce and aspen are growing so fast, becoming actual trees." A pause. "One of the best views in town." Simmering there, unspecified but also unavoidable, in all their thoughts and words, she knew, was the recollection that this very place had been high on their list of spots for a wedding reception. So indeed had the fountain and pond area with its broad paved plaza along the southern shore. It was a Saturday afternoon at the onset of fall, only a few weeks hence, the mountainside turning to bronze, red, and gold, the aspens and locusts like yellow laughter against the deep, abiding green of the grass, the fountain frothing and pluming upward, the circulation of white, calling gulls. It had seemed a very fitting place, there at the same institution from which she had graduated, where she was now employed and so highly regarded. Practically everybody's darling.

Then, off for a week-long honeymoon in Peru, his old mission field, with a night or two at the heights of Machu Picchu. Lon had been there, even had in mind the hotel room high among the clouds on the very brink of that ancient fortress city. He had shown her slides of the vertiginous green slopes, swordlike summits, plunging chasms that literally took some of her breath and made her brain swirl a little. "It's incredible," she had said. "So magnificent, but I'm afraid I'd die of vertigo."

"Naw, you'll love it," he had promised, "There's literally nothing like it anywhere else in the world. You'll feel so *alive*—well, there's absolutely nothing to compare, I'll guarantee."

"I'll probably be clinging onto you like a scared monkey every minute of the day and night."

He had waggled his eyebrows, grinned almost maliciously. "Sometimes a guy just has to take a chance." Later, driving together in the night, he had talked knowingly of South and Central America, the Mayans, Incas, and Aztecs, played on his car stereo compact disc recordings of Rodrigo, Villa Lobos, and de Falla, ending with his passionate "Ritual Fire Dance." It was all very heady stuff, typically Lon Yeager. Romantic overkill for some, maybe, and yet . . . that kind of thing was his essence, it *was* exciting, it *was* thrilling, and why *not* seize onto it instead of settling for the dull status quo–ism of Mr. Average?

"Hey, you're not eating your salad," he said. "Where've you been, girl?"

"Oh," she said and blinked. "Just . . . just . . . ah, letting my little mind wander a bit. It has a habit of doing that lately."

"Hmmmm," he mused, nodding faintly and watching her steadily. "Interesting coincidence." She definitely shouldn't have given him that sort of lead. It was simply the unlatching of a door she wasn't prepared to open again.

"Know what I was thinking?" he asked. She failed to reply, but for an instant their gazes met and held. When she glanced down at her plate a moment afterward it was too late. "About Machu Picchu," he added. She felt the flare of heat inside, excitingly, but also painfully like a bad case of heartburn. It was uncanny, either the weirdest coincidence, or the man could read her mind, and the latter alternative actually seemed more rational at the moment. Too many times before he had anticipated her so perfectly, tuned in on exactly the same wavelength. And of course that had been a plus in many respects, more of the Yeager mystique. The heat was rising less painfully into her neck and cheeks. "And you were too, beautiful, admit it." Her skin was suddenly pink.

Eventually she looked up at him, knowing her eyes glistened, but so what? He already knew her every thought and feeling before she did anyway. "Yes," she said. The very restraint of their reactions, the quietness of their words, was so intense it seemed to elicit glances from the few people present at other tables.

"Look," he said and frowned, gazing down. "I've had a couple of months to live with this now, and believe me—"

"Lon," she began warningly, "I don't think we'd—"

"No, wait." He held up his hands almost as though she had confronted him at gunpoint. "This might be my only chance." His smile and tone were again so vulnerable, so utterly winning, that all her hard-earned resolve melted.

"Okay," she sighed, "but we've been all through—"

"I know, doll, I know. Just bear with me one more time, one more shot, I promise. And then . . . if that's it, well, that's it. I'll never bug you again—cross my heart and hope to die." He sighed too, and his own eyes glistened, something that could hardly be faked. There was a long pause. "Now," he laughed, "I don't even know what I'm going to say."

"So appealing," she thought, "why did he have to be so fantastically *endearing*?"

"Anyway, I've had over two months to think about this," he continued, "and believe me, that's *all* I've thought about."

"Oh," Marilyn said and tried to make it breezy, "I suspect you managed to find a few small distractions."

"Yeah, sure," he admitted contritely, "I've still been going out a little." Her smile was cynical, and he tuned in on it immediately. "So, okay, maybe a lot—but that's been a good thing. It's just confirmed the fact that nobody else means anything. All the time I'm with some other girl, I'm only thinking about one person." The cynical smile increased. "Okay, touché." He laughed a little. "About Lon Yeager—that's what you were thinking."

Marilyn laughed too. "I didn't say a word."

"You didn't need to, but anyhow, you were wrong. Marilyn Cannon—that's the name . . . that's the face, that's the everything."

"Very flattering." She was trying to keep it light, but her voice was more quavery than she intended. "But you think that's really fair to the other girls you're with?"

"Maybe not, but it's not a question of fairness," he said, "it's a matter of fact—of how I feel, and I'm just trying my best to tell you how things are. Okay?"

She nodded, lowering her lids, penitent. "Okay, I'm sorry, but Lon, let's both be agonizingly honest, all right?" Her gaze was frank and imploring.

"That's the plan," he replied, "and I'm sure trying—what else can I say?"

"Okay, but if you've been thinking 'Marilyn' all the time, isn't that mainly because she's not available?" He began to frown and shake his head. "Seriously now, isn't it the old cat-and-mouse game to some extent for practically all of us? I mean, back when I started wearing the ring, what was the first thing that happened?"

Lon's head fell forward in an act of surrender. "Maybe there was some of that, I admit, but it was basically just stupidity on my part, thinking I could still play the field a little, just for fun, just for the heck of it. I mean, well, I've been going out a lot for about the past ten years now. And I guess the old habit was sort of hard to break. For some idiotic reason I thought it wouldn't be all that serious. Now I realize that I made the worst mistake of my life."

"I wish I could be sure of that," she said, hating her own voice for sounding so shaky.

The pause was potent. "So how are you ever going to be sure if you don't give me another chance?" To that she had no reply. "Look," he said, "I'm not asking you to make a permanent commitment. Just say you'll go *out* with me—even once or twice a week for a while—and see what develops. The rest of the time, no strings attached for either of us." He leaned forward, looking into her face. "Fair or not?"

"You oughta be a lawyer," she said.

He shrugged. "There are worse professions." And Marilyn knew without question that he was referring to her own father.

Twenty-Six

"So you're actually going to start wearing it again," Kelly said. It was technically a question but in practical reality an observation.

Marilyn took a deep breath, feeling rather irritated and defensive. "No, not necessarily. I—I haven't made up my mind for sure."

"Well," her mother said gently, "obviously it has to be your decision, sweetheart. I just don't want you to be pressured into anything, and I know how persuasive he can be."

"You can say that again," a little voice in her mind chimed. The tone was ironically humorous, a bit suggestive.

It was a beautiful Sunday afternoon in mid-August. Marilyn had attended church meetings in her home ward and, as usual on that day, was dining with her family. As was also usual in the summertime, they were eating on the back patio, shaded by the branches of an ancient apple tree with the view of the reservoir just beyond.

"But the thing is," her brother said. He was buttering an ear of corn very meticulously, each kernel practically, and frowning.

"The thing is what?" She was beginning to wish she'd never mentioned the idea, never even admitted she was seeing Lon again at all.

"If you ever start wearing the crummy thing again—"

"Kel," she said, "I wish you wouldn't keep referring to it that way. It sounds as if it's nothing but a piece of junk."

"Okay," he said, "I'm sorry. But once you put that ring on your finger again you're announcing to the whole world that everything's just great now, and you're saying *sayonara* to other guys for good."

His tone seemed patronizing, and it vexed her. "I think I can figure that one out for myself," she said.

"Hey, don't be defensive," he intoned, a bit airily, and that irked her too. "All I'm saying, I guess, is why rush it? I mean, you've only been going with the guy again for two or three weeks on and off, and you know perfectly well—"

"And I wish you wouldn't always call him 'the guy,' or 'Yeager,' " Marilyn said, quite forgetting that she had referred to him in the same way more than once.

"Okay—how about 'Lawrence' then?" he continued, and she laughed despite herself. That was indeed Lon's actual name, although nobody ever called him that—at his own insistence. "But you know perfectly well he's going to keep coming around," Kelly persisted, "so what have you got to lose by at least keeping the rock in its box, going out with other guys and circulating a while longer?"

"That's another word that bugs me," Marilyn said, " 'circulate —circulating.' "

Maria laughed good-naturedly and raised her eyebrows. "Dear me, I guess we'll all just have to choose our words a lot more carefully."

"I'm sorry," Marilyn said and began to feel rather foolish. She really was becoming temperamental lately, no denying it. "Maybe I'm getting battle fatigue or something. It's just that I'm so tired of going out to be going out. The same old get-acquainted routines, going the same kinds of places, and doing, well, essentially the same things. Know what I mean?" Even as the words left her mouth she knew how many people would be happy "just to be going out." Shannon was watching her with a sweet-sad smile, one that seemed to emanate great empathy, nodding her head. "Terrific sister and friend," Marilyn thought, "Tunes in on darned near everything."

But Kelly had decided to keep it light. "You mean you haven't been going wild over your new heartthrob Joe Doaks of the Utah Highway Patrol?" He grinned, gave her a wink. Marilyn laughed, shaking her head in disbelief, and Shannon joined her.

"Is that really his name?" Maria asked. "Actually? Or has Kelly just been putting me on as usual?"

"That's really and truly his name!" Marilyn assured her. "Joseph P. Doaks. Seriously! He read that newspaper article about the triathlon and came by to tell me congratulations. Said he'd be keeping the lab for his own hunting dog unless he could find the owner or unless I wanted it. Then, that night, he called up and asked me for a date. Well, I told him okay even though I wasn't exactly enthralled over the idea—and you'll never believe where we went!"

"Where?" Shannon asked.

"It was this crazy place called The Hanging Tree up in the mountains by Logan. You grind your way up a narrow little winding road that's so dusty you can't tell half the time whether you're going over the edge or not. All the way to this so-called restaurant practically at the top that has all sorts of animal heads on the walls and lots of freaky fake stuff like jackrabbits with horns and fish covered with fur or feathers."

"Sounds marvelous!" Shannon giggled.

"Really! And lots of corny, lewd postcards and paintings you're embarrassed to even glance at. And the band! It's called the Lynch Mob. Most of them look and sound like either Willie Nelson or John Denver—as if they'd both gone psycho—and they pound on bent saws and washtubs, even scrape this stiff wire brush up and down on a scrub board." Everybody was laughing now. "This one guy's a perfect double for Turk Broadhead and plays about five different harmonicas. Another one plays the banjo and guitar with the amp up so high it practically fries your brains . . . and every so often he starts leaping around as if he's walked into a nest of rattlers or something." The laughter, in fact, was becoming slightly hysterical. "And he actually . . . actually starts doing flips!"

Kelly was chuckling, shaking his head. "Really flips out, right?"

"Literally!"

"Probably all so high they needed oxygen tanks," Kelly said.

"Maybe, but the guitarist is really in fantastic condition—quite the gymnast. And all of it, get this, in cowboy boots and spurs!"

"Come on!" Kelly said.

"No, for real—and when he comes down it sounds like thunder, like the whole place is going to collapse under a load of logs!"

"And you were just telling us how tired you are of the same old thing," Shannon said.

"Well, this was different," Marilyn confessed and wiped her eyes. "I have to admit."

"And how was Joseph P. Doaks?" her mother inquired.

"Oh . . ." Marilyn looked reflective. "If your only interests are restoring old cars or ham radio, you're in. Well, hunting and fishing too. But otherwise there's not much to talk about . . . except that he keeps calling me Little Darlin'. " She giggled. "This is on our first date, and he's really not that much bigger than I am, even though he's pretty husky. In fact, I don't think he's as old. The first time I saw him out by Willard in his uniform and dark glasses and everything I thought he was at least thirty, but he's not. He actually talks and acts like a teenager a lot of the time. In some ways he's pretty funny, though. He was telling me all about this great deal he can get on a radar detector so I can drive over the speed limit without being caught!"

"A highway patrolman?" Shannon trilled.

Marilyn nodded emphatically. "Says a car like mine actually functions better and gets better gas consumption *over* fifty-five."

"You'd better take his advice," Kelly said, "the way you collect tickets."

"She never collects them," Shannon laughed. "Always sweet-talks them out of it."

"She'd better just learn to obey the law," her mother insisted.

Out over Pine View Reservoir someone was parasailing. They could see the red chute swinging wide above the nearby cove behind a surging powerboat. The chute was seventy or eighty feet in the air, and a figure dangled doll-like beneath, tracing its way above the long finger of Cemetery Point.

"So how was your date with Mark Aldous?" Kelly asked.

"It wasn't a date," Marilyn replied. "It was only one of our friendly—well, visits. He just took me out to dinner at Berconi's to show his appreciation for the extra hours I've been putting in on that series of profiles for the *Standard*. He just ended up listening and really being sweet and understanding while I poured it all out about Lon again." She glanced down at her plate and realized that the mashed potatoes were getting cold along with her mother's famed chicken gravy. "I actually wanted to have him talk about Karen if he felt like it, and how the kids are getting along without a mom, but he kept coming back to my problems, and he's really such a great listener. You know, all the time it's lots more than just the outer ear, too."

"Who takes care of his kids while he's at work?" Shannon asked.

"His mom and dad," Marilyn said. "They're retired now. I told him I'd be glad to keep an eye on them evenings every so often or a whole weekend if he wants to get away somewhere."

"That was nice," Maria said.

Her brother's eyes squinted knowingly. "Nice offer, but I've a hunch he'd also like to have you keep an eye on him."

Marilyn shook her head. "No, Kel, it's not that way, and I doubt he'll be wanting to go out with anybody for quite a while."

Kelly made no reply, but his expression didn't alter. He merely continued to appraise her with that faintly amused smile, laugh wrinkles deepening at the corners of his eye a lot the way their dad's so often did. "Anyway, I'm glad you've still been . . ." He cupped his hand over his mouth, leaning toward Shannon's ear. "Dare I say 'circulating'?" It was a loud stage whisper.

"Nut!" Marilyn said, and began thinking for the thousandth time about Lon Yeager. It was an almost hopeless addiction. She hadn't quite been serious about wearing the ring again, not in her earlier comments to her family, merely testing the waters to obtain a reaction. Well, they'd given it all right. But the fact was, Lon had treated her beautifully, now that they'd been together again, and how *could* she possibly know, as he had argued, what kind of life he was going to lead if she wrote him off entirely, refused any association again under any conditions? And after all—it wasn't as if he'd gone out and committed some heinous crime against humanity.

Kelly was devouring more chicken, and Shannon had gone inside momentarily to check on her napping infants. Maybe, Marilyn decided, it could just be a sort of undeclared engagement. That would give her a chance to test him out, see if he'd really be true without having to make a big production of it and involve anybody else. Then . . . then, if things went bad a second time, well, so be it. That would definitely be the real and final end.

The thing nobody else knew, though—even her family—was what he had said to her on their date the night previous, his very final words: "Remember when you were talking one time," Lon had said, "about what we'd be doing a million years from now?" He spoke very quietly and confidentially, even though there was no one else to hear. "I've been thinking about that a lot lately, and it really *is* exciting."

Twenty-Seven

The following morning he had flown once more to Mexico and then on to South America to make further contacts regarding his import business. The Enterprise, as Lon and his partners called it, was looking more prosperous all the time, especially regarding jade and turquoise jewelry, which they were obtaining at remarkably low prices for a growing market throughout the Intermountain West.

Everything considered, it was an absence that could scarcely have been more perfectly timed to make the heart grow fonder or the mind more fertile. The leaven of his final words had sent her imagination into frequent ecstatic flights, some a bit fantastic. If, on the other hand, Lon Yeager was thinking in terms of a million years and beyond . . . well, she assured herself, it really *wasn't* so childish to suppose that it might make a profound difference in his sense of commitment, eliminate his need to play the field once and for all.

For the hundredth time her mind turned to the wide-windowed hotel room floating there above the world at Machu Picchu. In the late-night solitude of her room at Canyon Cove near the golf course she listened to the conversation of blackbirds through her open window, felt life surging in the undergrowth along the moon-streaming hollow and hillside, and thought of Lon and South America. She played Rodrigo and de Falla very softly on her stereo, the sound little more than a pulse beat, dreaming of pyramids, ruined temples, bronzed Indian women with scarlet headbands—women clad in green and indigo like the shimmering, streamer-tailed quetzal birds—spotted jaguars, cable cars ascending to colossal and perilous heights. And she dreamed of love.

The cable broke only one night before Lon's return, plunging her into an abyss. She had completed an evening jog on the golf course and was napping with the doors to her balcony open, smelling the pungent-sweet odor of willows, when the call came. "Hi, babe," Kelly said. "Have you by any chance seen the evening paper?"

"No," she said brightly. "Why? Is one of my brilliant profiles on Weber State professors in there?"

"Afraid not." He sounded strangely solemn. "It's about your pal Lon."

"Lon?" She felt the surge of alarm like the tugging shock from a light socket. "What? Has something—"

"No, he's all right—hasn't been hurt or anything. But . . . there's quite a write-up on that diamond investment program he's involved with in Salt Lake. Says they've been accused of operating a scam."

"*What*?" she repeated. Her brow was furrowed achingly, incredulously. For a few moments none of it registered. Even though she understood the term, it somehow sounded like a nonsense syllable or even an acronym.

"Maybe it's not a scam," Kelly was saying. "But the article says that the matter is going to court, and it lists Yeager as a kingpin in the operation."

"It's all some kind of fraud?" she said faintly. Her insides felt like a plastic squeeze bottle clasped in a strong, tightening fist.

"That's the charge," he replied. His tone was gentle and temporizing, as if he didn't want to hurt her. "But nothing's been proven in court, and even if it's a big swindle, you never know—Lon himself might be innocent."

"Oh, wow!" She pressed the palm of her left hand to her cheek and felt the heat. "Does it give any details? I mean, what does it say they were doing?"

"Not a lot," he said, "and I don't know how much Lon ever told you about the program in the first place."

"Hardly anything—he always has all these different deals going. Just that it was supposedly a great investment that everybody should have been in on." She closed her eyes dumbfounded, pressed a hand to her cheek even harder.

"Yeah," Kelly said wryly, "sure sounds like it. Anyway, the paper says it was one of these multilevel deals. You invest in diamonds which not only undergo a lot of appreciation, supposedly, but you make a percentage on everybody else you bring in. At the end of a year's time you could sell if you wanted to for a 'guaranteed' sixty percent increase in value. That was the pitch, and any time you start getting claims like that . . . well, you can be positive the whole thing's phony to begin with. But in reality there wasn't anywhere near that much appreciation even though diamonds per se can sometimes be a pretty decent investment." His words weren't fully registering even now, but she was certainly getting the drift. It was hardly fragrant. "The people who wanted out after a year were actually *getting* sixty percent profit for a while, but what they didn't know—it was all being siphoned from the principal. They were just being handed other people's investments, and the guys at the top have apparently been pocketing the rest, at least a couple of million according to the article."

"Oh, no," she groaned. "I think I'd better sit down for a minute."

"It's the same old game," Kelly continued. "Been used right in this area a hundred times over, but nobody ever gets wise. It's almost like, well, I dunno—like some people *want* to get taken."

Marilyn was standing there in the apartment kitchenette, literally feeling her knees wobble. She groped for a chair with one hand, easing herself down cautiously as if it might collapse. Janie and Carla were in the front room watching a TV comedy, shrilling every few seconds with laughter, and momentarily she was actually thankful for the clamor, not wanting them in on what was happening. "This is a little more than I can assimilate," she said. "Maybe I'll drive on up. Gotta have a little air or something."

"Yeah," Kelly said quietly, "come on up—just don't drive like a wild woman. I know what happens when you get a lot on your mind."

"Yeah, okay." She scarcely heard her own reply.

"And, hey, one other thing." It was a pregnant pause. "Still got your diamond?"

"Yes," Marilyn said, a bit startled. "It's just burning a hole there in the back of my drawer." She gave a mirthless little laugh. "Why? Think that's part of the big scam or something?"

"Naw, not likely, but . . . well, bring it along, okay?"

"I guess," she began, "but I don't really see—"

"Just bring it—I wanna check something just for the heck of it. And wear your seat belt!"

Thirty minutes later she had arrived at her Huntsville home, her place of origin and constant sanctuary, yet she was still dazed.

There she read the newspaper article, feeling strangely myopic, struggling to keep the print from blurring; but despite all that, there was the name indelibly imprinted for thousands of readers to see, not only in Ogden's *Standard Examiner* but undoubtedly in the Salt Lake City papers and others throughout the state as well: "Lawrence W. Yeager, vice president of The Enterprise Investment Company." Only one faint bit of comfort there—hardly anybody knew him as Lawrence. Listed just ahead of it was the name of the president himself, one Albert Corelli, along with two other vice presidents. The word *vice*, in fact, clung to her mind with ironic tenacity.

Following was the explanation to which Kelly had referred earlier, along with a brief accompanying article titled "Utah—Scam Capital of the World," which quoted the head of the Criminal Justice Division in the State Attorney General's Office and excerpts from a recently published book on the subject. The central idea was that Utahns—members of the Church in particular—were often too naive and trusting. "If it sounds too good to be true," the write-up concluded, "it probably is."

"You can say that again," Marilyn murmured glumly. She was sitting there in the front room with her mother and Kelly.

"Well, hon," Maria said, "try not to become too agitated. After all, nobody's been proven guilty in a court of law yet. Maybe Lon's completely innocent. Maybe they all are."

Kelly shook his head. "I wouldn't bet the ranch on it, Mom, not even the flower garden." Simultaneously, Marilyn saw her mother glance at him warningly, and that single instant conveyed the entire message. "That may be true," it said, "but why get her more upset than we have to?"

For some reason, though, that irritated her. "Mom, I know you have my best interest at heart, but I'm not a little girl anymore. I know the facts of life."

"I realize that," Maria replied. "But the *facts* in this case remain that we really *don't* know whether the accusations are true or not, and there's still a lot to be said for innocent till proven guilty."

"True," Marilyn said resignedly and felt angry at everyone in the world, especially herself for the rising tears of bitterness and self-pity. In the silence an August wind hushed through the cottonwoods. Robins called. Munster, the striped cat, slunk rapidly across the front yard, heading for the sound. "Well . . ." Marilyn sighed, shrugged, held out her hands, then reached for her shoulder bag. "I brought the doorknob." She handed Kelly the box. It was dark red velvet trimmed with gold. "Want to see if we can sell it for a sixty percent profit?"

Her brother grinned sardonically. "That might just be the smartest move you ever made." Then more seriously, "No, I just want to check on something. I used to sell a few of these babies myself, in case you've forgotten, back when I was trying to come up with some extra bucks for my mission." His big, strong hands extracted it from the box carefully, and for a moment she averted her gaze, not knowing why. When she looked again, there it was on the tip of his little finger, and he was scrutinizing it intensely. Frowning, he held it up to the glow of the window, then switched on the table lamp beside him, presented the ring to brighter light, squinted one eye at it as though sighting a rifle.

"Well?" she demanded. For an instant he glanced at her strangely as if trying to recollect something he didn't quite like to. "Kel, don't just stare at me like I'm some kind of weirdo. What's going on?"

"You're not the weirdo," he muttered, "but I can just about guarantee you who is." Reaching into his pocket, he extracted a leather case from which he removed a small magnifying glass. Briefly she recalled seeing it before, back in the pre-mission days to which he had just referred. More casually now, he examined the ring with expanded vision, finally nodded and regarded her frankly. "Absolutely flawless," he said, "too flawless. Even at sixty percent profit, you'd probably get about thirty bucks for this thing. Maybe not that much."

"*What*?" A simultaneous gasp from both mother and daughter.

"It's a piece of glass," he said. "Well, not glass exactly, but not much better. It's a crummy zircon."

Twenty-Eight

She watched her feet in their new white Adidas joggers, pacing steadily, rhythmically along the meandering back road. The road was red-brown clay, but it left pink dust on her shoes. Only now was the shock and disbelief beginning to dissipate, giving way to bitterness and anger. The bizarre zircon business had been bad enough, but now . . . something far worse, something she had learned less than two hours earlier.

Sagebrush rimmed the road, blue-graying out across the ruddy, rolling landscape. Her good old faithful friend—the homely-yet-beautiful sage. The giant kind, averaging two to three feet high—*artemisia tridentata*. In the midst of her very bitterness, she felt a flicker of satisfaction at being able to remember the nomenclature, something learned in a freshman botany class. Despite everything, the smell of the sage itself was bracing and comforting, and it was good to be alone there against the early September sky. For now, call it an opiate, escape—call it anything—it was good to be running. It was better than anything else, at least. That way the emotion could somehow be released a little without quite choking her.

Here and there were junipers gradually congregating more heavily on the drifting landscape beyond. All about her lay hills and dales, and off to her left a quarter of a mile or so the terrain dipped westward in the direction she had come, bathed in tremulous expanses of aspen, the green awash with blendings of faint yellow like an immense watercolor still slightly dripping. She was moving along the backbone of Monte Cristo, having driven the twenty miles from her Huntsville home, feeling the first exhalations of autumn, subtle freshets even among the final heat waves of summer. Blending with it all was the subdued chanting of crickets and occasionally the shrill chirp of a ground squirrel.

No question, the wild land, and becoming an organic part of it all—moving, using her legs, heart, and lungs—that indeed seemed her only salvation at the moment. That and prayer, talking informally and at random to someone who might be watching, maybe even caring, up there somewhere through the infinitude of blue. And yet, ironically, the only voice she could clearly hear at present was that of Lon Yeager going on and on, almost obsessively, over the phone a few days before, in a long and labyrinthine explanation as to why The Enterprise was "*really* in trouble."

Nobody had done anything wrong, he kept insisting; it was all supposedly "some big vendetta" on the part of an overzealous "lunkhead" on the Attorney General's staff. Though why a vendetta—which word Lon used to the point of infatuation—she never got clear. "But the point is," he insisted, "nobody including Al Corelli has been making off with anybody's investment. The funds were all removed from Sunset Bank because we had some serious questions about its stability, and as you probably know, it's now insolvent. Gone belly-up. *Those* are the guys they should be prosecuting!" His unhappiness sounded genuine, somewhat shrill with indignation and incredulity.

"So what did happen to the funds?" she asked. "Are they all safe and sound in some other bank or what?" Well, no, not exactly, he told her. They had been transferred to more lucrative investments, but highly reliable, definitely highly reliable—"blue-chip stock." What that meant, Marilyn wasn't quite certain, but she wondered aloud whether such action had been taken with the permission of the investors or at least with their awareness. No, but it had been done at the advice of The Enterprise's board of directors, some of whom were allegedly staunch pillars in the Church.

The explanation mollified her somewhat. "You can't make money for your investors by leaving stuff in the bank anyway," he continued. "The only reason we put it there in the first place was to give us time to lay the groundwork for something more lucrative, and now we've got it. We're working through one of the finest investment firms around, and Con Underwood, who heads it all up, is probably the biggest name in the business, especially when it comes to mutual funds."

The questions and answers continued, with seeming enlightenment one moment and bewilderment the next. "But Lon," she said at last, "that still doesn't explain one thing." It was a question she had been reserving, partly perhaps out of fear, partly to catch him off guard.

"What's that?" The loss of assurance in his voice was barely discernible, something very subtle in its timbre.

"It doesn't quite explain why the ring I was almost ready to start wearing again is a beautiful, flawless . . ." Despite the tremors in her throat, she felt an almost sadistic satisfaction in pacing it just perfectly. "One carat zircon."

The silence was concussive. Momentarily she actually wondered if the line had gone dead. "Lon?"

"A *what*?" Either the shock was genuine or he was certainly one terrific actor. Now, jogging the ruddy back road of Monte Cristo, she decided that those two words alone should have earned him an Oscar. "You've gotta be kidding!" He had sounded dumbfounded.

"No, Lon." She heard her own words with strange objectivity, like a patient but weary mother dealing with a rambunctious child.

"Hey, look, Lyn, this is crazy," he said. "Are you absolutely positive? I mean, where—?"

"Of course I'm positive. You think I'd say something like that if I didn't know for certain?" Even then, however, part of her mind exuded doubt because it all seemed so preposterous.

"Hey, look," he repeated at last. "I know how weird this must seem, but if it's really a zircon I think maybe I've got the answer. Let me check something, and I'll get right back to you."

There had been little more to say at the moment, but after she hung up the phone she began thinking of her mother's question immediately after the discovery, and of Kelly's reply. "But what ever made you think of it in the first place?" Maria hd asked. The blue-green eyes were full of perplexity, the rather large, full lips remaining parted in question.

Kelly shrugged, shook his head. "Partly just a wild guess, but partly because I've heard a couple of rumors that some of the investors were winding up with zircons. One of the guys at med school was talking about it today, in fact."

"But why would anybody be so stupid?" Maria's brow pleated. "And why, especially, would a person as shrewd as Lon Yeager let himself in for such a dead giveaway where Marilyn is concerned?"

Kelly puffed out his upper lip with air and flipped up his thumbs in concession to mystery. "Search me. Why was he dumb enough to keep messing around with other women after he was engaged? Why even get engaged in the first place? Looks to me as if we're dealing with a highly irrational character here—maybe a split personality or something."

"Oh, I think he was serious enough about the engagement itself," Maria mused, "probably even the marriage. He just wanted to lead a double life."

"Lots more than double," Kelly said.

"But he wasn't even subtle about it." Marilyn shook her head. "I mean, he had to know that sooner or later it would all get back to me, or at least a lot of it." By then it was definitely old ground; they had been through the whole thing before, yet the mystery remained, and in a strangely perverse way she somehow enjoyed agonizing over it.

"Well," Kelly sighed, "he's one weird character." That sort of thing had all been said before as well. It was as close as they had come, though, to an explanation until Lon's return from South America, despite his promise to "get right back" to Marilyn with the answer. The whole thing was just a ridiculous mistake, he finally told her. The fact was, he actually kept several zircons on hand strictly for display purposes. One of them had been the same size and cut as her own diamond—even contained the same setting because that was obviously his favorite. But for some reason he'd never understand, the real McCoy and its cheap imitation had gotten switched.

"Don't ask me how," he kept repeating. "It was just one big, stupid boo-boo, and I'm really mortified . . . on top of everything else, especially."

On the surface it made a certain amount of sense, she decided. Hadn't even stranger things happened in her own life? Items of real importance sometimes vanishing, practically from her fingertips, then showing up unexpectedly somewhere else without the slightest rhyme or reason? Sometimes in situations that made her question her own sanity? Kelly, however, was far more skeptical. "Oh sure, he probably does keep a few zircons on hand," he admitted. "I used to have some, so girls who were looking for a ring could try them on. But I never kept them in a permanent setting—just used those cheap clamps that you can adjust to different finger sizes."

That, however, was hardly the end of her problems. In relating the matter to Janie and Carla a short while later, only two hours or so earlier, in fact,—before fleeing to Monte Cristo—she had received a worse jolt. Worse than anything since the actual breakup three months earlier.

"It all fits in, Lyn Girl," Jan had said solemnly. They were sitting together in the front room of their apartment, and she remembered staring at the blank gray screen of the TV as though it were a computer panel, feeling somehow that by punching the right buttons she could have it all spelled out—the whole big mess edited, lined up and enumerated in nice little neon green letters.

Marilyn shrugged, feeling gray like the screen. "I guess."

"You know about South America, then."

"He just flew down there on business, yes." She looked a bit perplexed. "Why?"

"And you know who went with him," Carla said, watching her face intently.

"Marve Gilbert," she said and caught her friends exchanging glances. "One of the guys he's in business with." Then, less certainly: "At least that's what he told me. Why?"

"Marilyn . . . ," Carla said, her gray eyes unexpectedly compassionate. "He took Taunya Barrymore."

"Taunya Barrymore!" She gave a little laugh of disbelief. "Just *Taunya*? Nobody else?" Jan nodded, looking very certain.

Taunya Barrymore! It was indeed like pushing a button, on the screen of her own mind: The provocatively reclining, scantily attired, desperately grinning female figure—an ad for a local reducing salon called Beautiful Bodies. Taunya Barrymore, not only appearing daily in the newspaper but plastered on billboards throughout the area as well—bonfire hair and leopard-skin bikini. Caption: "Would this body lie to you?"

"Oh, wild!" She clapped a hand to her brow, dazed. "You guys have got to be kidding!"

"We kid you not, Lyn-Lyn," Carla said ominously. Her head was canted slightly to the side, and her stare itself seemed irrefutable, boring right between the eyes for an instant.

"That's *frantic*!" Marilyn said. She shook her head slowly, still in shock, yet feeling a ridiculous sense of hysteria. "And just where did you obtain that fascinating bit of news?"

"Connie Alvord," Jan replied, "and you know Connie—she doesn't go out tossing around rumors. She got it direct from Marve Gilbert himself and thought you ought to know. Marve had to have an operation at the last minute for a ruptured appendix."

By now she was too distracted to consider the condition of Marve himself. "And Taunya hasn't even finalized her divorce yet, right?"

Jan shrugged. "I doubt it, but why worry about trivial details?"

"Oh," Marilyn said weakly, "no way—it's really too horrid!" It was a Saturday morning, and she gazed through the window off their deck to see a swath of yellowing leaves in the hollow, all aflutter with laughter. "Oh . . ." She whimpered with disbelief before succumbing to the welling hysteria. For a full minute or more she shook with her own strange noise—half laughter, half sobs and wails, while her two roommates hugged and patted her, joining at times in a kind of sympathetic vibration.

"So where are you going?" Jan called afterward. "We'll kill 'em both!"

"I don't know," she said. "Out away somewhere for a while. Gotta have space."

Twenty-Nine

She had stopped at her home in Huntsville long enough to collect the new jogging shoes inadvertently left there a day or two earlier. "I'll be back later, Mom!" she had shouted.

"A call came for you just a few minutes ago, hon," Maria replied. She appeared at the top of the stairs looking worried and inquisitive. "It was Lon . . . he said if you came by to phone him back at Snow King."

"Tell him to go take a wild leap!" she yelled.

Maria was descending the stairs rapidly. "What now? Is it still that crazy zircon business?"

"It's funny business. I just found out that his only 'partner' on the South American trip was one of the most predatory females around. She's going through her second divorce right now for that exact reason."

"What?" Her mother's face fairly swirled with bewilderment.

"I'll tell you more about it later." She finished lacing her shoes. "I've got to break loose for a while—really get out somewhere and move."

"Okay, hon, I understand." Maria gave her a quick hug. "Are you just going out along the reservoir?"

"I don't know—just following my nose," she said. Even the arms of her mother seemed too confining at the moment. "Maybe up on Monte."

"All by yourself?" The words were full of consternation. "I really don't like having you off up there all alone. Couldn't you just—"

"I'll be fine, Mom, just fine," she insisted, gave an impatient hug in return, and headed for the car. As she backed from the drive, Maria was standing on the front walk in her blue terry cloth robe, her brow knit with anxiety. "Don't *worry*, Mom!" Marilyn gave a fluttery little wave from the open window. "I'll be okay, I promise—love ya!"

That was how she came to be jogging along a remote back road on the top of Monte Cristo. She had been at it steadily now for about half an hour, clad in purple trunks and a white T-shirt that said "WEBER STATE" on the front. It also contained a snarling wildcat on the back. The patriotic young alumna sporting her school emblem and colors, even to the purple headband and wristbands. She had won another race recently, a six-miler near Logan, and that too had helped bolster her often-faltering morale. It made her a little happier, in fact, to be wearing the colors of her alma mater and place of employment, and even though she was far from happy at the moment, it always helped a bit to sport the right attire.

There was no one to see it, of course, but a couple of passing bow hunters in a white, pink-dusted pickup, questing for deer. The season was about over, and for that Marilyn was thankful. She had always hated to have creatures pursued, molested, and killed, wondering how people—even her own brother along with pals like Gordie and Daws—could be so oblivious to the animals' terror and suffering.

Far off, several miles, was a conical peak that looked like a small volcano, wreathed along the top in faint blue mist and brush-stroked below with reds and oranges. Yes, fall was beginning to claim the land, and she detected from somewhere traces of wood smoke. Maybe, she thought, I'll jog all the way to the volcano and back—a round trip of perhaps fifteen miles—soaking up the whole sky, the land, everything. Being absorbed by them in turn. Once again she was listening for the music, that curious, blood-tingling vibration from the heart of nature that she had heard at Powell and from the remote regions west of the Great Salt Lake. Like her brother Kelly, she was panoramic, revelled in vastness and immensity, in the sense of God's handiwork with all its endless variety.

Yet none of it at the moment could extinguish her combined disbelief and outrage—the thoughts and images of Lon Yeager with Taunya Barrymore. "Believe me, Marilyn," Carla had assured her, "this guy isn't worth zilch, not another spare second of your time. He's utterly incorrigible, just like Mick." Reference to her former husband, who two years earlier had dumped her in a helpless sprawl for "some complete airhead" built like Dolly Parton.

Well, Taunya not only had the general build, she also had some brains and apparently knew how to acquire anything her greedy little heart desired. Marilyn thought of the health salon ad, grinning triumphantly away in the daily newspaper, flinging itself salaciously, larger-than-life, from the billboards, and felt a wild surge of jealousy, nearly hatred.

Then, gradually, she began to wonder about Lon's call only a short while earlier. Apparently he had phoned her apartment first, just a few minutes late, and Huntsville just before her arrival, a few minutes too early. Did he know she was also aware of his latest in the way of fun and games? And if so, what sort of clever, phony explanation would he pull out of the hat this time? Always, always, always that disarming innocence, the words that initially seemed so convincing, even though they usually lacked rationality under the glass of objective analysis.

So what would he say to this one? That it was all strictly on the up-and-up, that Taunya Girl was willing to invest "big bucks" in the business? Rumor had it that she now owned a substantial portion of the Beautiful Bodies enterprise. Would he maintain that she had lots of contacts and was interested in becoming a partner in his South American import venture as well? That she needed to see firsthand what was available? Oh yes indeed! Needed to see what was available, all right!

"In fact," Carla Bonner had added, "Lon's *worse* than Mick"—and that was quite a concession—"because he not only kills every woman who lays eyes on him with his gorgeous looks, he's even a bigger con artist. And lots more slippery."

Again she felt the anger and jealousy, and her mind launched on a series of wild flights, one of which uncovered Lon and darling, ravenous Taunya there together in the hotel room at Machu Picchu. Immediately she felt the hot-wire sensation in her stomach, seemed literally to see within her brain the searing red-orange glow. So, all right, she would have to get ahold of herself, control her thoughts, but it was an endless, almost hopeless battle these days. Now, especially. "Impossible," a voice said. "you just can't fight it anymore." And besides she was so blasted *angry*! Why did he have to be such a stupid fool? So incredibly, willfully stupid when he was basically so intelligent? Being such an abysmal idiot when they had such a great thing going! And . . . the smug feeling insinuated itself . . . wasn't she actually the ideal mate for him, the best he could possibly get? And weren't all the others just a bunch of conniving females out for all they could lay their greedy little hands on?

Another part of her mind dismissed the entire thought as absurd and childish, egotistical beyond belief, but it was not replaced by anything better, only more jealousy and bitterness. Well, she told herself glumly, one of these fine days when everybody around knew him for exactly what he was, when he was right down there crawling, maybe he'd get wise, realize you couldn't have your cake and hog everybody else's too. Yes, one of these fine days he'd come crawling to her on his belly like a man dying in the desert, reach out with desperation and pleading in his eyes, beg in a croaking voice, then collapse, flat on his big, gorgeous, stupid face. And . . . Her expression was malignant. And she'd just keep running, right on over the top of him without missing a stride. Tough deal, Super Jerk!

"Oh, Lyn Girl," she thought, "what a fool! What a poor excuse of a human being you're becoming! How utterly *corny* can you get! You've come all the way up here on Monte to . . . to what? Who knows? To get some kind of surcease, some kind of healing. To cleanse your mind and spirit, better still, to talk a little with God —and instead you're practically becoming a homicidal maniac."

Her side was aching again, just as it often had before during her other runs when she started dwelling on the negative. "Heavenly Father," she prayed, "help me to control my thoughts. Help me to appreciate all my endless blessings and quit being—" Another ground squirrel shrilled. "Being my own worst enemy." A dragonfly entranced the air just ahead, shifting, hovering, zigzagging erratically, once again hovering, in full command of its every instinctive desire. And suddenly others were materializing as well. Spontaneous mitosis? Magical cloning? But they were different sizes and colors—sea greens, blues, pale translucent gold—a slender "darning needle" variety—pale red, such creatures as she had never seen before. Maybe it would try to sew her lips shut; that was the old myth, going clear back to the days of her grandparents. Possibly far longer, who knew?

The "volcano" was gradually growing. As she rounded a long curve in the road Marilyn glanced back and saw a swirling horizontal dust plume, one that steadily lengthened, sprawling wider and wider at the far end. At the other, generating it all, was a tiny vehicle, a mere plastic toy like those owned by her nephew Rone. But it somehow looked familiar, and even then she was beginning to suspect who was behind the wheel. Ah yes, somehow he had found out; never discount persistence when it came to Lover Boy Lon. Her mother had probably given it away, inadvertently mentioning something about the top of Monte, and he had lucked out, his bird-dog instincts heading him straight for the target as usual. So now—now her face filled with long-suffering, her body with excitement—so now, another impetuous, futile, stupid confrontation. And for what?

The vehicle was rapidly approaching and looked indeed like the Suzuki Samurai he always drove to Snow King, that they had journeyed the backcountry in together so often. Yes, somehow he had known just where to come—found her car even though she had parked it somewhat out of view to discourage theft or vandalism. Partly just logic, having been in the general area with her more than once, partly a kind of unnerving ESP that always enabled him to zero in on people, especially women, like a heat-seeking missile. Especially dearest little Lyn-Lyn. More and more she could feel herself acquiring Carla's cynicism, her penchant for acid parody, even when it came to parodying herself.

So? She heaved a sigh of resignation. What would his pitch be this time? Maybe he didn't yet realize that she knew about beloved Taunya Bare-It-More. How, in that case, would she break it to him? Certainly not with great emotion—no, definitely not that. He did not deserve the satisfaction. Indifferently, that was how. Clearly, yet with glacial indifference. "Glacial indifference"—fine! Maybe she would put it in a story some day. But what would she actually say to him now? There wasn't much time. "Lon, I know all about Taunya, and I'm not going to make a big deal out of it." Or maybe "big production." Still trite, but somehow a little more aloof and sophisticated. "But let's face it once and for all and quit kidding ourselves—you're obviously just not a one-woman man, and from the looks of things you never—" No, not quite what she ought to say. "You obviously just have this fatal addiction for women—*women*, plural—and I'm absolutely not going to be a part of . . ." The word processor of her mind was purring, searching for some deft bit of metaphor that would place him permanently, irrefutably just where he belonged.

And the whole thing was completely phony. It was merely one more of the endless games people play. Just be completely honest, Marilyn, completely honest—don't try to sound clever or impressive. If there is the slightest room at all in your mind for the Spirit, now's the time. Let it go to work. Let it speak, quietly and frankly without rancor but without compromising yourself.

She could hear the growing growl of the motor, rising and falling as the vehicle took its dips and curves, drawing nearer. Regardless, though, she was not going to grant him the benefit of a backward glance, merely move off the side of the road a little as she would for anyone else—into the breeze to avoid being smothered within the following dust. Its sound was enveloping now. The vehicle was pulling alongside her, slowing. She swallowed. Her body tingled. And what would *he* say? Let Lon Yeager make the first move.

Then it was passing by! Not the cream-toned Suzuki at all but rather an old-time combat jeep, an ugly olive drab specimen with three wild-eyed raunchos inside. That at least was her initial disillusioning impression. Dismaying, in fact, because a part of her had actually been *courting* one more "big final" encounter after all. Dismaying also because she hardly thrilled to their grubbiness; she resented their leers, the eyes that seemed to cluster upon her like horseflies. From the corner of her own eye she glimpsed a battered gray stetson and bearded face on the driver's side with wiry bristles that even sprouted from his cheekbones . . . on the other side, a lime green baseball cap, tapirlike snout and nonexistent chin beneath, Adam's apple the size of a golf ball. A third figure hulked in the rear, back broad and rounded, beefy, face nondescript like a giant onion.

All three heads turned, synchronized, as though controlled by the same button, eyes gorging, the jeep running off the margin of road and tilting slightly as it collided with a clump of sage. "Hey, hey—honey! You're a long way from home!" Soused, all three. She even saw a beer can in the driver's left hand, saw it slosh as he veered back onto the road, heard him yip and cackle like a hyena.

Well, at least they hadn't hassled her much. She could certainly have expected worse under the circumstances. The dust billowed up behind, blessedly obliterating the whole stupid mess, stares and all, leaving only uneasiness, disappointment that it had not been Lon Yeager after all, humiliation for having assumed so much so easily.

But anyway, she would not be jogging all the way to the volcano now. It simply wouldn't be very smart under the circumstances.

Besides, she had been going for nearly forty minutes already, would have to make the return trip, and the road no longer seemed her own. The whole atmosphere had changed as though a storm were in the making. About three hundred yards ahead, in fact, the dust was thinning and settling. Within its pale, ruddy haze the jeep had stopped and was turning around. She could hear it snort, hear the harsh, spinning rip of knobby tires as it backed into a rut and struggled out. Yes, it was definitely less comfortable now, and again she felt the electric inner twinge, this time from apprehension.

One thing was certain, in any case—whatever their plans, she wasn't quite dumb enough to keep running along the roadside. Instead, she gradually angled left into the sage, trying to increase her pace steadily yet imperceptibly. She did not want to encourage pursuit with wild flight, nor did she want to squander her energy. Ahead were a few scraggly juniper, and as the sound of the motor expanded she began to wish greatly that they were larger and much denser. Because . . . yes, the idiots were veering from the road now, grinding after her through the sage. Suddenly, she was feeling waves of panic.

"Don't look back," she told herself, "don't look back." Flitting through her mind was the advice Kelly had once tendered a bit laughingly, something about never looking a drunk in the eye or he was your friend for life—"just like Cuddles, like Velcro." Well, she'd gladly take anybody now, Cuddles included. The panic increased. If only she had Kel or good old Turk.

They were yelling something now. "Hey, Blondie, wait up—we're lost, no kiddin'! Where the devil ya goin'?" This to the accompaniment of more cackles and snickering little he-he-he's as though they had just said something agonizingly clever. Despite the sage, and now more rabbit brush, they were actually gaining on her from the sound of the motor, but still she refused to look back. Act as if they aren't even there, Lyn, don't give them an inch, not one sliver of encouragement. She swung around another juniper, glanced black fleetingly despite her own advice, and saw that she was momentarily concealed. A second somewhat larger tree stood fifty yards away slightly to her left, and she headed for it, really loping, wishing desperately that the sage itself were higher.

If only there were more cover! But a quarter of a mile beyond was an immense, unending expanse of aspen, billions of yellowing leaves alive and beckoning. The jeep was swinging wide, bouncing and jostling, and she could hear the scritch and snap of branches against its fenders. "Hey, Blondie—we *see* you!" a voice bawled moronically. The sage was scratching her legs, leaving a few red streaks, but no time to bother about that. Before long, in fact, the jeep was trundling along beside her, thumping and creaking over flat rocks, crushing the dry branches, and the yahoos were bellowing at her. "Hey, lover girl, hold up—you're gettin' all strung out, gettin' them be-ooo-tiful laigs all scratched up!"

Suddenly the jeep accelerated, veering sharply in front of her. Whether it was done to avoid a rock or clump of brush, or merely to scare her, she didn't know, but the rear fender grazed her right hip terrifyingly, jarring her off balance. "Oh, baby!" the voice blared, "Watch where yer goin'! You almost run us down!"

Again the jeep cut in front of her, less precariously this time, but far too close, choking her in billows of dust, almost blinding her for a moment. Marilyn gasped and shouted through the panting of her lungs, scarcely realizing it. "What are you *doing*? Stay *away* from me!" The jeep zigzagged, circled, roaring directly at her. She saw the bumper and headlights, a sudden mechanical monster, the lurch and leap as churning tires hit a high spot, and for the first time she felt the stark sense of malevolence, felt that death was actually coming. For an instant she skidded to a stop, then dodged to the side as the vehicle swerved away, missing her by inches.

"You're insane!" she shrilled, as much in anger as terror. A bunch of stupid, leering raunches, drunken bums who didn't even care if—The jeep was fishhooking again, heading back fiendishly amid whoops and shouts, but meanwhile she had taken refuge behind another juniper. Thank the Lord for junipers! No sense running now. They couldn't circle the tree as fast as she could, and despite her excellent physical condition, her knees were nearly buckling. Her lungs torched and her heart lurched wildly.

The jeep came on, snorting, galloping, tilting from side to side, and she could smell the volatile odor of gasoline, hear it sloshing hungrily in the ugly black auxiliary tank clamped to the side. Terror now, yes, but also growing outrage. Her face and arms were sweat-caked with dust, her legs stinging from scratches. The jeep crushed on by, and she circled the tree, crouching and crowding its branches for protection. Gulping air, she found herself searching for something, only half aware of what it might be. A weapon of some kind, however meager—rock, stick, anything . . . but there was only the loose dry earth, a curving gash of red dust churned up moments earlier by the tires. Stooping, she seized a fistful, and as the jeep grundled by once more, she flung it against the windshield. A pitiful effort, but it helped. She heard curses of surprise and saw the jeep swing wide, weaving a little.

As it returned she collected another supply, a bit larger this time. Nothing except a meager handful of dust against a relentless monster of metal and hard, grinding rubber, but as they went for her again she knew where the dust had to go, the kind of timing it would take. For an instant she moved into view, only partly concealed by the branches, using her body as bait, and as the jeep slowed, pivoting, she flung more dust, lobbing it over the roofless windshield—directly into the driver's face.

She heard the shouts of amazed complaint, saw the jeep winnow blindly and lurch to a halt, almost throwing its occupants from their seats, much like dummies in a vehicle crash test. But something was wrong—there were only two of them. The hulk in the rear seat was gone. Thrown out? Jumped? Maybe fallen and—She whirled frantically as the hands grabbed at her, saw the face like a giant blister, the sparse tufted hair, eyes squinty like bee stings. "No! Stay *away* from me!" One hand grabbed her upper arm, wrenching her off balance, the other her shoulder, almost dragging her down. She gasped, writhing. "Keep your rotten hands—"

"Feisty little devil, aren't ya!" He was even bigger than she had realized, nearly twice her own weight and far stronger. But it simply couldn't be happening. This was merely something you read about in the newspaper, names of people you didn't know. "Yeah, feisty!" There was no holding him off at all. He reeked with dirt and sweat, and his breath was rancid, almost burning with the odor of booze and tobacco. "Well, that's just how I like it, baby—so put up a good one." The arms encircled, crushing the breath from her lungs, and she flung her head to avoid his mouth, felt it fasten leechlike to the side of her neck.

"Hey, *baby*," he wheezed, half gloating, half reproving, "don't *fight* it—okay?" The hand knotted her hair, wrenching her head back as the mouth groped and slobbered against her own. She hissed, spitting, baring her teeth, ducking and twisting her neck.

"Ooooh—hey, you *are* a wildcat!" The hands fumbled, the beard bristles rasped, and only then did the realization assert itself—things taught by her brother and the old man. For an instant she seized the hairy forearms, clinging on for balance, to keep from collapsing. Then, summoning all her waning strength, she drove a knee directly into his groin. There was a muffled groan of astonishment and agony, an instant of paralysis as if someone had punched the stop button on a video.

Then he was slumping forward in slow motion, going down and almost taking her with him in the process, crushing and crackling into a clump of dead sage, rolling fetal position into the dirt. "It works, it really works!" the voice in her mind shrilled even as she struggled to extricate herself from the juniper branches, broke free and began running. Momentarily she stumbled and fell, scrambled on all fours, then regained her feet and kept going. Once she flung a backward glance, saw the jeep stalled, motionless, the driver still fisting his eyes. The tapir-nose with the green cap was running after her, bellowing filth, weaving spraddle-legged . . . falling.

Once again, Marilyn fell partway down herself, half tripping from dizziness and exhaustion. She arose, feeling her injured left knee area turn numb except for a sharp surface stinging like a spray of tiny needles—hopped and hitched, sucking in air between her teeth. Then, she limped her way ahead, pleading with her legs, entire body, not to wilt. Exhorting her mind to function and somehow use good sense.

Thirty seconds later she was passing through spots of golden-furred rabbit brush and entering the great mantle of quaking aspen, their pale trunks greeting her like a host of kindly friends. The land before her was gradually inclining downward toward a little valley not far beyond, and that would be all to the good, even greater concealment. Gasping for air, from relief and persisting fear, she kept going. At least they could never get through a forest this dense in their stinking jeep, couldn't even see into it very far because of fallen trees and the undergrowth.

Yet even so, it was vital to keep moving, take no chances, increase the distance even though her body felt as if it had just lost a quart of blood. Yes, deeper and deeper into it, the denser the better—places they could never follow. Madmen! Lousy, dirty, putrid . . . Coming out of nowhere, a total nightmare! And for no reason, no reason in the world, actually trying to run her down, not even caring whether they killed her, actually *destroyed another human being*! Even now, only minutes away, she couldn't quite believe that it had happened. She was still enveloped in a nightmare. Simultaneously, she could still smell and taste the flavor of beer, stale tar, and nicotine on her mouth. She spat savagely, thrust at her lips with the back of her hand and forearm, but the essence of it all remained, turning her stomach.

The sense of violation increased, and for the first time she truly empathized with victims of rape. Despite being a woman, despite having always abhorred the very prospect, it had all remained comparatively abstract until minutes earlier. It was not until now that she realized, truly comprehended deep within that there were people in the world—even the cloistered hills and valleys of Utah—who would use you in any way they desired—violate your body and soul, crush out your life, without a qualm, without the faintest compunction.

But forget that now, she thought, just keep moving, take no chances. Steadily, steadily, despite her enervation, she trot-limped on through dapples of sunlight and shadow, skirting underbrush, surmounting fallen trees, gradually feeling the pain in her knee diminish. Irrelevantly, so that it barely registered, she realized that the aspen bark was not truly white after all, the way it appeared at a distance, but rather a muted gray-green. The white was merely a pale residue as if the trunks had been sloshed with milk. And the circular patches of black were the healed wounds left by branches that had died and sloughed away. The black spot on one trunk, in fact, seemed abnormally large, rather bulging and fragile, like papier-maché daubed with mud. She glimpsed it from the corner of one eye, barely brushed it with her elbow in passing, and suddenly saw it crumble, exploding a swarm of yellow.

An instant later the first stings were coming, viciously like tiny white-hot needles—electric needles, needles dipped in acid—her arm, thigh, side of her neck—her cheek, and brow almost on the eyelid. Yellow jackets! Marilyn cried out, slapping and clutching at herself, blundered downhill into the underbrush. Branches whipped her face, ripped off her headband, tugged her hair, tore her shirt, and another electric needle struck her in the calf, another viciously on one thumb. Grinding the attacker against her chest, she stumbled blindly onward, feeling as if her thumb had been held in a candle flame. Slipping over a mossy log, she staggered, going down onto her hands, scuffed her left palm on the jagged stub of a small limb, ploughed blindly into a thicket of wreathing vines, heard the startled whir of a pine hen, when suddenly the earth collapsed from under her, and she was hurtling downward, sprawling in space amid a flood of leaves and snapping branches.

For a long moment, once again, there was suspension, and her mind cried out. "Not now, Lord—I'm too young!" She landed on her back and shoulder with a relentless thump that crushed the air from her lungs, cried out voiceless, rolled and bounced, seeing the valley floor coming up to meet her—the placid trickle of a stream, a slope dotted with stones, one the size of a melon that somehow turned white, belly up, and bounded from the earth at her.

A bone-jarring concussion in the side of her head, then nothing.

Thirty

Light returned gradually, sporadically, like a morning full of fast-shifting clouds. If the camera had been slow motion as she began her fall, it was now on fast speed, yet even then the right half of her world remained in darkness. It required a full minute or more for her to comprehend that the eye on that side was swollen shut. Her head throbbed, seeming to expand and contract with every pulse beat. Part of it also felt dead except for a faint tingling, prickling sensation like an arm gone to sleep.

Turning her head painfully to the side, she saw a rock-studded slope and tried to recall what had happened. Her upper lip felt immense, throbbing with an itchy, acidic burning. She tried to touch it, struggled to reach out . . . and nothing happened. For a moment it made no sense. Again, trying to reach out, simply move one arm. Nothing. Utter bafflement that suddenly transformed to terror. Paralysis! She could not move—neither her arms nor . . . She struggled to bend her knees, raise them. Nothing! Nothing! Neither arms *nor* legs! Her head fell to the side, the one still dark, and she gave a small, rasping cry of despair. *Paralyzed.* The word repeated itself passionately, only to die at length from futility and sheer monotony.

Her brain surged and her ears roared with a sound like wind blowing through treetops, or maybe a waterfall. Was she near a waterfall? It was impossible to tell, but gradually recollection began to return, groping its way from present to past. She saw the rock, felt the implacable impact and flare of pain in her head, even seemed to see it like the ruddy announcement of an explosion, and she suddenly realized that nature, in its own mindless way, could also be brutal. She felt herself sprawling, trunk twisting helplessly in space like a scarecrow, saw branches and the swarm of yellow. Yes, it was coming back now, even the chase and her escape.

Again she tried to move but without success. She closed her good eye and felt another spurt of fear. It was becoming hard to breathe; her lungs weren't working properly. Oh, no, please! She opened her mouth, panting shallowly, and gradually began to wheeze on each inhalation like someone battling emphysema. An allergic reaction—toxic shock! Something similar had happened once before, after she had been stung by a single honeybee. Her mind reeled, and she found herself going downward into the dark and spinning vortex of a whirlpool, convinced in her desperation that death might now be the best alternative.

On her second awakening, light came more rapidly and recollection was more sudden. The breathing was a bit less labored. Reaching up, she touched her swollen eye. Sunlight blurred through the lid very faintly, a dull red blackening into maroon. But wait . . . *hand*! Hand, reaching up—*moving*! Her foot twitched. The opposite knee shifted slightly, bending.

She gasped in relief. Thank you, Lord—thank you, thank you. Thanks so very much! Soundlessly she began to weep, little racking sobs that hurt too much, caused her to fight once more for air, lapsing again toward unconsciousness. But maybe that was the right thing, nature taking its course. Maybe the next awakening would be still better.

On the other hand, she couldn't remain there helpless—not if locomotion was possible. Maybe they were still after her, searching despite their drunkenness like hunters after a wounded deer. From only a short distance off came a shrill cry, almost a cheer, and she jerked convulsively, catching her breath. A flicker watched her from the branch of a tiny aspen. She saw its gray-white breast, the dun-colored wings decorated with neat little bars of black, the rapierlike bill and red throat patch. It canted its head at alert, ever-shifting angles, the eyes blinking rapidly several times a second. It was something she had never noticed before and wondered if the same were true with all birds. The flicker watched her with remarkable alertness, cheered again, then flew. Or was it a jeer? For an instant she felt a surge of envy over its fantastic mobility.

So, all right—maybe she could at least get a little mobility herself. Both arms and legs were functional now but with a deep, tingle-throbbing ache like the sensation in a banged elbow, the crazy bone, after the worst had faded a little. It was only then that she realized that the tiny stream glimpsed during her fall lay only a few feet away. She was, in fact, sprawled in a slightly boggy spot, her back and hair caked with muck. Gradually, very cautiously, she wriggled onto her side and felt a stab of pain in her ribs. The waterfall sound returned, mounted and subsided. The thumb of her left hand looked like a boiled hot dog. Her entire hand was swollen so badly it appeared to have no knuckles, not even the dimpled spots. Carefully, superstitiously, shifting her body with infinite discretion, she struggled from her side to a sitting position, and for a moment nearly blacked out again, falling backward onto her elbows. It was as though the earth had suddenly tilted, as if the spirit had left her body temporarily and executed a perfect little loop-the-loop before returning. Fascinating, yet frightening, and accompanied by a belly-clenching sense of nausea.

Yet she had to have water. Her body craved it desperately. Slowly, ever so slowly, she wriggled toward the stream, and eventually, after much struggle and misery, was groveling on her belly at its edge, bathing her swollen hand in the coolness. Clumsily, she applied its silt to her neck, calf, arm . . . wherever the demons had struck. Her right leg was swollen badly from the knee down to the foot, the foot seemingly ready to burst from her shoe. The side of her head throbbed with migraine intensity, and when she placed her fingertips there ever so gently, she discovered a kind of sponginess. The hair was matted and sticky, and her fingers came away daubed with red. Something for everyone, she thought, anywhere you want to look.

Her shoulder and back were scraped and bruised, and her right ankle throbbed, seemed to be sprained. Her entire body was such a mass of bewildered misery it was impossible to distinguish one injury fully from another, or in some cases to decide which had been inflicted by her fall and which had resulted from the hornets. "Lyn Baby," she told herself, "you're one sad case." Then, with a series of pain-wracked contortions, she drank from the stream, oblivious to the smokelike drifting of silt she was creating, the tiny particles of bark and leaves in their gentle rise and swirl, mildly surprised at how difficult it was to drink at all with such a swollen and rubbery upper lip. Almost ludicrous.

She remembered now, a time at about age ten when she had been struck in the mouth with a golf club, had blundered directly into brother Kelly's wild backswing there on the front lawn. For days her upper lip and part of her cheek had been a swollen mass of awfulness, turned black and blue and finally a sickening tallow color as it reluctantly healed. Full of remorse, Kelly had supplied her with daily milk shakes and had even depleted his precious paper route savings to buy her a little red bicycle.

Having slaked her thirst, she glanced about and saw a dead sapling. It lay next to the one from which the flicker had flown, and she crawled to it. There, after much painful struggle, she broke off the brittle upper end with its remaining branches, creating a crude walking staff. Then, using it as a brace, she struggled to regain her feet, halfway up lost her balance, and fell backward to strike the earth with a cry of agony. For several minutes she merely lay there moaning, then tried again. This time she made it, clinging to the staff with one hand and hauling herself up the live sapling, clutching and half climbing it with the other. By now she was wheezing again, struggling for air and wondering whether it was wise to move at all. Her neck felt as though it had been wrapped in a blood pressure cuff, the pressure gradually increasing. Once she caught her breath as a lone hornet traced yellow squiggles against the hillside a short distance away. More hornets—that was all she'd need. Marilyn closed her eyes in a plea for clemency, opened them, and the marauder was gone.

Relief itself seemed to leave her trembling, but it was time to go, keep moving no matter what the struggle, even if only a few feet per minute. And to begin with, that was truly about it—a few yards at best. Tough enough, she thought, having one bad leg, but two—both pulsing with pain—made it absurd. Still, she crippled onward, groaning with each breath, gasping, clinging, eyes clenched shut, to her staff while everything about her reeled. She was heading downstream in the general direction of her car, a destination that now seemed a hundred miles away.

Four hours later she had covered about half a mile, her lungs still wheezing, head throbbing, spinning as though a gyroscope inside were losing momentum, bobbling and ready to go down. Her ankles were twice their normal size, one from the sprain, the other from a sting. The entire calf was so swollen, in fact, that she could not see the shin bone. Her skin had taken on a baked and glassy sheen, looking as though it were ready to split. Time after time, she had crumpled to all fours, crawling along the grassy edge of the stream, collapsing to bathe her face, her arms and legs, in its coolness—to drink, slurping ludicrously because of her wounded upper lip. The stream was only two or three feet wide in spots and only inches deep. A bare trickle, and the water was undoubtedly far from pure, but that mattered little. It was her friend. It was life.

Gradually the valley had widened, becoming flatter. The forest of aspen had attenuated and lost altitude, a dwindling peninsula now in a sea of sage. Soon she would have to desert the watercourse, for it was gradually meandering westward, luring her away from the road along which she had come. Thus far she had seen no signs of human life except for a distant plane droning monotonously over the hills a long way off, slowly circling into nonexistence. Anonymous and gray, barely moving, it obviously had no interest in her little predicament.

A faint breeze bore a whiff of something rancid. Momentarily it faded, then came on stronger—something dead. Marilyn stopped, clinging to her staff, hunched and haggard, the Witch of Endor, peering at the sage and squinting. The afternoon was hot, and sweat smarted in her eyes, both of them even though one had long since swollen shut. It took several seconds for her to realize that she was actually staring at a dead cow, a red and white Hereford, its belly bloated monstrously, two visible legs, front and rear, projecting stiffly toward the horizon. Flies swarmed, clustering blackly—several of the larger ones dark lacquered blues and greens about the cow's eyes and nostrils. Her stomach churned and she battled the urge to vomit.

The cow lay partially in the water, damming its flow, but it was downstream, and despite her roily stomach it seemed vital that she drink once more before heading into the open country. Again on her hands and knees, she peered into the placid, barely flowing surface and saw her reflection all too clearly. Porky Pig or Donald Duck? The face looking back was a pitiful yet frightening blend of both. Her shirt was filthy and torn, barely clinging to one shoulder, her hair matted with leaves and mud. "You're a real beauty," she mumbled, and the reflection mumbled back in mockery.

Then, flat on her belly, she slurped greedily, caught the stench of death again, and gagged. Time to head for the road.

Thirty-One

The computerized numbers on her little red watch, the plastic special she used for running and swimming, said seven forty-nine. It had been three more hours of struggle, some of it on her hands and knees, and now at last she had almost reached the road.

Occasionally a lone car or pickup had trundled up and down that road, casting its dusty spin-trail, but each time her response had been too frail and distant. Or too late, as she struggled to arise with the aid of her staff, tottering and waving feebly without success. Once, on the verge of waving, she had panicked, convinced that the vehicle was a jeep, the very monstrosity she had encountered before, such a short-long time ago. At the last moment she had dropped to one knee, peering through the rabbit brush, feeling an acrimonious twinge of pain in her neck. Every move she made spawned retaliation.

Once a chopper had passed over, circled widely, catching her in a near coma, huddled in the shade of a dying juniper. By the time she had revived and struggled to her feet it had drifted off into the haze, the battering of its blades still loud in her ears but steadily muffling into memory. "Wait!" she croaked. "Oh, please wait! Come back!" It ended in a parched moan of despair. But her plight remained unheeded. Only the indifferent gaze of a lizard which suddenly zipped away, vanishing with phenomenal speed. That and an oblivious flitting of sparrows somewhere across the road ahead.

"They'll have to find me before long," she promised herself. "It's not as if I'm lost in Alaska or someplace. All I have to do is get on the road and start following it back toward my car. Sooner or later someone will come along." But the night was also coming along, and the hot afternoon had faded swiftly, almost treacherously. Already the cold exhalations of early fall in the high country were expanding and coalescing, and she was hardly dressed for a night in the open. At that altitude and season, the temperature might drop to freezing. That very morning, in fact, when all had seemed so amiable and summery, she had spotted the frost's first victims—curling, black-brown leaves on the sunflowers, some of the heads already deprived of their petals. That and the chitinous carcasses of grasshoppers still embracing the dried yard-long stems of wild clover.

By now it seemed incredible that she could move at all. Never, without having to strictly for survival, would she have been able to persevere in such a condition. But there simply was no choice. No, more than ever, she would have to continue, more to avoid chill and possible hypothermia than to reach her destination. At her present rate of locomotion, only ten or fifteen feet per minute, she would not arrive at her car for days or even be able to drive it. Collapse seemed inevitable. Furthermore, it now appeared that the road would remain empty for a long time, that it had seen its rare and random traffic for the day. If they were looking for her, the search had drifted to other areas. It was doubtful that anyone had even discovered her car since she had parked it off the road in a deserted campground for the very purpose of keeping it hidden, concealed from thieves or vandals. On the other hand, she thought, maybe no one was really concerned. Jan and Carla had probably just assumed that she was at her home in Huntsville, and maybe her mom . . . her mother thought she had returned directly to her apartment. She hadn't given anyone the slightest idea how long she'd be gone. Very little, anyway. She closed her eyes. "Oh, Marilyn," she murmured, "you've really done it this time." Then, eyes still closed—"Lord, forgive me for being so stupid. Maybe I don't even deserve any help, but if there's the slightest chance that I do . . . please get me out of this mess."

Well, the Lord helped those who helped themselves, and she still had her staff, a mere dried stick that had broken off a time or two at one end, but it was still long enough that she could cling to it for support. She could not have survived thus far without it.

Slowly, like an old crone with advanced arthritis, she hunched and hitched along the darkening road as the shadows lengthened, her own shadow casting grotesque patterns eastward to her left as she dwindled through the remaining veils of light, through fading streamers from the dying sun, a red-gold cauldron now, receding beyond the distant hills. And already, despite her exertions, she was beginning to shiver. Once a tiny, singing cloud of gnats converged, exploring her face and swollen eye, her blood-matted hair, the gash on her head. One even invaded her nostril, and she choked, spitting, flailing, and croaking with outrage. Too much, truly the last straw, an indignity she utterly refused to tolerate.

Moments later, however, they were carried away in the gathering cold. The sun had vanished and darkness was dominating the landscape. Once she saw or perhaps merely imagined a flicker of light miles ahead, possibly the high beam from a car painting the trees or a hillside, maybe heat lightning. Seconds later, she stopped suddenly and caught her breath. Was someone calling? No, it was only the remote lowing of a stray Hereford, and her shivering increased.

Not far ahead the road looped, forming a broad, lopsided U, and within its embrace was a stand of scrub oak interspersed with maple. Instinctively she increased her pace, hitching and limping along, stabbing weakly at the road with her stick. Despite all the pain and exhaustion, she had developed a certain rhythm. If only, she thought, I had a single match. One flimsy little match, and she could start a fire with dead sage branches, perhaps even better fuel from the grove ahead. But there was no match, and she was no Indian capable of starting a fire in more primitive ways.

She merely knew that it was impossible to continue much farther, that it might be a little warmer within the trees. On the other hand, what would happen if she stopped moving? It was increasingly obvious. She was shaking harder now, teeth literally chattering, and the whole thing sharpened her pain. "Heavenly Father," she prayed, "I don't know how . . ." Her wheezing was continuous. "How I ever got into this mess, or if I'll ever get out." Her swollen mouth barely moved. The words pulsed hopelessly in her mind. "Maybe I deserve it, and if that's the case . . ." It required a little effort for her to add, "Thy will be done," and even then she slurred over it a bit halfheartedly. "But I . . . I've honestly about had it. And I do need thy help—I mean I *really need* it if I'm going to last the night." She was trying desperately not to cry, to avoid collapsing for good.

Moments later, her toe caught something. She felt the tug, heard a rustle and clatter, tripped and sprawled with a croak of agony and surrender. For a time she simply lay there feeling the cold, alien hardness of the roadside, panting and sobbing into the darkness. This was it, really the end. Really and truly the end. Strange, strange life—that it could shift so suddenly from good to bad, so irrationally. But at least they'd be able to find what remained of her without much search. Somebody would just about have to come by the following day, and hopefully there would be no "viewing" at the funeral. Surely her family would have the compassion not to display her in such a condition.

The very possibility was almost more frightening than that of death itself. Marilyn stirred and realized that whatever had tripped her was still hooked to her toe. She also realized what it was, hearing the rustle of plastic, the clatter of cans, the clink of bottles. A pale tan trash bag full of garbage, a gift from some litterbug. "Well, girl, there's your answer," the voice in her mind said. "You pray for help, and you get a sack of garbage. Either God's not listening or he's got quite a sense of humor." Bitterly she kicked the bag aside, smelling beer fumes and the stench of damp cigarette butts. They were much like the breath of her assailant that morning, and again her stomach was in turmoil. Maybe even refuse cast off by the same bunch of lunatics. It was something, regardless, that she could do without. Bad enough to die from exposure without being asphyxiated at the same time.

Then, completely unexpectedly, something said she was making a mistake. A strange prompting was creeping over her, urging her to lay hold of the bag and empty it. "Empty the stupid bag?" she countered. "What am I supposed to find in there—Aladdin's lamp? A magic carpet?"

"Empty the bag!" the voice in her mind commanded. "Just do as you're told." Again she resisted—the thought was ridiculous, repelling. And again, the voice insisted, literally commanded. Squirming backward with a sigh, half crawling, half dragging, she groped for it, tugged blindly at one corner, spilling its contents. Nothing there but cans and bottles, cigarette butts, paper plates . . . and what? Melon rinds? Yes, she could smell those too, almost feel them. A terrific find. So much for inspired promptings. But wait . . . one other item; her hand reached out and touched it. A folded newspaper. Well, great. Nothing like keeping up on the day's news.

Wonderful, though, for starting a fire if only she had a match, a single precious match. Scarcely realizing it, she reached for the paper, thinking vaguely that perhaps it would make a pillow of sorts, something better than the rutted, dusty road for her head. But wait . . . if paper could make a pillow . . . Suddenly she remembered something her dad had once said long ago, something about how hoboes and drifters occasionally wrapped their bodies with newspaper, wearing it under their shirts or coats for insulation. "Paper's a lot warmer than most people realize." The words returned clearly almost as though he were speaking at the exact moment. For the first time in nearly an hour she felt a faint throb of hope.

It required a full minute merely to sit up and about five more in the growing breeze to wrap the paper around her trembling body, a body that sometimes shook so violently it undid her own clumsy handiwork. At last, however, she had accomplished the task, working the paper in under her tattered shirt and tucking it beneath the band of her running trunks.

Gradually, in the process, she began to feel slightly warmer. Warm enough to struggle on a bit farther. No, too much effort, too painful to stand. The breeze ruffled the garbage bag, drifting it across her side, and immediately she felt an added shielding effect. Yes, shielding. So? "So why not wear it?" the voice in her mind inquired. "Wear it?" she wondered. "What am I supposed to do—climb into it?" No, no—ridiculous. "No, Lyn, just wear it, put it on." And with that, she clearly understood what had to be done. Carefully, gently tearing and working with her teeth, she ripped an opening in the bottom large enough to put her head through. After that, she made two smaller holes in front for her forearms. Then she pulled the bag over her head a bit like a poncho. It was longer than she had hoped, hanging all the way to her knees, and she hugged herself, clasping her arms together, astonished at the increased warmth.

It was a dramatic change that eventually gave her the courage to rise again and hobble on a little way with the aid of her faithful staff. By now, it had become a part of her, one she would not relinquish no matter what remained. "Thank you, Lord," she sighed. "Forgive me for being so stupid and ungrateful. I am in thy hands, whatever happens. Thy will be done." The pain in her ankles was still intense, and it lanced through her neck each time she turned her head or lost balance, tore at her ribs. Her head throbbed. She could feel the wound expand, then clench, leechlike, with each pulse beat. And yet, none of it seemed quite as bad now. Somehow her mind interpreted it differently. Her body could contain it all a little better.

From the east now came a faint, ethereal glow that subtly expanded, gradually outlining the distant peaks and a nearby ridge scraggled with pines. The mountains were yielding the moon. Slowly the blackened landscape filled with light like an endless outpouring of quicksilver, and she could see the grove of scrub oak clearly again. It lay just ahead to her right, seemed to beckon. For a moment she hesitated, saw glowing rocks along the roadside ranging in size from lemons to potatoes. Gradually, agonizingly, she collected enough to span the road with a crude arrow design, one pointing toward the grove, and beside it, nearly two feet tall, the letter *M*. The entire process was outlandishly awkward, adding considerably to her misery, especially now with the terrific pain in her ribs, but it gave her a sense of accomplishment. It added hope, increased her warmth.

Then she left the road and entered the trees, feeling her way among their gnarled trunks, hearing her feet stir the thick carpet of oak leaves from seasons past. Scaly bark and branches tugged and scraped at her, but she moved with utmost care, taking every precaution to avoid ripping her special plastic coat. The leaves spilled and crunched about her ankles as she went, and moonlight filtered through the branches in places, illuminating the rough spots, showing a depression just ahead drifted deep with leaves. It was there that Marilyn knew she would spend her night.

Slowly she lowered herself into the noisy, spilling carpet at her feet and sat there tucking the bag about her legs. Then, with gentle scooping motions, she began piling leaves over her feet and shins, gradually mounding them over her thighs and around her waist. Wincing and groaning, she lay back and eventually covered her torso all the way to the neck. Slowly, with infinite care, she wriggled her arms in through the holes of her plastic bag, gradually working them up beneath the bottom of her shirt.

Thousands of little, scalloped oak brush leaves, brown and curling, emanated a faint, musty, earthen odor. They had combined in wondrous abundance to become her friend, her security blanket, trapping the night air and converting it into insulation against the gathering cold. Marilyn groaned, more in relief now than in pain, issued a long, tremulous sigh, saw particles of the moon among the branches, dappling downward about her like a benediction.

Her left eye was still swollen shut. The right felt grainy, the lid immensely heavy, helpless against the weight of gravity. One ear sang wildly as though a tiny locust had lodged inside it. The other was filled with a faint roaring, muffled and measured like the beating of her own heart. Her lips struggled to move. "Thank you . . ." The word was scarcely audible or even decipherable through her suffering mouth. Yet it was there for a single, pulsating moment before she melted into unconsciousness.

Thirty-Two

The moon had gone, deferring to the pearl-colored light of dawn, when she emerged from her sleep, bemused and reluctant, surfacing from the womb of night, of time. Something had drawn her forth, though what she didn't know. A sudden loud stirring among the leaves, a crashing and snapping of limbs, something passing nearby. Her heart leapt, burning, but her body remained motionless. Perhaps, she told herself, it had only been a dream, and yet it seemed very real and lingered frustratingly like an echo along with the continued ringing and muffled implosions within her ears. She could, in fact, smell something strange yet vaguely familiar, a musky animal scent.

Cautiously she struggled to raise her head, feeling a dart of pain in the neck, a vicious gnaw in the ribs, another spasm of fear. Maybe she was again paralyzed, maybe this time for good. But no, she could shift her arms and legs despite the pain and stiffness. Even though it felt as if her entire body had been beaten with a club. For a time the effort to rise, even to one elbow, seemed insuperable. Better to simply remain in her little niche and sink back again into the goodness of oblivion. On the other hand, she knew that it was essential to reach the road, that people would definitely be searching for her by now regardless of what might have happened the day before. Suddenly she felt a pang of guilt over the anxiety her family would be undergoing, especially her mother. Until now she had been so engrossed in her struggle for survival that such thoughts had been remote at best.

Slowly she worked her forearms through the holes in her plastic coat, dubiously, fearing retaliation from every part of her body, still apprehensive over the sound heard earlier. Rolling awkwardly to the side, she struggled to one elbow. It was literal agony. She remained in that position for several seconds, listening, summoning her willpower. At last, gripping her staff in one hand and the trunk of an adjacent oak in the other, she struggled, groaning, to a mere crouch and gradually straightened up.

It was then that she heard something behind her, a snapping branch, stealthy crunchings within the carpet of leaves. Again, she felt the burning little heart spasm. Unable to turn her head, she shifted her entire body, reversing hands on the tree and staff with utmost awkwardness. What she saw made her gasp—a bizarre figure only thirty feet away, a man in a visored cap and coat that seemed to be made from the very leaves themselves. His left arm was extended, the clenched fist pointing directly at her. One eye was closed as though sighting, drawing a bead, and suddenly she saw the flexing surface of the bow, the gleam of lacquer, and the head of a hunting arrow with razorlike flanges. Her mouth opened in disbelief, sought to cry out, barely croaked.

The man hesitated, lowering the bow very slightly. Vaguely, she realized that the coat and cap of leaves were simply mottled camouflaging. He swore softly but profoundly in great disbelief. The bow string relaxed. The arrow withdrew. "You're the *one*!" He stared. "You're the girl they're *lookin'* for!"

She nodded weakly, issued a tiny gasp of acknowledgement.

Again the man swore, this time with the wildest surmise. "And here I thought you was a *deer*! Wounded one a little ways back and it come right through here."

Thirty-Three

The summer had ended technically on September twenty-first, but the transition into fall had been so subtle and tranquil as to be scarcely recognizable. True, the mountains had splurged in yellow and red, even washed out to dun and faded pink in the higher regions of Mount Ogden. Yet now, as the first week of October drifted to a close, the Huntsville afternoon was seventy degrees.

Walking slowly along the shore of Pine View Reservoir, Marilyn Richards Cannon felt the sunlight caressing her skin and saw it blending with the water. She still limped a little, her right ankle mummied in stretch wrap. The ligament had been badly torn and now, even a month later, was unable to take much stress. The three broken ribs had about healed, but her neck remained rather stiff and she felt an electric twang of pain whenever she turned it too sharply. The gash in her scalp had healed with the help of seventeen stitches, and a new crop of downy hair an inch long covered the area they had shaved. Her allergic reactions to the hornet stings had been neutralized quite effectively with antihistamines, but there was still a ringing in her left ear. Her doctor had explained that it might be there forever—pleasant thought—then added rather nonchalantly that she was one of millions with the same general affliction. Some people, in fact, had listened to the sound until, in the good doctor's words, they "wigged right out." All very comforting. The trick, obviously—she kept reminding herself—was simply not to listen, not even to *think* about listening. Otherwise . . . No, don't think! Think about what? Nothing, nothing at all–never mind!

Well, anyway, she had made a lot of progress the past month. Despite the aftereffects, despite the fact that she still carried her special walking stick, wondered at times whether she would ever dare part with it, she was no longer the pitiable, moaning creature paramedics had transported via helicopter to the McKay-Dee emergency ward in Ogden. A creature with its face, mouth, and left eye swollen beyond recognition, hair a tangled mass of blood, mud, leaves, and burrs, her body battered black and blue and clad in a plastic trash bag. And newspaper underwear!

What a sight she had been! For nearly two weeks afterward she could scarcely bear to glance at herself in the mirror. Gradually, gradually, though, she had returned to normal, or nearly. "So now you're pretty as ever," Lije Marriott had said. "Happy?" Yes, oh yes, definitely! "Grateful?" Yes . . . very. But moving slowly now along that empty shoreline, seeing her constant reflection in the watery surface, hair flowing down her back like the tail of a palomino, she wondered. And she saw old Lije's eye, the one with the surrounding scar tissue that always scrutinized so penetratingly. Hadn't it contained a touch of skepticism? Kindly, a bit amused even—yet skeptical. Comprehension that went so far beyond her own. Was she really and significantly grateful? Humble? Could she even *begin* to empathize with those condemned to spend their lives looking homely, a bit strange? Ugly? Even frightening? What if that "leaping rock" had caught her directly in the face, crushed and scrambled her features forever? The thought was still too terrible to contemplate.

For a moment she thought of her friend Cuddles, his baglike body, laughable gawkiness; it was a little as though he had been constructed of leftovers, mismatching parts. Laughable? Yes, even now she felt guilty for still thinking of him in that light. At times, admittedly, Cuddles seemed almost to strive for the ludicrous, fairly begging for uncharitable reactions. The outlandish wearing apparel, for example, like someone costumed for a roadshow comedy. But even so . . . had she the right to think of him condescendingly? To think of *anyone* condescendingly? What about some of her obese women friends at the college, the one whose entire epidermis seemed to be filled with oil, who moved with a "blubbery, oleaginous waddle." That, in fact, was precisely how Marilyn had described the girl to herself, gazing from the pleasant one-way window there in her comfortable air-conditioned office. She had regarded her friend with literal disdain, belittling her mentally as a "slob" as she struggled along the hot, empty walkway toward the LDS Institute just north of the campus.

How did it go? "Though I speak with the tongues of men and of angels, and have not charity . . ." What? Something about brass and cymbals. Yes, "I am become as sounding brass, or a tinkling cymbal." She felt the old blood pressure cuff around her throat again, this time from sheer emotion. "Help me, Father," she prayed, "help me to be full of kindness and love, full of gratitude and humility." Scarcely realizing it, she was shaking her head a little, feeling her eyes moisten, trying hard to rid her mind and heart of their impurities, the vanities of the world that managed to collect so persistently. At the moment it seemed an almost hopeless battle. "Be thou humble; and the Lord thy God shall lead thee by the hand, and give thee answer to thy prayers." Another scripture. She wasn't sure where it came from, but oh—her eyes melted—was it ever true! Yes, yes—humility, prayer, unconditional love.

Once a chopper chattered by, swinging her way as though for a better view, banking and climbing against a tiny school of clouds. Marilyn thought of the search and rescue effort a month before, greater and prompter than she had initially supposed. By midafternoon her mom, always vigilant and often extrasensory, had become worried enough to start making calls. Kelly, Gordie and Daws, Jan and Carla, even The Turk and his motley collection of pals—all were soon enlisted. Toward evening members of the Sheriff's Jeep Patrol had also joined in the search.

But Monte Cristo was a big place, and no one had ever spotted her well-secluded car. Several of the searchers, Gordie and Daws included, thought that they had traversed her same little jogging road during the late afternoon, but if so she either hadn't seen or hadn't recognized them. Perhaps she had been lying exhausted, even unconscious somewhere along the stream or hidden within the shade of a juniper. Nor had anyone ever seen her special arrow and initial. As fate or divine providence had ordained, the roving bow hunter had discovered her instead, had mistakenly almost taken her life in the process.

Life in general was so fraught with unpredictables, such an endless proliferation of senseless mishaps and disasters. Or so it surely seemed. Only a week earlier now, one of her friends, a returned missionary who had served in Holland, had died in a car accident on Harrison Boulevard near the college, in almost the exact spot where her old VW had broken down that spring. Apparently he had been following too closely or had taken his eyes off the road for a moment and had slammed into the rear of a large semi that had braked unexpectedly to avoid a dog. Why, on the other hand, had her brother Kelly miraculously survived his own encounter with a truck in Japan, preserved by the healing hand of the priesthood, the fasting and prayers of members in a little branch outside Kobe? Why had her father died in an auto wreck and the drunk responsible survived with only minor bruises? Was someone up there actually programming it all? Every earthquake, bullet, knife blade, every little bug that might prove fatal, deadly snake-bite, heart attack, drowning, drug overdose, strangulation on a chicken bone or unchewed piece of meat?

That was the question she had posed to Lije Marriott during her visit to his home a few evenings earlier. "Well now, I'm inclined to doubt it," the old patriarch had mused. This, following a lengthy, cogitative pause. "To my way of thinking—and I may be a hundred and one percent wrong—but many of these things come strictly by chance, in my book." They had been sitting in the quiet of his living room with her mother, Kelly, and Shannon. "For now, we see through a glass darkly. I reckon all the answers won't be in on that one till the life to come, and even then—who knows? May even take a spell after that." Lije sat gazing out the window, locked his hands together—those gnarled hands that always looked as if they belonged to a larger body—and reflected for some time in silence. "But this I do know. Sometimes the good Lord enters in—either to take us or leave us—for his own good reasons. For now, I'm content to live with that, and to always remember that each new day is a gift."

"But why so little certainty?" Shannon asked, voicing verbatim Marilyn's very thoughts.

"Oh," Lije replied placidly. "There are plenty of certainties." The laugh crinkles deepened around the corners of his eyes. "After all, what's more certain than change?"

They all laughed, Marilyn with a bit of frustration. "Yes, but . . . ," she began.

The old man, however, continued. "Death and taxes!" Then, in a more serious vein: "There are the great eternal verities, my girl—the Atonement and resurrection for one thing, and a whole big grand system all spelled out in clear and beautiful detail for our exaltation." He paused portentously. "It's called the restored gospel, and there are divine promises that can never be abrogated as long as we live up to our end of the bargain. It's just that God's time frame may be a bit different from ours, and his manner of doing things doesn't always happen to coincide with our own little notions of just what should and shouldn't be. Now, granted . . ." He massaged the dewlap under his chin, cleared his throat. "Within that great and certain framework there are plenty of unanswered questions, plenty of variables. Maybe that's part of why we came here—to cope with a pretty good dose of uncertainty along the way and still keep our cool. Still maintain our humanity, our dignity, without ever surcumbing to bitterness and self-pity." Marilyn smiled inwardly, caught Kelly's glance, and knew exactly what he was thinking. For all his wisdom and, often, natural eloquence, the old man had never relinquished his share of colloquialisms and occasional, half-intended mispronunciations. Like *surcumbing*. "And we came here," he continued, "among other things, for the right to struggle, for the privilege of suffering."

Privilege? she thought. *Privilege?* Her soul recoiled as bare skin shrinks at the touch of iron in winter. The old man's countenance, however, remained confident and serene. Furthermore, his message had credibility because Elijah Marriott had "been there" if anyone had.

Lije watched her, one eyebrow tenting quizzically. "Hard doctrine, isn't it?"

"Yes, it is," she said. Her voice was high, fracturing slightly on the final word with a touch of resentment.

"And yet," he observed, "there isn't anyone here who hasn't already had a pretty fair serving of it. Your lovely momma included." Momentarily she looked at each of them and saw the confirmation. Gazing into her mother's eyes, she even felt a twinge of guilt, a sudden sense of insight. How often had she truly empathized with her mother's plight, her aloneness, even acknowledged that there might be a continuing struggle? Momentarily, too, she actually felt a little vexed at her for bearing up under it all with such unremitting stoicism, for sharing her own pain so rarely. "Look into the face of a person who knows no suffering," Lije continued quietly, "and you see a face without any character, no more personality than a boiled egg."

"I keep thinking of a statement somewhere," Kelly said, "about people who were 'arrayed in white,' and singing 'a new song.' Revelations, I guess."

"Ah!" the patriarch exclaimed, his face becoming even more luminous. "Ah!" He paused. "And why were they arrayed in white, singing a new song?"

"Because they had been exalted," Kelly replied quietly.

"Absolutely. And why had they been exalted?"

"Because they had come through 'great tribulation' and had overcome all things." This time the old man merely nodded steadily, almost imperceptibly. His smile warmed steadily as well with a growing tinge of pride. His young protégé was coming along.

"So!" he said at last. "So now our Marilyn has been having her own share of tribulation in the past while—correct?" The gentle eye was watching her from under its heavy lid, the eye of wisdom. "Maybe even a little extra portion, right?" Marilyn began to demur, but the patriarch persisted. "Don't sell yourself short, child; you've known a bit of the refiner's fire, and now I have a question or two. Ready?" His expression seemed a bit mischievous yet also highly sincere.

"I don't know," she said smiling and looking, without realizing it, very sweet and timorous and vulnerable.

"Question is . . ." The grandfather clock in Lije's hall tick-tocked steadily, suddenly quite insistently. "And it's a question for all of us, one that we should ought to be asking a whole lot more often." Their gazes fused, her own nervous yet unwavering. "Question is, what have you learned?"

Marilyn took a deep breath, wondering frantically for a moment whether she had ever learned anything, anything at all in her entire life. "I'm not sure," she managed at last, "but maybe I've learned a little more about hanging in."

"Aha! Hangin' in! You most surely have, and it's a grand virtue. Tell us about it—share the wealth."

"Well," she said slowly, "up there on Monte I made a couple of bad mistakes." She hesitated. "I made a bad one going up there all alone in the first place, I guess. Not listening to my mom."

"Don't guess!" Maria chided, but she was smiling. "And don't do it again!"

"It's just that I needed space, freedom in a bad way . . . and, well, maybe I still resent not being able to go anywhere I want strictly on my own . . . the way a man can."

"Just take Braun," Kelly said, referring to his hunting dog, a large and powerful Chesapeake Bay retriever that was also highly protective. "He'd have shredded those buzzards. You just have to make a few practical compromises, Lyn-Lyn. We all do, one way or another."

"Yes, I guess," she said wryly and reflected on the fact that her assailants were still at large despite efforts by the law to track them down. It was a disquieting thought at best, and whether they were ever apprehended or not, the fact remained that there would always and forever be people like that—even worse if possible—"out there somewhere." And besides, Braun was only a partial solution. She couldn't go traipsing to her brother's place to collect his dog every time she wanted to go anyplace.

"And we'd better keep working on the karate—all three of you guys," Kelly had continued. The "guys" in this instance happened to be the three women present, and Marilyn was considerably more enthusiastic about that suggestion than about being assigned a permanent canine escort. Skill in self-defense, she had now decided, would impart the confidence and freedom she desired more than anything else.

"You're right," she said. "In fact, if it hadn't been for those basic techniques you kept drumming into me, I'd—" It was still impossible to relive the experience without great agitation and revulsion. The prospect of what might have happened was even worse, continued to make her ill at times, a bit paranoid. Simultaneously there was also the sense of triumph over the way she had laid her attacker low. Despite his superior size and strength, she had *not* merely been a "poor helpless woman."

The old man nodded knowingly. "So maybe you made an initial mistake," he allowed, "but then you rallied strong and fought the good fight. Showed a tremendous amount of courage and determination, in my book." He paused. "So tell us a little more about hanging in."

"Well"—she sighed and felt embarrassed, knowing how often she'd been on the brink of surrender—"I also made a bad mistake along the way—after I got myself into that whole big mess. I really panicked with those yellow jackets, completely freaked out, and nearly ended it all as a result."

"Yes, but I don't think anybody can put you down for that," Shannon said. "You just did everything you could to get away. I'd have done exactly the same thing—almost anybody would have, especially people who are allergic to them."

"Yes, but *blindly*," Marilyn insisted. "I mean, there are good instinctive reactions, and there are bad ones. That's something I don't exactly understand, but somehow . . . you have to, well, work on the bad ones with your mind, with lots of effort and discipline, until you can substitute the right ones."

"Now you're a-learning something," Lije rasped happily. "You're really *thinking,* and that's hard work." He paused, raising the usual tutorial forefinger. "Now! What happens when and if you have another run-in with those little yellow critters?"

"Hmmm . . . well, somehow I'm going to watch where I'm going better—I hope. Not have a run-in to begin with."

"Good, but don't just hope—plan."

"I'll try."

"Don't just try—do!" They were all laughing, Kelly especially. He had been the old man's disciple for a long time, and Lije Marriott was nothing if not pragmatic. "Make up your mind strong enough right now, then *live* it in your imagination, in all your actions, every time you get the chance, until it becomes that kind of correct instinct you're talking about."

She nodded, smiling, taking it all to heart. "And if I'm on a slope without much visibility . . ." The others watched her expectantly. "I'll go uphill instead of down, even if it's slower."

"Why's that?" Lije inquired.

"Less chance of falling over a cliff."

"Aha!" the old man exclaimed. His eyebrows sprang exuberantly. "Now you've taught us *all* something."

Thirty-Four

Marilyn's reflections on the family visit with Elijah H. Marriott were interrupted by a loud and sudden panting, the sound of something rushing along the sandy shoreline, closing in fast from the rear. Startled, she turned, ready to wield her staff, and felt a twinge of pain in her neck. She also felt a flood of relief. It was only Braun, so named because his name meant "brown" in German, because it also tied in with brawn and was definitely consistent with the animal's size and strength. "Braun!" It was a half sigh, half exclamation. Good old Brawny. Good old Wernher von Braun —that was where Kelly had acquired his actual inspiration for the name, from the famed German-American physicist and rocket expert.

The dog's coat was a rich chocolate color with just a touch of honey and rust, thick and slightly curly, a bit marcelled along the back and shoulders, and he nearly bowled her over in his enthusiasm. More than once on other occasions he had picked up her tracks and come gallumphing along to join her. Well, it was nice to be wanted, but she also suspected a little conspiracy was afoot on the part of her family. His appearances of late seemed more than coincidental.

He reminded her a lot of the golden lab that had emerged from nowhere during her triathlon adventure, even the supernatural yellow eyes. The lab's owner had never been found, and it was still in the possession of her friend from the highway patrol—one Joseph P. Doaks. He had continued to ask her out from time to time, and occasionally she had gone. Quite a good-looking guy, actually, sturdy and permanently tanned with his thick, dark hair and handsome mustache. Yet somehow he seemed rather clonelike, too, nothing very salient or distinguishable. The same was true of his personality. He loved cars, CB and ham radio, and was quite the avid outdoorsman. He relished his work with the highway patrol, looked sharp in his uniform, pretty cool, in fact, when he donned his amber-colored shades—which, however, also rendered him even more anonymous. At times Marilyn wondered, in fact, if he didn't relish the uniform and shades even more than the job per se.

Joe Doaks was still little more than a kid in some ways. But the real problem in dating him was that they rarely had anything to discuss, nothing to talk about but *things*, never the meaning of things. As for religion . . . well, they both belonged to the same church, and he even attended his meetings, when not off hunting or fishing, but there was little about the doctrine that appeared to excite him. It was largely an uninquiring, passive kind of acceptance.

Braun was in one of his most rambunctious moods—dashing up and down the shore, cavorting about, and occasionally spraying her with sand from his paws. Periodically he would also shoulder against her, thrashing his tail and making strange little coaxing sounds deep in his throat, muted combinations of a growl and whimper, pleading to be petted, begging with eyes the color of lemonade. Once he brought her a piece of driftwood, prancing ingratiatingly and arching his neck a bit like a circus pony, obviously proud of his offering and eager for her to make use of it. "Oh, so you want to retrieve, want to do a little swimming, huh?" Extracting the stick from his mouth, she flung it sidearm into the reservoir, and immediately the dog was after it, chesting into the tranquil water with a great splash and swimming vigorously. Seconds later he had seized it in his powerful jaws and was returning, leaving a slight wake that cut through the concentric rings he had already generated, snuffling happily.

Clearly, it was a game she would now have to repeat a good many times, until he became winded enough to lose interest. Otherwise he would pester her to distraction. Well, why not give him his fun? Why not let him wring all the delight and joy from life he possibly could? Heaven knew such options weren't always available to man or beast. Moments later he presented her the stick again, but not before shaking his coat free of water and spraying her new white walking shorts and golf shirt with muddy droplets. Berating him loudly, she hurled the stick again, this time much farther. She had reached the narrow peninsula that extended from Huntsville, partially dividing the south arm of Pine View from the rest of it and terminating at Cemetery Point half a mile distant.

Sitting down on a low bluff, she perused the water and found it, as always, somewhat healing. It was the reservoir's low point for the year, water having descended from its height at mid-June in a series of small terraces and dropping a total of ten feet in the process. Even so, it still possessed a kind of plentitude, and except for

Braun's localized disruptions it lay smooth as a mirror, meditative and rich with reflection. Nothing else stirred the surface, not even a solitary fishing boat.

Somehow the serenity of it all reminded her of Mark Aldous, her supervisor at the college. It had been several months now since the loss of his wife, and despite it all he continued to meet life with his usual grace and courage. An affectionate, attentive father to his three young children, responsible in his occupation, and never descending to the bitterness of self-pity of which Lije Marriott had spoken, never at least so far as she had observed or heard. A spiritual man with natural dignity, but fun-loving too. Gentle sense of humor, the ability above all to laugh at himself.

He had visited her, bearing flowers, during her stay in the hospital and had been highly attentive throughout her recovery, insisting that she take all the necessary time off, even more, actually. He had recently treated her to dinner at a Greek restaurant just off campus. At the time she had received an offer from Utah State in Logan for a position similar to the one she held at Weber State, though at a substantial salary increase. The public relations office there, in fact, had been courting her strongly, and it was all quite exciting and flattering. Simultaneously, Weber State—Mark Aldous especially—wanted greatly to retain her.

"Let's face it," he had said, "we definitely want to hold onto you if at all possible, and even though we can't match the offer from our friends up north, not for a while at least, I've consulted The Powers That Be . . ." He paused, eyes blue like Yeager's though devoid of the uncanny electricity, serene instead, utterly guileless. Now too, however, they contained a glimmer of mischief, as though some of his words, including the "Powers That Be" allusion, might possess a slight double entendre. "And, well, let's just say I suspect we could get you a decent increase—say at, oh—at least two-thirds what they're offering, anyway."

"That's wonderful, Mark," she said, "really sweet of you."

He chuckled, his face warm and empathic. Loving? Immediately she had squelched the thought, yet there was something a bit beyond the brotherly in his glance, some sort of chemistry. She could feel it simmering throughout her skin, along her neck and arms. Then he had suddenly become more serious, but it hadn't diminished the initial sensation. "We'd really hate to lose you," he said quietly. For an instant their gazes traced each other, the merest instant, but the effervescence increased, and she could feel her cheekbones glow. Just as quickly his glance had flicked down at the table, then up again, direct and casual. "On the other hand, I definitely want what's best for you. It just might be a great opportunity up there at Logan . . . in a lot of ways. Maybe a good change of scene."

"Thanks," she said, "I really appreciate that, Mark, and I hope you know I'm not playing any little games to see how much I can squeeze from anyone. I want what's best for everybody, and I really have mixed feelings about—" Unexpectedly her voice fractured a little, and her left eye blurred. Perhaps it was partly just aftermath reaction from the hornet sting, the swelling which had at last gone away.

"Sure, I know," he said.

"Oh," she gasped simultaneously and gave a little laugh, a quick shake of the head. "I don't know what's the *matter* with me lately!" Two of her former professors from the English department were seated a few tables away. Momentarily they glanced in her direction, then politely resumed their conversation. One of them, Royden Eldredge, had helped her obtain her current position, writing quite a glowing letter of recommendation. Eldredge was as bald as an ostrich egg and was fondly known by certain of his students as Daddy Warbucks. "I'm such a crummy little wimp about practically everything lately," she continued more quietly.

"Hey," Mark said gently, reached out and gave her hand a little squeeze. Merely fatherly? "I understand, believe me."

"It's just that everything's so up in the air."

"Sure," he said, "*sure.*" The words, though almost inaudible, resonated compassion. "You've been through an awful lot for quite a spell now."

Marilyn looked up, her lips flowing and unstable, trying to smile. "Yeah," she gasped and suddenly felt mortified. "Tell *you* about it, right?" How trivial her own concerns still seemed compared to his! Yet there she was blubbering on his shoulder and receiving generous commiseration.

"You're a really great man, Mark," she said. "I truly mean that."

"Thanks, Lyn-Lyn," he replied.

Braun had returned from the water for the fifth or sixth time with his beloved chunk of driftwood, showing little loss of enthusiasm, and she warded him off with her staff to avoid another shower bath. "All right, Wernher," she said, fondly weary, "one more toss and that's it." Sudden, vigorous motions were still hard on her constitution, especially her neck.

Once again the chopper appeared and circled as if, possibly, she bore watching. For an instant her heart faintly fibrillated with the childish thought that Lon Yeager might be up there, the ridiculous fantasy that soon the strange and strident sky monster would land where the peninsula was flat and level just above the slope to her right. A mechanical dragonfly. Its huge bulbous eye would explode sunlight, and out would come The Yeager, Mr. Charisma, Inc. Dressed in what? Maybe a brilliant blue-green shirt, open at the throat, and white denims. Yes. Standing there, hands on hips, head playfully cocked to one side a bit as if to say, "Well-well-well . . . sneaking off on our own again, eh?" Then, he'd descend, cascading sand in that easy, fluent manner, seat himself beside her and say . . . Say what? Maybe nothing for quite a while. Eventually: "Hey, look, ah—" They would both be gazing out across the water. "I understand completely how you feel, and I can't blame you one little sliver for it." One little sliver. It was another Yeagerism, something out of his family background she'd heard him use before. He would clear his throat, and his eyes? Merely the faintest glistening like her own? He'd be wearing white canvas beach shoes, no socks, just the strong, tanned ankles, the bones and tendon stark and masculine. Forearms bulging as he clasped his knees, the heavy silver watchband on his wrist with its jade inlays contrasting starkly. "So . . . I'm not asking for a thing, really. I wouldn't even expect you to believe me if I said I was trying with everything I've got left to turn my life around, and . . ." For an instant his eyes would caress her face, drawing her own eyes toward them. Momentarily, she would half succumb, but her own glance would simply be full of immense regret for all that might have been. And he would utter an explosive little laugh of surrender, head bowing. "See? You don't believe me—not one little sliver, right? And why should you, right?"

She would offer no reply, her throat too parched. "But it's true, Lyn, the Lord as my witness."

Two avocets skimmed whitely across the inlet, whimpering through their slender upturned bills, long legs trailing. And for a moment he actually seemed to be there. "So, I'm not asking a thing—just not to hate me any more than you have to. Okay? And maybe . . . well, a little prayer once and a while?" A gentle squeeze on her shoulder as he arose and headed back for the chopper. That would be all. Unless of course, she decided to open her mouth and give one little call . . . just one little call before . . .

And this time Braun really gave her a shower bath. She had been utterly lost in her dream. "Idiot!" She whacked his rear with her staff, wrenched her neck in a spasm of pain, and he shied off with a squeal of dismay. Arising somewhat stiffly, she continued slowly along the shore, still peeved at the dog for decimating her tender, foolish illusion. In reality, however, he had done her a favor, brought her back to her senses. The reality was that Lon Yeager had visited her in the hospital, bearing flowers of his own, full of the usual old charm and devotion, touchingly sympathetic, and offering all kinds of plausible explanations for his recent actions. And the most important reality of all was that she had somehow managed to reject them, had told him, eyes almost dry, that it was over—finally, irrevocably over and done, that she simply could not, would not maintain a relationship that demoralizing. What did the psychologists call it. "Emotionally disequilibrating"? Well, whatever, too much was too much.

It was a very painful experience, like the breaking of adhesions in a bad wound, and she had been amazed at her own determination. Afterward, of course, countless doubts, sleepless hours wondering whether by some remote possibility everything he had said in his own defense might be true after all. Restless, sometimes passionate dreams and fantasies. But she had made the right decision, as various trusted friends "in the know" continued to assure her. Lon Yeager's was unquestionably the classic case of "bad to worse." And now . . . only a few days earlier, there was the final irrefutable truth that he had vanished in the wake of mounting accusations regarding the big diamond scam in Salt Lake City, amid growing rumors that his role as Mormon Casanova had landed him in serious trouble with several different women, including a prominent divorcee and political figure old enough to be his mother.

Gone too was the voluptuous Taunya of Beautiful Bodies fame —nothing left but her sensual ten-foot replica with its dazzlingly narcissistic smile, bronze-skinned in its zebra-striped bikini— gracing the highway billboards. A lingering threat to safe driving.

"Would this body lie to you?" It was a great temptation to improvise on that one.

According to the latest glad tidings, Lon and Taun had gone winging off together again in his private plane—the plane to which he merely held one-third ownership, actually—and were somewhere in South America. Most likely the two of them were now wildly trysting high above the world in the cloudlands of Machu Picchu. Yes, Marilyn assured herself, little doubt. Well, they definitely deserved each other—and maybe, just maybe, if she really prayed hard an earthquake would hit the area in the midst of their most rapturous moment. She clenched her eyelids tight for an instant almost painfully, realizing that such reflections were little short of blasphemous, downright vicious, that such unalloyed bitterness was a canker to the soul. Change the *k* to *c*, in fact.

But what *was* the man, really? How did you explain him?

Coldly calculating villain and con man? Helpless woman addict? Split personality? Or in her brother's words, simply "one weird customer"?

"Well, Lyn Girl," she told herself, "it's about time to quit agonizing. Kiss the obsession good-bye and chalk it up to experience." And yet . . . it never quite worked that way. It was never that easy in real life.

Thirty-Five

So what now? She really didn't know. She had arrived at the end of her summer and did not know what lay ahead. No James Bond floating down from out of Timbuktu in a parachute, and who in the world could ever make a life with the likes of James B. anyhow? No El Cid rounding the shoreline on a mighty white charger, pennant flying from the tip of his upraised lance. And even if he were to appear, the Cid would no doubt be dead, only the corpse secured to his saddle with a wooden back support at the movie's end. Besides, even in death he belonged to the exotic Xemene, otherwise known as Sophia Loren.

Right now, there was absolutely nobody on the horizon. Utterly zilch. Here she was almost twenty-six years old and nobody there. What was it her dad used to sing? Sometimes in the morning while he was shaving. "Last night I saw upon the stair, the little man who wasn't there. He wasn't there again today. Oh, how I wish he'd go away!" Well, he *had* gone now. Nobody there—never was, maybe never would be. All right—tough, so *what?* There were tons of others twice her age, three times, and more, with nobody there. Millions inside the Church and out who had to sit on their hands and wait, partly because of some stupid, assinine chauvinistic tradition. And the problem was . . . well, it actually amounted to a kind of mutual conspiracy. In all honesty, it wasn't entirely some sinister plot hatched up by males alone. Too many women simply acquiesced and consequently perpetuated their own victimization.

She was frowning deeply, almost scowling. Too few, when actually challenged or even exhorted by men themselves, had the courage—that was the best word for it—to seize the initiative. They were simply too darned timid, too fearful of being considered "aggressive" or "plain Janes" who couldn't hope for a date or marriage in any other way. Kelly himself had decried the whole business more than once. "If you really like some guy, why not let him know? You don't have to grovel at his feet. Just be cool and let him know. Pay him a visit, ask him out. What have you got to lose?" Well, yes—in theory—but in reality she wasn't sure she had that much courage herself. Maybe just too much pride, maybe just fear of rejection. "It's good-looking, on-the-ball girls like you who still have some options," Kelly insisted, "that oughta be taking the lead. Set the style and make it easier for everybody."

Well, okay, maybe so. She heaved a sigh and kept walking. Stalks of mullein clustered in a little swale above the beach to her right, projecting long, conical heads of tightly packed green buds, tiny yellow blossoms blipping into life like popcorn. A part of her mind noticed with pleasure, and yet . . . she remained preoccupied. The problem now—even if she accepted Kel's challenge with literally open arms—was where to start looking. At the moment she couldn't even think of anybody who really appealed to her except for a couple of teachers on campus, and they were both married. One, in fact, was old enough to be her father. And maybe . . . she had to admit, Mark Aldous. The feeling had grown subtly, and it was something a bit more than platonic now. Why not admit it? Yet in reality, she again reminded herself, Mark was still married "for all eternity," to one of the loveliest women she had ever known. Maybe Karen Aldous really had been too good for this earth, actually had been taken for that very reason. Conversely, maybe Marilyn Cannon had survived for the very opposite reason, that she needed lots more hard-knocks schooling before she'd be ready.

Life was virtually writhing with such ironic little imponderables. Anyway, she truly loved Karen, held her in the highest esteem. Also resented her a little for being so wonderful? Was there actually a tinge of jealousy? Oh, come on now, Lyn-Lyn, how ridiculous can you get? But sharing a man with anyone, including someone so nearly perfect who is beyond this veil of tears—*that* would take some terrific attitude adjustment indeed.

Besides, she wasn't really alone. Wernher von Braun was still there, too much so today, and so—bless his soul—was Cuddles Eskelson. Not today, but often lately. Definitely a good and loyal friend with a kind of puppy-dog lovableness himself. Now that she had recuperated enough to start work again, he had begun visiting her office almost daily to gripe about certain teachers who allegedly had it in for him, but mostly to reminisce on the summer past, the memorable Lake Powell days, the Golden Spike Triathlon, and other races, often to the point of exhaustion, insensitive to the fact that she might have work to do. He had, additionally, rehearsed in endless and childish delight the plans of his stake Special Interest group to create a haunted house for the Halloween season just ahead—all proceeds going to help support missionary work.

It was a laudable idea, yet somehow the prospect of such involvement made her feel all the more trapped. Church Special Interest programs in general still turned her off. The thought of becoming a participant made her feel labeled, living in limbo with a bunch of matrimonial losers. That thought, also, another part of her mind admitted, was—well, not quite in league with praying for an earthquake, yet anything but Christlike. As bad, perhaps, as looking down upon those who were homely or "looked comical." Where, for heaven's sake, was her sense of caring? she wondered. Of service? Of being her brother's keeper? *Sister's* keeper? It vexed her no small degree that almost all language was so sexist. That every pronoun referring to mankind—ha, *mankind* itself!—fell under the umbrella of the masculine. Why? And why, for that matter, did she allow so many things to bug her? After all, she was *alive*! She had been preserved. One way or another, she had been granted more time upon the earth. And as for Special Interest, hadn't she heard some beautiful things in that connection? Had it not provided many people an added sense of belonging and purpose? Hadn't it produced some truly happy marriages?

No doubt about it; in her struggles for emotional survival she had indeed become pretty self-centered in many respects. There had not been enough giving, not enough selflessness, empathy, and compassion. And service? Oh, she subscribed to the idea in theory, all right. "Whosoever will be great among you, let him be your minister." The words themselves seemed strangely paradoxical if you really thought about them, but the basic message was abundantly clear. And she seemed to have become so entangled in her own problems of late she could scarcely summon the will to give except in rather superficial ways. She thought about her friend Janie Johnson—Janie's almost constant support. Above all, the radiance of her countenance a few days earlier when she broke the news, proudly displayed the long white envelope with its impressive return address in the upper left-hand corner: "Office of the First Presidency, The Church of Jesus Christ of Latter-day Saints." Janie had been called as a missionary for eighteen months to Italy, and she was utterly ecstatic.

Truly, Marilyn was happy for her, shared her joy, and certainly thought that a mission in Janie's case was no mere consolation prize. Come what may, whoever might or might not be "out there" some day, matrimonially speaking, regardless of where or when, Janie would not be denied her year and a half mission. Momentarily Marilyn felt a twinge of envy at her friend's sense of assurance, her irrepressible cheeriness and positivism. She squinted, scanning the horizon. Was it possible? Was a mission for the Church perhaps her own answer? How could she really know? Abandon a fulfilling job, maybe her career, her work? Return home at age twenty-seven, chances for finding somebody steadily diminishing? But of course, she had never even pondered the possibility very seriously, never once prayed about it, in fact. Strange. Was it more lethargy or fear of a positive answer?

Well, maybe at the very least she could make a contribution. The spook alley wasn't a bad idea actually. Daws and Gordie were getting into the act at Cuddles's request. So was Tami Oda. Even The Turk, having consented to double as Black Beard's Ghost or something. Suddenly she was smiling, almost laughing aloud. What a splendid, perfect Black Beard! Too bad she herself couldn't star exactly as she had appeared a month earlier as one of the living dead.

Anyway, what about personally giving Janie a hand? She apparently hadn't been able to save a lot, having just paid her way through four years of college, and her parents were sending her on the mission. So why not a monthly contribution to help them out and keep her friend afloat? After all, she was making a decent salary now with a raise coming up, and the truth was that she spent nearly all of it on herself—car, clothes almost lavishly, meals out, her apartment. Of course, she did pay her tithing and fast offerings, and felt that ought to count for something, but oddly enough the act had become so habitual, performed with so little thought, she had almost ceased to realize what she was giving or why.

Marilyn paused, eyes closed, leaning upon her staff. So what to do? The answer was incredibly obvious. Impart even more, more of her "substance" to those in need, and much, much more of herself. People with needs were all over the place, almost anywhere one wanted to look if the eye was at all discerning. And pray, more earnestly, more often. Everything to gain that way. Nothing to lose.

Once more her thoughts reverted to the previous night in Lije's living room. The old man had been expounding upon one of his favorite themes, namely that "attitude is everything," and that decisions rather than conditions were ultimately the determining factor regarding sadness or happiness. "Do you actually realize," he had said and looked each of them directly in the eye, one after another, "that you can literally *decide*—make a conscious decision—whether you want to be happy or sad?"

For a moment Marilyn had doubted his words, and she realized immediately that he knew it. "True, my girl! Absolutely true. Now you take, for instance, my little granddaughter Tessa—wonderful child just turned eight years old. Youngest grandchild. Got *great* grandkids considerably older! But anyway, the other night I was over to her place for dinner, and Tessa was a-looking pretty down in the mouth. Lower lip sticking out so far a chicken like-ta hatch eggs on it. Well, turns out her sister Sally won't play with her. Sally's an old sophisticated ten-year-old, by the way, and she's got a playmate on hand her same age who's lots more interesting than Tessie girl—even though Tessie invited the friend over in the first place! Got the picture?"

They were all smiling; it was a familiar scenario in most households. "Just keeps happening, doesn't it?" Lije chuckled. "Sure as hoppers in August. But there's Little Tessie all worked into a lather, a-whining and a-pouting like the whole world's nothing but castor oil. Having quite the love affair with her own misery." He paused, crossed his knees, locked his hands behind his neck, and regarded the ceiling. "Well sir, I got her aside after a while, had her come sit on Grampa's lap; that's always the first step. Then I told her, yeah, it was a dirty deal all right, but that I knew for sure she had more grit than to make a racket over it. 'Besides,' I says, 'I can smell a real fine dinner in there, and you don't need to plan your life around Sally Gally or anybody else. You're my Tessa Ann Marriott, the girl with the billion dollar sunshine smile. Ya know,' I says, 'That smile's one of the things I like most about this place—that and the fact that you're pretty near always happy as a meadowlark in May. Why, that's a whole lot of what makes *me* happy, and plenty of other folks too.'

" 'What other people?' she wants to know. Still hasn't quite bought the idea, and there's a tear on her cheek, but the lower lip's only out far enough now for a blackbird. 'Well now,' I tell her, 'you're whole big ever-lovin' family for one thing, and how about all your little school chums?' About then, her lip pooches way out again. 'Not Eric,' she says, 'he puts worms in my hair!' " The old man cackled. " 'Well, most of 'em,' I tell her, 'about ninety-nine percent, and that's more than most of us would ever dare ask for in this mortal probation. In fact, your momma was just a-telling me what the teacher said on your report card—remember? About how Tessa Ann Marriott helps make everybody else happy and looks out for them who have it tough.' "

Lije smiled and stretched. "So anyway, we go on like that for a while, and pretty soon she's a-coming around. She's decided to be happy again instead of sad."

"But she had some wonderful help," Shannon said.

"Oh, we all need help—nobody's an island." The room itself had assumed an even warmer atmosphere. "But still and all, in the end happiness or sadness is up to us. Even though the conditions can't always be changed, least not for quite a spell by mortal reckoning. But outlook can, even in the salt mines of Siberia."

"Yeah," Kelly laughed, "you can always be glad they're not pepper."

"*There* you go," the old man said, "absolutely! Salt mines are tough, but we all have 'em one way or another if we stick around long enough. And we can do far, far more for ourselves than is ever dreamed of in your philosophy, Horatio, by standing back and asking four simple, magical little words." Lije waited, pursing his lips thoughtfully. He was indeed the master of the dramatic pause. "Very simple." His brow rippled up well past the one-time hairline. " 'What do I want?' " Again, he paused. "That's correct. You just sort of stand back from the *you* havin' all its troubles and ask that simple little question as honest as possible. Think, ponder. That's when your Wise Counselor Self goes to work. What I call it, anyhow." He squinted one eye, gave his head a little twist to the side. "Now that alone can accomplish a surprising lot, but if you want full impact, the real stuff, you go one step farther. You say a little prayer and try to picture the Savior himself in your mind. Imagine he's right there beside you and that you're a-gonna think and do to the very best of your ability what *he* would think and do." The grandfather clock in the hall tick-tocked steadily away.

"Oh, you're not a-gonna find a gold mine in the backyard if that's your ambition, and most likely you won't have all your problems solved. Why, that would be the biggest problem of all. But you'll be able to cope better, I'll guarantee, and any of the really great godly virtues—love, faith, courage, wisdom, kindness, etc., etc., will begin to come on immediately, *instantly!*" Instantly? Marilyn wondered, but glancing into her mother's eyes she had seen the confirmation, and that combined with Lije's words made her a believer.

"Now, of course," Lije continued, "we all know a lot of these things, but sometimes we forget. Helps to be reminded. And isn't it a wonderful and ironic fact"—his face glowed—"that these marvelous gifts—which in the end are maybe the greatest of all—are right there for the asking. 'Ask, and ye shall receive; knock, and it shall be opened unto you.' "

Marilyn nodded, head slightly bowed for the moment. "I think I'm getting the message, " she murmured and felt the tingling. "If only . . ."

"If only what?" Maria asked gently.

She frowned, trying somehow to peer within her own mind. "If only I could keep from vacillating so much. Lots of times lately I don't know how I'm going to react from one minute to the next. If only I could, well, just hang fast and keep from wimping out."

"Wimping *out*?" The old man stared at her incredulously. "Why, don't even *think* about it!" He actually sounded a bit scandalized. "Don't even think the crummy little *words*!"

They were all laughing again. Elijah Marriott could be so delightfully theatrical when he wanted to, yet simultaneously, somehow, so utterly genuine.

"Just keep counting my blessings, instead—correct?"

"Absolutely!"

Thirty-Six

The conversation had ended there, but she had visited with Lije again unexpectedly, only a short time earlier at the onset of her walk along the beach. The old man was sitting under an apple tree in his backyard as she strolled by, and he hailed her, beckoning. "Best you come set a minute," he declared, gesturing toward the empty lawn chair beside him. "Have yourself a right nice apple and tell old gramps here how things are goin'."

A ladder leaned against the branches overhead. Just below were two bushel baskets brimming and fragrant with yellow apples. "Here now . . . ," Lije said, searching out a large and handsome one, buffing it on his trousers. "Golden delicious."

"Oooh, wonderful! Thanks." She settled back in the chair beside him. "My very favorite."

"Well," he said and selected another for himself. "So you're out for a stroll."

Marilyn nodded. "I can't jog yet, or even bike much, but I can walk if I take it easy on my bad ankle."

"Bravo," Lije said, "that's the spirit!"

She bit into the apple. "Hmmmm—absolutely delectable."

"Verily," he replied and took a substantial chonk on his own, flashing a gold eyetooth in the process. The bite was so large it cracked the core, revealing some of the seeds. "Amazing creation." He continued to chew, looking thoughtful. "And just look at this little rascal." He probed at the apple's innards, extracted a seed, peered at it with growing pleasure. "What a miracle!" More chewing. "You can count the seeds within an apple . . . but who can ever count the apples within a seed?"

Marilyn smiled, shaking her head, feeling the sweet, mellow tang upon her tastebuds, and half closed her eyes, letting sunlight filter through the lashes. "Limitless."

"Right you are," came the reply. "Just like the offspring of Abraham . . . and the worlds of outer space."

She regarded him fondly, slightly amused, knowing the old man could no more resist observing and philosophizing on the results than birds could refrain from flight. "And you think maybe there are people on those other worlds?" Her question was a bit mischievous because she knew full well what his answer would be. What form it might take or how he would amplify was something else.

The shaggy eyebrows lofted, the chin tucked in, drawing back a little, hooked downward at the corners. Profound incredulity personified. "Why, of course!" For a time it seemed as though he had nothing more to say on the subject. "Sure as there's more apple trees than one—sure as they'll never stop a-growing and providing mankind the fruit thereof."

"I believe that," she said and suddenly felt very vulnerable yet very happy.

The old man was watching her. "Matter of fact, there never *was* a time when there were not worlds in the making, and when there were not people upon them, a-doing pretty much what the rest of us are. There never will be. Knowing all the fears and hopes, all the sorrows and the joys." He paused. "Hard to comprehend, isn't it? But as we come to—even to get the first few glimmers—it certainly puts our own little problems in a different perspective. Becomes a great consolation to the soul."

"Yes," she said. The words were very faint, yet for a few seconds the conviction was so complete it seemed as if she might rise and take wing.

They remained silent for some time. "Just one more thing—one of those 'little problems,' " Marilyn said at last. "Well, it's something I've wondered about lately." She hesitated. "I feel pretty silly asking about it in a way because . . . oh, I'm not exactly sure why. Maybe it sounds as if I'm doubting the Lord, or your own inspiration as patriarch, and I'm really not."

"Go ahead," Lije prodded. "You've got a question, fire at will." He chuckled. "That was the stale old joke clear back in my days with Uncle Sam. Nobody named Will could figure on lasting very long."

That made it easier although she was still apprehensive, feeling quite fragile over the matter. "Well, okay." She blinked and dabbed at the corner of her eye with her little finger. She was, in fact, feeling a near superstition, like the patient who fears to ask for the doctor's prognosis yet knows it must be done. "Remember when you gave me my patriarchal blessing? Just before I started college?"

"Certainly," Lije replied.

"Well, in that blessing you promised me an 'eternal companion who would love the Lord and honor and magnify his priesthood.' " She looked into his eyes, found them utterly serene and unwavering.

"That I did," he said.

"And you also told me that all the promises in my entire blessing depended upon faith and good works."

"That I did."

"So, lots of blessings are actually conditional, and in many cases they come to pass according to the Lord's time, not necessarily our own—right?"

"Right, absolutely correct."

"So, okay." She inhaled, held it, summoned a fluid and uncertain smile. "Does that mean I might not even find that person in this life at all? That maybe I'll have to wait till the next?" The old man inspected his gnarled hands, then glanced at the mellow fall sun, one eye squinched almost shut. "Tell me straight, Lije." She tried hard to keep her voice casual, everything in control. "I don't want you to just make me feel good."

Gently he reached over and patted her hand. "Possibly," he allowed. "Right this moment I don't have any further news on the matter, not direct from the Spirit. But if you're asking an old gaffer who still ain't totally blind, I sure as heck don't *think* it'll be that long of a wait—not from the looks of you, my dear girl."

"Thanks, Lije," she said. "I guess maybe I was hoping for some kind of little P.S., a footnote or something, but . . ." She shrugged and laughed. "That's not exactly the way with patriarchal blessings, is it?"

"Not usually," Lije replied. A hummingbird flitted among the branches, curtsied, flared its tail, throat scintillating rainbow colors, then trilled off toward the south. "And sometimes maybe it's better not to know everything, you stop and think about it. Why, just imagine, for instance, if we was to all know the exact day and manner of our passing." Marilyn nodded, closing her eyes momentarily. "On the other hand," Lije went on, "that's not to say more details can't come, about all kinds of things. A patriarchal blessing, in the main, is a road map. At least that's the way I picture it." He pursed his lips, following the track of the hummingbird with his eyes. "If anything else comes, you'll be the first to know in any event. Meanwhile, don't forget you've got your own prayers, your own inspiration to fill you in on a lot of questions."

"Thanks," she said. "But right now, I'm kind of drawing a blank, too. Maybe I just need to apply myself a little harder. Maybe I'm just praying in vain repetitions."

"Possibly," Lije allowed. "We all do at times. Could be the good Lord is just keeping some of it on ice a while yet, for his own good reasons. The only thing I know right now is what Paul said back a couple thousand years ago." She watched him, waiting. " 'All things work together for good to them that love God.' " Across the lawn in Lije's corral two horses munched hay contentedly and regarded them with calm curiosity.

"Well," Marilyn replied slowly and frowned. "I have to admit that the 'all things' part stretches my faith a little. All things? *Everything*—no matter how terrible?"

Lije Marriott regarded the sun once more, surveyed the sky as though reviewing his own history. Perhaps the horror of no-man's-land in far-off France, the desolation of the trenches where he was wounded by the mortar shell, bayonetted in the throat and left to die and rot among a thousand corpses. Back before the birth of her own parents! She had heard him talk about it in a Church fireside, once or twice to Kelly and his pals years before—"children ardent for some desperate glory." Or perhaps the automobile accident fifteen years earlier which had brought him once again to the brink and entailed months of physical therapy, disfigured his face, requiring operations and skin grafts. Perhaps the death of his wife, Carrie, following her years with advanced rheumatoid arthritis.

"Yes," the old man said. His tone was utterly uncompromising. Indeed, even triumphant. "That's a big order, isn't it? But our good friend Paul had been there; he knew whereof he spoke." Far, far above, a concourse of angels circled in the blue. So it almost seemed for a moment.

"Look," Marilyn said, "what are they?" Her lips parted in wonderment.

Lije shaded his eyes with one hand, peering. "Great white pelicans." He watched with knowing admiration. " 'There is a power whose care teaches thy way along the pathless coast,' " he mused, quoting from Bryant, " 'the desert and the illimitable air. Alone, wandering, yet not lost.' " Then he gave his head a little shake. "On dry land, gawkiest critters imaginable, but you get 'em up there in the heavens a-riding the thermals . . . my oh my, hardly anything to compare. Almost put the eagles to shame."

Then he reverted once more to the Apostle Paul and his remarkable promise. "Now to some folks, that statement about everything working for the good is nothing but a wild and foolish allegation. Either that or Santa Claus faith at its worst. And yet . . . properly conceived by the wise and spiritually minded, it becomes one of the greatest barometers of faith imaginable. Faith and courage."

For a moment she felt again the affirmation of his words, the effervescent thrilling in the veins. Mere imagination? Mere wishful thinking? "And, of course, the whole key is 'them that love God,' " Marilyn mused.

"Yep, that's the whole thing," the old man said and gave her arm a pat, a little squeeze that seemed to vibrate almost electrically. "You're getting the pictures. And I'll tell you something else that ties right in with it. Ready?"

"I think so"—she smiled—"hope so."

"Well, it's simply this—not one single thing, not one single blessing, however large or small, will be withheld. Not if it's truly deserved." He smiled at her and held up his finger. "Postscript: In the good Lord's own due time."

She closed her eyes, mind aswirl, yet still managed to return his smile. "I guess that's what scares me so much—the deserving part, but the time aspect too. God's time can be so much *longer* than ours! I honestly wonder about my endurance."

"Endure to the end," Lije said. "There's only one alternative, and you just throw the rascal out. Never give it a second thought. Never! You just keep a-putting one foot in front of the other like in that big triathlon. You keep moving forward, forging ahead, even if you have to do it on your belly, like that cold, dark road up there on Monte." He waited some time. "And the prize will ultimately be yours."

Walking the bright and empty shoreline now, she remembered his words, also recalled the prayer of her friend and sister-in-law Shannon. It had been offered at Lije's request as the family visit to his home had ended a few nights earlier. "And Heavenly Father," Shannon had concluded, "please, please bless Marilyn." Her voice was full of love and tears. "Marilyn and so many others out there—all those who must wait and wonder—who are still longing to find the right one."

For now the shoreline was vacant except for her pal Braun, who was at last content simply to trot by her side with an occasional excursion up along the nearby bluffs of Cemetery Point to her right. They too were vacant except for spans of sunflowers, russet-colored Indian tobacco, and the lilting flight of a monarch butterfly. Unexpectedly, she found herself humming a familiar tune, almost under her breath, then even a few of the words. Her voice fractured a little in the process, sounding unfamiliar and forlorn at first, a bit like whistling in the dark. "Count your blessings; name them one by one. Count your blessings; see what God hath done." It was part of an old gospel hymn which she had learned during earliest childhood in Sunday School.

Yes, she thought, why not actually count them, follow the very advice she had given herself so recently? And yet . . . in reality, it would be impossible to count them all, ever, like trying to count the apples within a seed. Because . . . well, because God not only bestowed blessings outright, he also gave his children the power to create their own. To create a blessing from virtually anything if they truly wanted to enough. Even if—she smiled—it sometimes required a pretty lively imagination. But imagination itself, that was another blessing—that and appreciation—limited only by one's reluctance to use them.

She paused to gaze at a young cottonwood, most of its leaves now a rich yellow, some of them scattered about the sand at her feet. For a moment she recalled her awakening among the leaves of Monte Cristo. And for a moment, too, something seemed to be rising within her. It was hard to articulate, but she felt the current of excitement, something she suddenly sensed as never before about human aspiration. For a few shimmering moments it welled thrillingly yet a bit frighteningly also. All those great challenges people were perennially presenting themselves—everything from running races to building pyramids and empires, writing great symphonies, and soon colonizing other worlds. They were but a type and shadow of what mere mortals, God's own offspring, might ultimately become, of their divine potential—the spirit and heart speaking of a promise the mind had yet to comprehend. That was the old man's great secret—one he had left for her to discover.

Turning homeward, she had no idea what to do for the rest of the day, but she knew that it would be a mistake, almost sacrilege, to sit and mope. Maybe a call to Cuddles about helping with the haunted house. Suddenly she was laughing inwardly, knowing how delighted his response would be, and how earsplitting! She would have to hold the receiver at arm's length. But why not become involved? It was something at least to be doing, in Lije's words, "just for openers." She thought about the blessing of family and friends, which many people did not have, the blessing of a good cause even if for the moment it seemed a little blah.

But the sun itself did not seem blah, nor did her surroundings—the land with all its life, the mountains and sky, or the water reflecting them. They never had. And it was definitely better, yes, to keep putting one foot ahead of the other than to remain forever in one place. High above, the great white pelicans had reappeared, slowly circling with the day, the light, and the wind beneath their wings.